ALAINA CLAIBORNE

A British Agent Novel

MK McCLINTOCK

Published in the United States of America
Trappers Peak Publishing
www.mkmcclintock.com

McClintock, MK
Alaina Claiborne; novel/MK McClintock
ISBN-13: 978-0615742502

Cover and book design by MK McClintock
Current cover released in 2024

PRINTED IN THE UNITED STATES OF AMERICA

PRAISE FOR
THE BRITISH AGENT NOVELS

"Ms. McClintock weaves a thick tapestry of mystery and romance in her historical setting . . . Multiple twists and unexpected alliances hook the reader into her complex tale . . . Bravo Ms. McClintock!"
—*InD'Tale Magazine* (on *Blackwood Crossing*)

"This is a wonderful book with suspense to keep me on the edge of my seat and surprises to keep me guessing. The main characters—a feisty heroine and a strong, gentle hero—are just the kind I love and the villains are worthy of being hated."
—Verna Mitchell, author of *Somewhere Beyond the Blue*

"Ms. McClintock succeeds in masterfully weaving both genres meticulously together until mystery lovers are sold on romance and romance lovers love the mystery!
—*InD'Tale Magazine* (on *Alaina Claiborne*)

"The balance between romance, mystery, and adventure was perfect. Usually one outweighs the other, so I was pleasantly surprised. In addition, the plot had some unexpected twists, which made the story that much more interesting. With memorable characters and an entertaining plot, *Alaina Claiborne* has it all. —*Readers' Favorite*

"A mystery entwined with an ongoing hopeful romance between Devon and Anne, *Clayton's Honor* is utterly enticing and captivating!" —*InD'tale Magazine*

Other Books by this Author

BRITISH AGENT NOVELS

Alaina Claiborne
Blackwood Crossing
Clayton's Honor
The Ghost of Greyson Hall

MONTANA GALLAGHER SERIES

Gallagher's Pride
Gallagher's Hope
Gallagher's Choice
An Angel Called Gallagher
Journey to Hawk's Peak
Wild Montana Winds
The Healer of Briarwood
Christmas in Briarwood

CROOKED CREEK SERIES

The Women of Crooked Creek
Christmas in Crooked Creek
The Trail to Crooked Creek

THE MCKENZIE SISTERS MYSTERY SERIES

The Case of the Copper King

Discover more at www.mkmcclintock.com

For April.
You were the best of us.

A special thanks to my editor, Lorraine Fico-White.
Your dedication, encouragement, and humor are a rare
combination.

AUTHOR'S NOTE

Dearest Reader,

This book was, to say the least, a journey. What began as a story I started more than ten years prior, ended with a love for characters to whom I wasn't willing to say goodbye. Alaina is as I believe heroines should be—strong, resilient, and ladylike. Of course, she has a few flaws, but who doesn't. Tristan is a gentleman hero, but he's not concerned about doing what others expect, and I love him for that. I hope you enjoy Alaina and Tristan's journey of romance and mystery.

It should also be known that I write fiction, not history. My stories are meant to entertain and offer the reader an escape into another time and place. While I remain true to the era and customs, there are times when I exercise a certain artistic license to find a balance between what we believe, what was, and what we can relate to in our modern day. It is never my intention to offend the historical purists.

Why did I make a duke a British Agent when they had no occupation in the standard sense? It's quite simple. Because I saw a man who although trapped by his station in life, wanted to be known as someone and something else . . . and so he was.

Happy Reading,

-MK

In the spring of life your cry prevailed,
Blossomed and flourished with every wail.
The bloom and blush of roses fair,
Each morning and night, an answer to prayer.
Blessed child within the heart,
From this love we'll never part.

—*MK McClintock*

One

Benbrook Ball, County Wicklow, Ireland
October 1880

The room sparkled, from the glistening chandeliers to the flickering light of the candles. Beautiful people in elegant clothes danced across the gleaming floor in grand style. Laughter and whispers mingled with the fluid music of Brahms, teasing young men and women into a dance of subtle seduction and promise. Never before had she been allowed to witness such grandeur. Her young mind processed every detail, every movement, every word. Images of herself ten years from now, dancing with the boy she loved, filled her imagination—until the boy spoke.

"I told you I did not dance, Alaina." Braden stepped on her foot for the second time.

"You are the smartest person I know, Braden Melbourne, and you are telling me you have danced not once?"

"I never said I didn't know how—I'm just not good at it." He danced on her foot again. "Do not say I did not warn you when your toes are bruised tomorrow."

Alaina smiled in response to his gruff reply and continued to dance. Alaina knew in her heart that Braden was the only man she would ever wish to marry. Best friends always made the best husbands, or so her mother once told her. For now, she was content to dance with him and think about racing him to the pond when they returned home to England. The song ended and Braden escorted her back to her watchful parents.

The evening continued to wear on as they were introduced to a seemingly never-ending line of people. Alaina gazed at every woman who waltzed past her and studied the way these ladies of society behaved.

Of course, the ladies in attendance were either married, widowed, or closer to her age. Alaina's perusal of the guests continued until a gentle hand pressed down on her shoulder. She turned to look up into the loving eyes of her father.

"Would you pleasure me with this dance?" He bent down to whisper.

Alaina smiled at her father and curtsied. "I would be delighted," she leaned over and whispered, "Papa."

Christopher smiled down at his daughter as she wrapped her arm through his, and he escorted her to the dance floor for a waltz.

Christopher Claiborne excelled at almost everything he attempted, and dancing was one of his many talents. Alaina imagined she danced on air as they glided across the ballroom. She felt like a fairy tale princess, and this was her magical night in the arms of her father and in the company of those she loved the most. This was a night for her to remember.

A ten-year-old girl who had known only love in her life failed to believe anything would ever change.

Melody after melody continued lilting through the air as the band played on. Alaina glanced up at her six-foot-tall father. Her neck cramped, but she didn't mind.

"Papa, is life always this wonderful?"

Her parents had taught their daughter to be honest and to respect that virtue, but her father did not want to erase her joyful smile with life's truths. He looked into the innocent eyes of his daughter and answered carefully.

"I want to tell you something, Alaina, something my father told me a very long time ago, when I was about your age." The music carried on and he continued. "We were fishing in the small pond near the house, and I caught my very first fish. When I reeled my line in, I grew excited until I saw the fish coming closer. I saw it struggling against the hook in its mouth. My father held up the net to catch the fish, and then he laid it on the ground until the fish stopped fighting. I had never seen anything struggle for life before and it upset me. I wanted to put the fish back in the pond, and when my father asked me why, I told him I didn't want to eat something I killed." Christopher continued the dance as he held his daughter, his voice covered by the music.

"My father loved me very much, as I love you, but he wanted me to understand something that day, a truth I didn't understand until many years later. He told me life is a circle and in the circle exist hate, love, happiness, sorrow, and death, and in order to appreciate one, we must experience the others. Without those experiences, we are not whole and live only a part of the life we are given, and it is up to us to make our lives full, for only within ourselves can we find peace."

Christopher paused to study his daughter's face and saw confusion and an innocent kind of wisdom. He feared someday she would understand his words far more than he desired and prayed for that time to come later rather than sooner.

"Papa? Was what your papa told you really about the fish?"

Her perception never ceased to amaze him. "No, my sweet, it was not about the fish, but I didn't realize it at the time. Someday you too will understand what he meant, but not now. Tonight we only remember this dance, and how much your mother and I love you."

"I love you too, Papa." She hugged her father as the music ended, and they returned to Clara and Braden, who stood on the side, enjoying the view of husband and friend.

The evening's entertainments slowly ended, and the foursome bid their hosts farewell. They had been offered a room for the night, but they did not have far to travel, and elected to return home. The moon lit up the night sky, and moments after the carriage departed the old castle, the two younger passengers slumbered peacefully. Christopher gazed up at the moon through the window, his wife's head resting on his shoulder.

"Christopher?"

"Yes, my love?"

"Thank you."

"For what, my dear?" He pulled her closer to his side.

"For bringing us here and giving us your time and love. You're a wonderful husband and father." She placed her hand on his knee, and he covered it with his own.

"My darling, I will love you both forever."

"As will I, my love. As will I." She raised her lips, and all the love in his heart poured into her. The kiss ended, and she ran her fingers softly up and down the length of his arm as they drifted into a companionable silence until something jostled the carriage occupants.

Braden awakened abruptly and scanned the carriage. "What is happening?"

"Nothing to alarm yourself over, son. It was just a deep rut in the road."

The horses quickened their pace, and one of the footmen lowered himself partially over the side until the passengers inside the conveyance heard him. The footman was young, and Christopher clearly recognized the young man's panic.

"My lord, we have trouble," he managed to say before the carriage reached a dangerous speed and he had to return to his perch.

"Christopher." The panic-filled word forced him to look at his wife, and a deep pain clenched his heart.

Everything he loved and everything worth living for were with him inside the carriage. He smoothed his hand over his wife's cheek and kissed her brow. She did not need words to know what his eyes freely spoke, but he said them anyway.

"I love you, Clara."

"Do not even think what you're thinking, Christopher."

They both glanced over at their daughter, who had not been disturbed. Braden held the young girl carefully in his protective embrace. He was young, but he refused to allow any harm to come to her.

Christopher nodded to Braden and saw immediate understanding in the young man's eyes. The earl lifted the window flap aside and stuck his head out to speak with the driver. The carriage had reached maximum speed, and he found it difficult to speak with the wind blowing ferociously in his face. Finally, he gained the driver's attention, who motioned behind them.

He turned his upper body to look behind the carriage and saw what he feared the most—riders. There appeared to be half a dozen, but this area was not usually frequented by highwaymen—they tended to stay closer to the shipping ports and the more traveled roads to ensure a bigger purse.

Christopher pulled himself back into the carriage, grabbed a gun from a small box behind his seat, and then took one more look at his wife and silently prayed.

The chase continued for another half a mile, but the riders, not burdened with luggage and passengers, slowly closed the distance between them. Braden continued to shelter Alaina from the jostling caused by the bumps in the road, but he felt her begin to stir.

A shot pierced the night sky and echoed through the valley. Alaina awoke, not mindful of the warm arms around her or the sudden lurching halt of the carriage. She noticed only her father holding her mother with one hand and a gun with the other.

Another shot.

The horses lurched forward, but as they attempted to once again move forward, a third shot rang out and the geldings reared back while the driver did his best to keep the team under control. The horses fought the reins, but too many piercing shots had frightened them, and the animals backed up perilously close to a slope in the hill. Shouts were heard as the passengers sat in silence, too fearful to even breathe loudly.

Their driver shouted at the men and again at the horses. Another man laughed a sickening laugh that brought a prickling of fear to Christopher. The carriage wheels teetered precariously on the decline, and the horses lacked the strength to pull the heavy conveyance back once it started to tip. The carriage toppled over and the woman screamed. The horses whinnied, and the driver yelled again as he jumped off his perch. Down they went, rolling over and over, the sound of cracking wood echoing inside.

The doors flew open and broke off. Christopher tried to shove Alaina through the portal as they continued to roll, but he was unable to reach her. Then he saw Braden try his best to hold onto the seat and reach for Alaina. With more strength than a young man of his age should have possessed, Braden grabbed his best friend and guided her to the opening, where there were only splinters from the broken door. Christopher watched as Braden pushed her from the carriage. He slipped and lost his hold in the same moment they hit the clearing and the carriage stopped, landing on the once open door.

Christopher braced himself to take his wife's fall, and they lay there, suspended in time.

Two

Scarce moments passed before they managed to relax their bodies enough to breathe properly, and with the carriage lying on its side, they had little room to maneuver. Christopher checked his wife, and though she looked bruised and shaken up, she appeared to be without serious injury. Hurriedly he reached over to Braden to check him for injuries, but the young man lay still. Christopher steadied his fingers above the young man's mouth, but no breath touched his skin.

Christopher slowly levered himself up and gently lifted the younger man's head on his lap as best he could, and he felt for a pulse. It was still—the fall had broken his neck. Christopher leaned over the boy as something wet dropped on Braden's face. Christopher reached up to wipe away another tear before it fell. He held the young man, who in the last moments of life had given his own for a friend. Clara wrapped her arms around him and Christopher heard her gentle sobs. They knelt over the friend their daughter loved more than life and prayed for him and for their daughter's safety.

The carriage rattled, and they heard mumbled voices outside. The only way out was above them, through the other broken door. A man's head appeared, but the light of the moon shone behind him, and they could not discern his features.

"Ye get yerselves ou' of that there carriage right now, or I'll get you ou' meself." There was no mistaking the threat in the guttural slur, and they had no choice but to comply.

Christopher laid Braden's head back down and turned to embrace his wife. He kissed her with all the love they had shared over the years, and it took more willpower than he knew himself to possess to pull away from her.

"Remember always, Clara."

The tears in her eyes flowed freely, and she kissed him once more. They heard an impatient pounding through the carriage wall.

"Enough! Remove yourself from the carriage at once."

This was a more formal and cultured voice. *Too cultured for these swindlers.* For the safety of his wife alone, Christopher lifted himself out of the door and studied the men. There on the ground were nine men, a few more than he had counted before, which led him to believe others had been waiting up the road and they had fired the shots.

The horses had broken free from the carriage and now lay lifeless on the slope. Exhaling deeply, he turned back toward the opening and leaned down inside to lift his wife out of the carriage. He maneuvered to the edge and lowered himself to the ground first. He then lifted his wife down to stand beside him. Christopher did his best to shield her from the men, but they were curious and moved around to get a better view. Clara was a smart woman and she knew that to say anything meant their death. She remained inside the protective embrace of her husband.

"Bobby, make sure there is no one else inside." This voice came from one of the men on horseback, an almost aristocratic voice.

The other man did as ordered and clumsily climbed up on the side of the carriage with the help of the wheels. He peered down inside. "Why, me lord, there's a boy down there."

"Well, then pull him out." The man kept his shadowed eyes on the couple.

"He 'pears to be dead, me lord."

The man on horseback turned back to the couple. "My condolences. I do detest the death of innocent children." The man offered no sympathy in his dry voice, and he pulled a thin cheroot from his breast pocket, lighting the end. He looked at the men and then back to the couple. He ordered for Clara to be brought to him.

"No!" Christopher and Clara yelled at the same time. Everyone paused as the leader continued to study the couple, and then he tried another approach.

"And who might you be? Other than an Englishman far from home."

The reply was not immediate as Christopher tried to remember where he had seen or heard this man before. "The Earl of Claiborne."

The leader's queer smile vanished instantly, and it was a moment before he spoke again, all pretenses of formality gone.

"Well, this is indeed a pleasure. It is not every day men such as us happen upon such a wealthy conveyance. I had no idea when I took this job, I would have the opportunity to settle a score between enemies."

Christopher was puzzled for a moment by the cryptic remark until realization of what the leader said hit him. Someone had wanted them attacked, and this was the man they had sent. Mindful of his wife still holding on to him but not speaking, he looked more closely at the man on the black mount.

"Croxley."

Clara gasped and her husband held her more tightly.

"I must say that I am pleased you both remember me. It has been many years, but I can see you have prospered. You have both changed. Why, Clara, you were a mere girl last I saw you. Tell me, Lord Claiborne, have you enjoyed bedding the woman who was supposed to have been my wife all of these years?"

"She was never yours."

"Oh, yes, I had great plans for us as did my father." Croxley ignored the last comment.

"You were a monster even then. Her father saw it, and it was why he refused your offer."

"Her father was a fool. She should have been my wife. Tell me, did she only breed the one son?"

Anger suffused Christopher, and he almost forgot the precarious position they were in as he stepped forward, fists clenched at his side.

"Now, now, we don't want any of that. I suggest, Lord Claiborne, you cooperate or you might find your regrets to surpass the death of the boy in the carriage." Croxley stared down at Clara with lust-filled eyes and spoke to the man she held tightly.

"I suggest you tell your wife to step forward, or I won't guarantee your safety."

Clara finally broke her silence. "You will never have me. Never."

She turned back to her husband, but not before she sensed the anger radiating from Croxley. Christopher pulled her with him and backed up as far as the fallen carriage allowed. Croxley laughed at their efforts, and then with the signal of his raised fist, four guns pointed directly at Christopher.

"Now, my dear, you have two choices. You either come with me now and we spare your husband, or he dies and I take you anyway. Only one way will save him, so choose wisely."

"I will kill myself before I ever let you touch me."

"I will eliminate your husband, my dear. You may decide if he will die slowly or painlessly. Now come here."

Christopher pushed his wife back behind him. "Never."

"Then you leave me little choice."

When she realized what was happening, Clara stepped out in front of her husband and hugged herself to him, even as he tried to push her back. It was too late. The sound of the bullet leaving the chamber permeated the air, and Christopher stood suspended in shock when his wife stiffened against him. He lowered her to the ground and smoothed his fingers across her cheek.

"Always, my love," she struggled to whisper before the breath left her body.

"No!" Christopher wrapped his arms around his dead wife and rocked back and forth, his tears flowing freely as he temporarily forgot the surrounding men. "No, no, no, no. Clara, come back to me."

It was the cry of a man whose heart had been torn from his chest. Croxley appeared surprised at the emotion the earl expressed for his dead wife.

Croxley turned to Bobby, who stood shocked at what he had done and never saw the bullet from Croxley's gun before it entered his back. The other men watched as one of their own fell limply to the hard ground.

Christopher kissed Clara's brow, smoothed back his wife's hair, and whispered for her and him alone. "Always, my Clara."

"Stand him up."

Unable to draw the strength to fight the men, Christopher allowed the men to drag him to his feet. They pulled him away from the still body and ordered him to kneel in front of their leader. Christopher complied, knowing his life ended with his wife's. He had no hope of escape. He prayed Alaina had survived and would someday forgive him for not protecting all of them.

"This brings me great pleasure, Lord Claiborne. You denied me her, and you shall have her no more. She should have been mine."

"She was never yours. She will always be mine. You and death cannot change that." And forgetting that three guns pointed at his head, he continued. "She never did anything to you. She only followed her heart. Now you will live, knowing she died rather than be with you. She reviled you that much."

The crack of the pistol and the smoke from the gun lingered. All three men with guns looked up to their leader, who still held his arm up, the grip on his pistol tight and unyielding.

Silence filled the air, broken only by the brush of wind as it moved through the trees. They watched the nobleman fall to the ground, and their leader put his gun back in the leather holster.

"Take everything you can carry from the carriage and mount up. Our job here is done." The men obeyed and moved in rapid fashion as the lord on the tall black gelding looked down at the two motionless bodies on the cold earth. His men waited for him to ride ahead, and with one last look, he turned his horse around and led the group up the hill to the country road.

Back in the clearing, where silence now engulfed the land and the animals lay quiet in the crisp late-autumn night, they had failed to notice the small form huddled behind a nearby bush, bright blue eyes staring out after them as they rode into the darkness.

Three

British Agent Safe House, Scottish Highlands
1887

Tristan stared at the stains covering his hands. He couldn't tell where the dirt ended and the blood began. From across the room, he watched as Devon took his turn at the washstand. Charles sat on a stool nearby, his blood-stained shirt partially unbuttoned, revealing his bandaged chest.

Devon Clayton and Charles Blackwood had been with him on every mission since they joined the agency after they had all finished their studies at Oxford. For three years, they worked side by side, mission after mission, with the highest success rate in the agency. The youngest, brightest, and best trained, they were called on by Britain because they succeeded where others had failed. However, they had not expected this.

Tristan had killed men before—it came with the work—but he had always believed those killings had been justified. At the tavern they had done everything possible with their combined knowledge to save the woman and child who had unknowingly fallen victim to their hunt. Their target—the woman's husband—had used her as a shield. Another man had used the child. They had never fired on a woman or child and had momentarily backed down—a mistake which cost too many lives, including two of their own.

Tristan replayed everything from the moment they had reached the tavern, attempting, in vain, to see any other way for a different outcome. There had been five agents and six men expected to be at the location. Their source had been mistaken or had betrayed them. There were eight men and the woman and child, sitting down to supper. Tristan and his agents did all they could to make the arrests without injury, but the men had refused to go peacefully.

He saw again the woman's husband throw her into the middle of the ruckus as he attempted to escape out the back door. Charles shot the man. The other, who had used the child as a shield, had held a knife to the boy's throat. As he tried to make his exit, the knife slipped.

Tristan remembered every man and every move. He had seen two of his agents go down, each taking a culprit with him. One had escaped, but he couldn't recall how. They might be the best at what they did, but they had made a deadly mistake. Tristan once again studied his partners and friends. Neither would forget what happened either. The woman and child's screams promised to haunt them all for years to come.

Tristan cleaned his hands, watching the blood darken the water. Some of it left a temporary stain on his hands, but a more permanent one stained his mind.

He nodded to his friends and they all left the room. They were due to return to England, and there were bodies to collect before they left.

Four

Claiborne Manor, Northamptonshire, England
Summer 1889

"Would you care to share your thoughts?"

"What? Oh, sorry, Aunt Charlotte, my mind wandered again." Alaina sat across from her aunt in the blue tearoom. It had been her mother's favorite room and held many memories from long ago.

The older woman glanced at the niece she and her husband had adopted ten years ago and watched Alaina sit lost in her own thoughts, gazing out the window of what was once her happy home. Alaina, now a woman of twenty years, had inherited her mother's beauty and her father's brains and wit, a combination of traits capable of catching any eligible young man. But rather than encourage the affection of suitors, she chose a life of solitude with only her gardens and horses for company.

Charlotte's childless state had not prepared her for Alaina. However, she and her husband, Sebastian, doted upon Alaina as a young girl. After that dreadful night, the couple had come to live with Alaina at Claiborne Manor because the young girl had refused to leave her home.

Charlotte thought and continued to study her departed sister's daughter. Alaina's golden hair lent her the image of her father and her sapphire blue eyes had brought more than one suitor to the door. Though ten long years had passed since her parents' death, Alaina refused to speak of the tragic night to anyone, avoiding conversation about how she managed to escape, claiming she did not remember. After a while, people stopped inquiring and the doctors thought it best to let her alone. Charlotte thought otherwise, wishing she knew what secrets Alaina's mind safeguarded. Charlotte continued to coax Alaina into sharing, but the young woman evaded the questions whenever someone mentioned that night.

"Are you well?" Charlotte sipped her lemon tea and stared at her niece. "Your complexion could do with a little color."

"I am British, Aunt Charlotte. Pale is a curse which blights us all." Alaina sneaked a glance at her aunt and saw by the older woman's expression that she did not appreciate the sarcasm. "I'm quite well, thank you." And as though whatever she thought about vanished from existence, she forced a smile and continued her embroidery.

Alaina knew that Charlotte disliked the emotional barrier she raised whenever someone inquired into her feelings. Alaina had become a one-way mirror reflecting off only itself, allowing the world to see only what she allowed, and the effort to break through from either side had become a tedious effort.

"I heard Uncle Sebastian speak of a new stallion he procured while in Scotland last month. He's bringing the animal home today, is he not?"

Charlotte gave up further inquiry into Alaina's health, much to Alaina's relief. Charlotte did not share her husband or niece's love for the large animals, which was an oddity in the Claiborne household.

"Yes, your uncle should arrive this afternoon, and I believe he is bringing a gentleman from the tracks to watch this new beast run."

Alaina knew her aunt supported her husband in his enterprises but did not condone racing horses. She believed horses were a waste of one's time and money, even though her uncle generally walked away as the victor. Her aunt and uncle lacked the loving relationship her parents had shared, for their kind of love and devotion came rare in any society, but they appeared to be a devoted couple.

"Uncle Sebastian has a gift when it comes to the races, and I, for one, am pleased with his choice of hobbies. Otherwise I would not have new mounts to ride every year."

"What about your own stallion, Serendipity? Isn't he coming along in age?"

Alaina's longtime steed brought back fond memories of her parents and the afternoon they had gifted her the stallion. Despite her mother's misgivings, her father had chosen not to geld the animal, and he had taught Alaina how to handle and ride the spirited horse. "He is only eleven years with many more ahead of him, I imagine. He is full of life, even now." She paused a few moments and then turned a question on her aunt. "Why is it I never see you ride a horse, but Uncle Sebastian adores them as much as I do?"

"I've told you before, dear, horses and I simply don't suit."

"I remember, but surely there must be a reason."

"Well, it is simply because I am afraid of the ghastly beasts."

Alaina looked at her aunt with sincere surprise. "Why didn't you tell me you were afraid of horses? I've seen you around them all my life, and I just assumed you didn't enjoy riding."

Her aunt looked thoughtful for a moment as if choosing her words carefully. "I never told you how my brother Philip died."

"No, I don't recall that you have. Come to think of it, Mama never mentioned him often, either."

"Well, she wouldn't have. She was still just a baby at the time. You see, we were close, my brother and I, and did most everything together. I used to love my morning rides with him, but one day when we were out, Philip rode a newly broke stallion our father had recently purchased. Philip was a skilled rider, but the animal was skittish and much stronger. We always raced over the hills and avoided the cliffs, but one day we ventured too close. The horse stopped abruptly, and Philip fell off the back and hit his head on a jagged rock. He died almost instantly. I rode as fast as I dared back to the house for help, but by the time I had returned with my father and the groom, it was too late. I've been afraid of riding ever since."

Alaina stared at her aunt, her eyes full of sympathy, as she moved from her chair to sit beside the woman on the Chippendale chaise.

"I'm sorry, Aunt Charlotte. I had no idea."

"No reason to be sorry, girl. It was a long time ago."

Alaina laid her hand on her aunt's shoulder. "That shouldn't stop you from riding horses. I understand fear, but it can be overcome."

"Yes, it can, but not everyone has the courage to face their fears." Her eyes focused on her niece. "It takes the strongest to persevere and face their demons, no matter the cost."

Alaina caught the double meaning of the other woman's words and lowered her gaze, removing her hand to her own lap. The words she had tried to free so many times remained unspoken. For some reason she didn't trust even the people closest to her.

"Why do you want me to remember? Why can't you let the memories disappear with the past?"

Charlotte chose her words carefully, uncertain when it came to this topic. "For your own comfort, child, to finally put the memories to rest."

"The memories are long buried and forgotten, but never at rest." Alaina shook her head slightly and gazed out the window for some kind of distraction, grateful to find one.

"Uncle Sebastian is early, and he has the new stallion with him."

Alaina nearly bounded out of her seat and rushed from the room. Charlotte sighed and spoke to the now empty room. "Someday, my dear, I just pray your fear is realized before it destroys you . . . or anyone else."

Alaina's looks might be fashionable, but despite how beautiful she was, Alaina possessed a spirit and temper that contradicted the demure facade she showed society. Charlotte nodded in self-approval, conjured up her best smile, and walked outside to greet her husband.

Alaina's uncle permitted her to run the horse around the dirt track. She proved to everyone watching that the horse had potential champion status, but she also proved her capability of running a race as well as any jockey. Charlotte disapproved of Alaina's infatuation with the horses, but it was a pleasure Alaina refused to relinquish.

The cool wind caressed Alaina's face and whipped her hair out of the carefully arranged coiffure Daphne had created that morning. The wind and crack of thunder drowned out the sounds around her. The horse raced across the track, leaving a cloud of dust in his wake while peace replaced her shadowy thoughts.

She smiled as she slowed the stallion and climbed down to walk him around before handing him over to the waiting groom. Alaina generally preferred to brush down her own horses, but this stallion was not hers. Her thoughts turned to Serendipity— it was time to devote attention to her own stallion.

"WHAT IN HEAVEN is going on with you?"

"I beg your pardon?"

Charlotte and Sebastian prepared for bed that evening after an afternoon of watching the new stallion run and eating an early supper. She sat at her dressing table, brushing out her long gray-tinged hair while playing ignorant to her husband's question.

"I mean the smile you put on the moment you walked out of the house today. You're up to something, my dear, and I have a feeling you should forget the idea right now and let whatever it is alone." He glanced over her shoulder at her reflection in the mirror.

"Why, Sebastian, I am up to nothing I shouldn't be."

"You should leave her be. She's not ready."

Charlotte turned her focus to her husband, her expression now serious.

"My dear, she just isn't ready for what you have planned. She's a smart girl and will know when the time is right for her, and when it is time, the decision will be hers to make."

She sighed and caressed her husband's hand. "I just feel as though there is something more I should be doing to help her. She puts forth a facade for everyone she meets, and the only time she is truly happy is when she is with her horses or digging through dirt in the gardens." Charlotte turned to face her husband. "Do you not believe she deserves more?"

Her heartfelt words touched her husband because he too felt the same way about their niece, but it was not their decision. He stood by that with as much conviction as he had three years ago when Charlotte attempted to make a match for the girl.

"There is someone out there for her, but she needs to be the one to do the looking and the finding. If it's forced upon her, she'll feel trapped and betrayed."

"True, but it wouldn't be wrong if I helped a little." Her husband of thirty years raised a brow, and she continued before he responded. "I don't intend to force anyone upon her, but perhaps if I just nudged her in the right direction and introduced her to a few gentlemen . . ." She waited for him to say something because he wore his unreadable expression. When he finally spoke, his words brooked no argument.

"Introductions only, Charlotte." At her excited nod, he added, "And not so many that the poor girl is overwhelmed. Don't be obvious, and be careful of her heart. Ten years have passed, but she is not yet healed."

"It will never heal if she never allows herself to love again."

Sebastian studied his wife, uncertain as to why the girl's marriage was so important right now. He knew no good could come from any of this, but it did not matter because arguing would only release his wife's Irish stubbornness. He was too weary that night to fight it, but not too weary to protect his niece.

THE WIND WHIPPING THROUGH her unfettered hair invigorated her as she raced across the hills on her uncle's new stallion. He gave her leave to ride the horse whenever she desired, knowing the new stud needed the exercise and training. Alaina had a magical touch with the animals, and he needed her touch for his new racer. Sebastian named the animal Noble, a fitting name for such an animal that might someday outrace even Serendipity. From the first moment she had stroked the steed's neck, his raw power coursed through her, and now with every stride, she felt his strength beneath her.

The crisp morning brought with it cold, but even with the chill air and the cool wind wrapping around her body, she only knew pleasure. As she and Noble cut through the air, she experienced power and strength she'd been unable to find anywhere else. The tragic night many years ago haunted her dreams, but she forbade herself to forget because someday she intended to make those responsible pay for their crimes. Revenge had raced through her blood for ten long years, as fast as she raced the mighty Noble. Even so, no one else knew. She hid it well.

Alaina rounded a bend in the road and passed a glen of trees that broke off into the well-traveled meadow surrounding the lake she thought as her own. She needed these familiar surroundings in her life just to get by. Alaina's eyes absorbed her surroundings and she closed them, seeing everything the way she knew it to be. Beauty blossomed everywhere this time of year, with the summer bringing a vibrancy of color and beauty not found during any other season. The blooms on the trees burst from their leaves, and the green of the lush meadows promised good grazing for the deer that roamed the property. Her own gardens thrived, and she hoped this season would not meet an end.

Alaina slowed as she neared the lake and pulled Noble to a stop to dismount, leading the animal to drink of the clear water. She sat down on a nearby boulder and gazed out over the water, allowing her mind to wander back to the days when she and Braden would ride to this spot and wait for their frustrated groom, whomever the unlucky chap happened to be at the time, to catch up with them. She smiled to herself and let the memories flood over her. A tear hit the back of the hand upon her lap, and she reached up to wipe away the next one.

"Oh, Papa," she said to the sky. "Why did you have to leave me? I miss you all dearly, but as heaven is my witness, I will make them pay." She forced the tears to stop, anger choosing an inconvenient moment to consume her, but Noble's loud whinny interrupted her passionate thoughts. Alaina stood abruptly and moved next to the horse as she kept her eyes on the trees.

"I know someone is there. Show yourself immediately."

It took no further prodding. A man stepped out into the clearing not more than fifteen feet away from them with his horse's reins in his grasp.

"My apologies, my lady, but I was unaware anyone else frequented this spot. I did not mean to frighten you."

He took a leisurely perusal of her person—from the flaxen hair to the sun-kissed cheeks over a creamy complexion to the sensible riding boots. *She's a remarkably fetching woman.*

"You did not frighten me, and furthermore, I happen to come here often. If anyone is trespassing, sir, it is you." Alaina's senses heightened when the man slowly looked up and down her body. She wondered if she ought to demand that he stop. *Was that approval in his eyes?* she wondered. *Who is he? I will admit he is handsome. Very well, if I am to be completely honest, he is sinfully handsome.* The man continued to look at her with startling amber-colored eyes. His eyes possessed the look of liquid gold—unusual and almost pretty. *Listen to me,* she scolded herself, *this man is a stranger and he is trespassing. Rid him from my mind and be on my way.*

She was finishing the lecture in her own head when he spoke.

"I'm sure you've now had plenty of time to determine whether I plan to attack you and take you off into the woods, but I assure my lady that you are in no danger from me."

"That remains to be seen, sir." Alaina stepped back and studied him again, hoping for some recognition. "Who are you? This land belongs to Lord Melbourne, and you most certainly are not him."

His lips quirked into a smile, and he found her feistiness charming. He admired her beauty and bravery and continued to enjoy himself by humoring her.

"I am Tristan Sheffield, my lady." He bowed gallantly, the devilish grin still firmly planted on his mouth.

"I am not familiar with your name. You are visiting?"

"Not precisely."

"Pray tell then, what exactly are you doing here?" Her impatience and curiosity warred with each other.

Ignoring her question, he asked one of his own. "I have revealed myself to you, so I think it only fair you supply your name as well."

If it will get him out of here. "Lady Alaina Claiborne, and you are still trespassing." Alaina thought she saw a flicker of surprise on the man's face, but it must have been a trick of the light through the leaves.

"I assure you, my lady, I am not trespassing."

"Explain yourself, sir."

Tristan almost laughed at her haughtiness, but then he thought alienating this woman may not be the best of ideas, so he tried another tactic.

"When did you last speak with Lord Melbourne?"

Surprised by his question, it took Alaina a minute to respond. "Truthfully, it has been many years. Why is that important?"

She looked directly at him and the impact of her eyes took him again by surprise.

"Sir?"

He drew his attention back to her previous question. "I ask only because if you had spoken with Lord Melbourne recently, you should be aware he sold his properties, including the manor. The sale finalized a few months ago, but this is the first opportunity I've had to visit at my leisure."

His announcement evidently shocked her, which he had intended to do, but he didn't count on the pain he saw in those beautiful eyes. It was not the first time he provoked another's pain, yet he was unable to explain the uncomfortable ache her sadness caused him.

Unwilling to accept the news, she looked at him. "I believe I would have known if the Melbournes left. We have been neighbors all of my life. I would have known." She said the last with such conviction, and Tristan found he was oddly pleased that she had not had contact with the man in all this time.

Tristan had spent months negotiating with the lord, who decided to hold out for all he could the moment he realized who was interested in the property. Apparently, Lord Melbourne had been so deep in debt that he had no choice but to sell off his ancestral estates. Tristan knew a desperate man when he saw one, and Lord Melbourne had been desperate. He eventually yielded to Tristan's way of thinking and settled on a fair price. Tristan was happy to be rid of the man, and even more pleased to find the daughter of Melbourne's deceased neighbor in his own backyard. Tristan studied the object of his thoughts for a moment longer, trying to catch another glimpse of those revealing eyes. She declined to look at him, but he wanted a reaction from her—any kind of reaction would please him.

"It seems we will be neighbors." He realized he had blundered when her spine stiffened, and she turned toward him. Anger marred her lovely face, and he guessed she likely suffered from temper when the mood struck, as it seemed to be doing now.

"You, sir, may now own this property, but I assure you we will be neighbors in no other way except that we share a border. I see no cause why we should ever meet again." With her back stiff and head held high, she turned to her impressively large stallion and mounted with surprising ease, her riding habit no hindrance to her.

He wondered if she rode with as much confidence as she showed him right now—he thought she probably did. "There is no reason why we can't be civil to one another, Lady Alaina. After all, I now own half of your favorite lake." He couldn't seem to stop saying all of the wrong things, but he was enjoying himself. She stared down at him from her elevated height and looked him over with a mixture of what he thought to be disgust and perhaps admiration. But there was only anger behind her next words.

"I have plenty of ponds on my own property."

"Then why are you here?"

"That, sir, is none of your business." She turned the horse, spurred him forward, and once she broke through the trees, she sent the horse into a suicidal run, one which she surprisingly had complete control over. Tristan followed her with his eyes until she rode over the hill and out of sight.

"A most interesting woman." He turned to his horse and

stroked his muzzle. "What do you think, Admiral?"

The horse whinnied and nodded his head. "I agree, old boy." His gaze returned to the hill where she had been moments before. "I agree." Tristan mounted his horse with equal ease and turned to continue the inspection of his property.

Five

Alaina pulled Noble to a halt on top of the hill overlooking Claiborne Manor, her hair in complete disarray from the thunderous ride. Her face was still flushed with anger and brightened from the cool wind. She was not upset with the man named Tristan but disappointed she had not been aware of the sale. She should have known, but after she returned from Ireland and news reached Lord Melbourne about the murders, he had come to her in a fury. Youth and inexperience had been her enemies as she stared into space with blank eyes in her mother's parlor while he shouted every vile thing to her that he thought of. The servants had taken it upon themselves to remove the man from the house. Her aunt and uncle had not yet joined her in the country and thinking back to that time, she wondered why.

Alaina shook her head in an attempt to erase the awful memory from her mind and gazed out over the only place she had ever loved. Too much of life and the tragedies it brought filled her past, erasing her innocence and burdening her with responsibility that should not have been hers. She accepted the responsibility because she trusted no other to preserve her parents' legacy.

The manor remained tall and proud with the stone, brick, and mortar in a good state, and the fences mended regularly. The gardens continued to bloom under Alaina's skill and gentle encouragement, and once her uncle began racing and winning, she had expanded the stables to accommodate his additional horses.

The tenants whose families had lived on the land for generations continued to work their plots, and each year the rewards were great for all involved.

Her thoughts drifted back to the man she had met less than half an hour ago and realized her sorrow was not for the loss of her neighbor. She never liked Lord Melbourne, but she did not want to lose the one last hold she had with Braden. She might never have visited his home after he was gone, but knowing it was still his made her feel closer to him somehow. Now all of that had changed. She nudged Noble's flanks, setting him into a slow canter and rode up to the stables, where a groom waited. Alaina dismounted and rubbed the horse's forehead before leaving the stable.

Once inside the house, she headed directly for the staircase, but her progress was halted by the sound of her aunt's voice coming from the parlor.

"Alaina dear, have you returned?"

"Yes, Aunt Charlotte." She regretted that her hot bath would have to wait a while longer.

"Would you please come in here for a moment?"

Alaina turned to enter the parlor but stopped a passing chambermaid to ask her to ready a bath for her in her room. Whatever it was her aunt had to say, she was determined to be out of there in ten minutes or less. She entered the room and found her aunt sitting on her favorite chaise, partaking of her afternoon tea, a custom Alaina had not fully enjoyed since her mother's death. She glanced down at her dusty clothing and refused a seat. Instead, she stood near the window and waited for her aunt to speak.

"How was your ride, dear?"

"Eventful."

Noticing the lack of attention her niece was paying to her, Charlotte made no hesitation in making her point. "I merely wanted to remind you of the ball tomorrow night at Hillcrest. You had not mentioned anything about your dress, so I assumed you had forgotten."

Alaina had not forgotten. She just did not want to go. "I

thought you and Uncle Sebastian planned to leave for London tomorrow morning."

"Your uncle's plans have been postponed a fortnight. I was sure you wouldn't mind. We haven't been to a ball in months."

Alaina knew this was an old argument and one she preferred to accept rather than upset her aunt. With her stubbornness subdued, she reluctantly agreed to accompany them.

Her aunt nodded approvingly.

"On one condition, Aunt Charlotte."

Charlotte held her teacup suspended over the saucer. "Now Alaina—"

"No attempts to play matchmaker. I'll change my mind here and now unless I have your promise."

After a moment, Charlotte nodded her agreement.

"If there is nothing more, I have a bath being prepared." Alaina started for the door.

"Go, child. Relax. And I will see you at dinner."

With a dreary spirit and already regretting her decision to attend the ball, Alaina slowly walked up the stairs and down the long corridor to her suite of rooms. The decor had changed over the years to reflect her growing tastes, but the rooms still held the memories of childhood. Her large copper tub stood to the side of her dressing room, steam rising from the water that one of the young maidservants from the kitchen was still pouring from buckets. The maidservant left the room, quietly closing the door behind her. Alaina always preferred to bathe herself.

Alaina quickly undressed and sank down into the hot, soothing bath water. *Heaven.* The scent of lavender wafted from the steam, and she smiled to herself, mentally thanking Daphne for stocking her favorite oils.

She managed to show a little enthusiasm when her aunt spoke of the ball during supper, and it even seemed her uncle was looking forward to the event. Once she was able to escape back to her rooms, she quickly changed into her nightclothes, splashed her face with water, and sank her weary limbs into bed. Though her body begged for sleep, her mind remained painfully alert as she was plagued with thoughts of an amber-eyed gentleman on a tall stallion.

THE SUN PEEKED IN through the slightly open curtains covering the ornate French doors that opened to the second-story terrace. A light chill permeated the air, and Alaina curled up in a tighter ball under the covers in an attempt to ward off the morning cold. Someone rustled around in the room, and she knew it would be Daphne, preparing her clothes and hopefully bringing her breakfast. Hearing her own stomach rumble, Alaina withdrew from the comfort of her bed linens and with a mumbled "Good morning" to Daphne, spied her breakfast of hot chocolate, toast, and marmalade. Her stomach growled again, and this time Daphne heard the rumbling and turned to her mistress.

"Not enough to eat last night, my lady?"

"I was not hungry."

"A poor night's sleep as well, I see."

"Excuse me?"

"Well, it being so late, I figured you didn't sleep well and needed the extra time this morning."

Alaina looked outside again, noticing for the first time that the sun settled near the center of the sky. She panicked. "What time is it, Daphne?"

"It's almost eleven, my lady." Daphne walked around the bed to fluff a pillow and lay out Alaina's dressing robe. "The rest of the house has been up for a while now, but your aunt instructed me not to wake you."

"Daphne, you know I don't like to sleep late. You should have wakened me. I can't believe Aunt Charlotte allowed me to stay in bed." Alaina quickly poured a cup of chocolate and spread marmalade on her toast. She then inhaled her breakfast, stopping only long enough to talk when Daphne gave her an odd look.

"I'm hungry and I'm in a hurry. If someone had wakened me on time, I would not be in such a rush." She finished breaking her morning fast and wiped the crumbs from her face.

Daphne appeared not to be in the least affected. *This is what happens when servants have been in a family's employ for so long that they have no worry of dismissal.* It was lucky she had been ill and unable to accompany them to the ball that dreadful night ten years ago. Otherwise, Alaina might not have her now.

Daphne finished with her mistress's clothing and left the room with the empty breakfast tray.

Refusing to waste one more minute of the day, Alaina walked to the French doors and opened them wide, stepping out to the terrace to breathe in the brisk fresh air. She gazed out over her gardens and the hills behind the manor, taking in all the beauty the day promised.

"A nice ride is just what I need," she said aloud, grateful that the ball was nearby and she had plenty of time to prepare. Alaina was about to turn into the room when she spotted someone walking around in the garden—her garden—and it was not the gardener. The man stood with his back to her, and from that distance, all she noticed was the soft brown color of his hair, his straight back, and a confident walk.

"Wait a minute." She watched as the man began to turn around. "Why that odious man." Realizing she was talking to herself, Alaina took one last look at Tristan and rushed inside to dress, not caring that her hair hung down her back in wild disarray. The ice-blue dress she pulled on tied in front so she managed at least to do that by herself. She was more concerned with why he was here, and why no one had informed her.

What was he doing here anyway? She thought it possible that her aunt had learned of their new neighbor and invited him over, but it would have been unusual to do so without telling her. While she mulled this over, Daphne walked in as Alaina slipped her feet into dark blue slippers.

"You will not leave this room looking that way." The maid dragged Alaina back to the vanity table and pushed her onto the bench.

"Daphne, I do not have time for this. There is a man in my gardens."

"Yes, there is and he is here to see you. I came up to inform you of his arrival, but you will not leave this room until we have done something with this hair." Daphne brushed Alaina's long flaxen locks, making them shiny and the curl more prominent, and in the interest of time, brought up the sides with pearl-encrusted pins. Daphne looked her mistress over, nodded her approval, and before she said a word, Alaina hurried out the door and rushed down the stairs.

Goodness. With the way they treat me, I may as well still be a child. Alaina thought about the man she was about to approach and decided to give him a few points in his favor, for anyone who favored waiting outdoors rather than in the confines of a parlor could not be without some redeeming qualities.

Tristan enjoyed the morning sunshine and admired the gardens he had been walking through for the past fifteen minutes. He did not mind the wait, as this was an unexpected visit, and he loved spending the time outdoors to enjoy the workings of a talented gardener. His own mother excelled as an avid gardener, and he remembered spending countless days as a child, playing outside while his mother applied her gentle touch to the plants. Tristan leaned over to inspect a particularly lovely and unusual rose when he heard the soft footsteps on the stone walkway behind him.

"I see you've discovered my new roses."

Tristan turned at the sound of the voice he clearly remembered and stopped short as his admiring eyes moved up and down the woman standing before him. Her hair shone in the morning sun and the contrast to her blue dress made her the most beautiful creation in the garden.

"Good day, my lady, a pleasure to see you again."

"Good day to you, sir."

"You are free to call me Tristan."

"And you are free to call me Lady Alaina."

The twinkle in his eye lent him a boyish charm, and she found she could not glare at him when he looked so adorable. "What prompted this visit today?"

"The nature is for pleasure. I realized after your abrupt departure yesterday that I wanted to see you again, so here I am. Now about these roses . . ." He turned his attention back to the flowering bushes, not giving her a chance to reply. "Where did you find such a color?"

Curious now more than ever as to the real nature of his business, she entered the conversation. "I created them." She smiled at the surprise on his face. "It's a hobby of mine. That particular shade of blue took me months of cultivating and cross-pollination."

"I'm impressed. It's beautiful."

Alaina believed he meant it, not just by the admiration in his voice, but by his simple appreciation for the rose as he bent to inspect it more closely. She giggled, the sound foreign to her ears.

"What's so funny, my lady?"

"You smelling the roses that way—it reminded me of my father."

Her voice took on a note of melancholy. He straightened up to take a closer look at her, but she quickly rid herself from whatever spell she'd temporarily fallen under.

"Alaina." He addressed her by her given name, ignoring her previous statement. "Have you always been interested in horticulture?"

"Very much so." She seemed to have forgotten she was talking with someone she did not like. "My mother started these gardens when she married my father and moved to Claiborne Manor. I loved spending time with her and soon found horticulture was something I loved as much as she did. Our growing gardens required us to hire two more gardeners just to keep up with the place, and it has become what you see now." She indicated the landscaping around her. "A few years ago, the staff declared it outshone even the finest parks in London and is known as 'The Park' to our neighbors. The rose you admired comes from a collection I keep in the greenhouse. It was the first one I attempted to bring outdoors to test its hardiness against our English weather."

Tristan noticed as she began her story of how the garden came to fruition, she took on a new demeanor and seemed momentarily lost in another time. He also noticed how she spoke of her mother and father, evidence of her love for them and sorrow for their loss. He tried to keep the conversation moving as they walked toward her greenhouse.

"My own mother loves gardening, and there isn't a day goes by when she's in residence that she doesn't spend a few hours digging in the gardens, dirtying her skirts with flowers up to her elbows. She was never much for the socializing whirlwind of the city." Tristan's smiling face and revelation of his mother's love of flowers eased her mind, and she found herself relaxing in his company. Today had been the first time she recalled speaking of her parents without waves of sorrow and guilt sweeping over her—sorrow for their loss and guilt because she survived.

She looked up at him and he added, "I admire a woman who is willing to wear a little dirt." He turned down to look at her and was pleased to note he didn't have to turn very far. He'd never realized the advantages of a taller woman until now. He felt the smile form and the newfound energy flow through his body. He realized what he was doing and mentally berated himself, taking a step back. *What am I thinking? I'm supposed to be gathering information, not mooning over the object of my questioning. Good saints. Mooning?* He cleared his thoughts and attempted to steer the conversation back in the necessary direction.

"And your father . . . does he enjoy gardening?" she asked him, though the question didn't sound as though it was asked easily.

"My father passed on some years back—a fever took him. My mother remarried shortly after, and she now has two younger ones at home to keep her busy—twin girls."

The intimate and unexpected confession aroused her sympathy.

"I was sorry to hear of your own parents' death."

Alaina looked at him with surprise. "Daphne certainly took a liking to you to have supplied that information."

He didn't correct her assumption that the maid had told him.

"It was long ago, and I suppose it no longer matters who knows." She spoke the words quickly as though they conjured painful memories she preferred not to discuss.

"How did your father catch fever, if you don't mind my asking?"

Tristan realized a desire to ease her discomfort, even if it brought forth his own painful memories. "One of our new foals at the time had found its way into the pasture and caught a hoof in a mud hole. It was storming at the time, but my father had refused to come in until he had set the foal free. He had been out there a long time and when he finally came in, he was soaked through. The cough developed the following morning and became worse over time."

The half-lie came as easily as it always did. Tristan felt her hand on his arm in condolence, but she quickly removed it when he looked down at where they joined.

Alaina's experience with intimate conversation between men and women was limited to those with Braden and her father, and she found that though she enjoyed it, she was unwilling to divulge equal amounts of information about herself. *I came out to scold this man and send him on his way*, she thought, *not make friends*. But somehow she was loathe to leave his company. They reached the greenhouse and he opened the door, allowing her to enter first. Once inside, he closed the glass door securely behind him and followed his guide while she walked calmly into the indoor gardens.

"One who enjoys the outdoors such as you may find the exotic plants beautiful."

"Exotic plants?"

"My parents traveled a great deal, and my mother fell in love with a variety of botanical species on some of the islands. My father brought some of them back as a gift to her. They are unable to survive our changeable climate outdoors, so she had a greenhouse constructed for them. I've added a few species of my own from acquaintances who have traveled abroad."

By the manner of her voice, he assumed she had never left their island.

"Why is it you have never traveled?"

"What makes you think I haven't?"

"You speak with longing, as though you wish you were the one to have discovered the plants and bring them back yourself."

His perceptiveness surprised her. "You're correct, I have not traveled except once to Ireland, but otherwise I have not ventured farther than London. This is where I am happy."

"When were you in Ireland?"

A shadowed look crossed her face and just as quickly, it was gone. *Perhaps I imagined it?* Tristan thought.

"A long time ago."

Her tone told him she would speak no more of it, but he pressed her. "Did you go with your parents?"

She was quiet, and he thought perhaps he had pushed her further than she was ready to go, but then she spoke.

"Yes."

That one word held a great deal of pain, and Tristan decided to let it be—for now. He found himself not wanting to depart from her company and took the time to study his surroundings. Overwhelmed by the beauty around him, he realized this was not an ordinary hothouse such as he had seen before, but rather it reflected an outdoor garden. He found himself walking on a cobbled pathway absent of long tables holding neatly potted plants. On either side of him grew rows of the exotic flowers she had mentioned from her parents' travels. Tristan had done some traveling himself but had never seen most of these species. He found himself in awe of the beauty and of the woman who stood beside him. A small wishing pond sat in the center of the structure with cobbled and dirt pathways leading in different directions, each path lined with rows of various flora and small trees.

Two stone benches had been placed near the small wishing pond, and he wondered if she sat there often. He saw no gardener inside the building, and Tristan discovered he was alone with her.

"This is amazing, Alaina. Absolutely beautiful. I've never seen such a thing."

Alaina seemed pleased with his reaction.

"Thank you, Lord Sheffield."

"Tristan."

"Excuse me?"

"My name is Tristan. I'd like you to use it."

She hesitated a moment. "It's hardly appropriate, but very well, Tristan. Does this make us friends now?"

His voice took on a soft timbre and his words sounded smooth like honey and hot tea. "I like to think so. I do not share such personal information as I have with you today to just anyone."

Pleased with his response, yet still wary of his delving into her own feelings, she battled her inner thoughts for a moment. She had been prepared to despise this man simply because he bought her childhood friend's home, but perhaps it was better to have it gone to a man like this than to stay in the care of Lord Melbourne. She longed for someone to talk with outside of the tea party gossip her aunt preferred and decided that having him for a friend could be wonderful.

Tristan waited patiently while she mulled over her thoughts, and he took the time to examine the fountain—a truly magnificent sculpture—of a fairy, her wings intricate and spanning, her long hair flowing, her hand holding a wand. It was remarkable workmanship and he wondered about the sculptor.

Alaina broke through his inspection of the art. "We should return to the house. Perhaps you'll consent to join me for lunch?"

Realizing he was famished, but only for the woman beside him, he regrettably declined. "I must be on my way. There are matters to attend to back home."

"What are your plans for the Melbourne residence?"

"I have a few changes I will be making to the grounds, but nothing unworthy of the property, I assure you."

"Of course, it will bear your name now, and I imagine conditions will improve for the tenants. Lord Melbourne was worthy to be neither a landowner nor landlord."

Tristan agreed with her, having seen for himself the condition of the tenants' homes and the poor use of land due to a lack of supplies and funds from the lord. All of that would now change.

They stepped outside into the dim light as it peeked through the clouds, and Tristan turned to Alaina.

"Will you be at the Hillcrest ball tonight?"

"Yes, why do you ask?"

"Curious nature."

"Are you acquainted with the marquis and his wife?"

"We've met." He gave her a smile capable of melting the heart of any debutante, and he bid her a good day.

Alaina walked slowly up to the house, confused as she watched him leap gracefully onto the saddle as he rode his beautiful steed down the drive and over the hill. She had no idea why he would have asked such a strange question and then be curt in his reply. Alaina wasn't paying attention when she walked into the hall and nearly collided with a young maid. Normally, the staff stopped and spoke with her for a moment, or at least acknowledged her, but this young maid curtsied and shimmied away before Alaina could apologize. *Strange*, she thought, for she didn't recall ever seeing the young girl before.

Six

andsome and mysterious. Alaina ran the comb through a curling section of her hair, her eyes turned away from the reflection in the mirror. *He is certainly charming. I would not be opposed to—*

"Alaina, dear, are you ready?" Charlotte walked into Alaina's room, impatient in her movements.

"Yes. Daphne is just finishing my hair. Is Uncle Sebastian waiting?"

"He was about ten minutes ago and then decided to call the carriage around. I'm certain he is down there with his coat and hat on in the foyer. Never was a patient man, your uncle."

Alaina noticed her aunt's unusually frantic behavior and watched as she rearranged items on Alaina's nightstand. She then walked over to the bed and smoothed out Alaina's silk cloak. *Aunt Charlotte seems to have an excess of energy tonight,* Alaina mused and watched in the mirror as Daphne tucked the last few strands of hair into a clip.

"My dear girl, you're lovely." Charlotte's nervous energy seemed to dissipate, and she walked over to her niece for a closer inspection, obviously pleased with what she saw.

Her aunt actually beamed. Alaina turned back to the mirror and had to admit she felt wonderful—more than she had in a long time. The carefully chosen gown of blue silk with a gossamer overlay fit her svelte form to perfection. The higher cut currently in fashion accented Alaina's smooth neck, and the clothier had cleverly draped the sleeves, allowing a hint of creamy shoulder to show. Daphne had skillfully pulled her hair up, leaving a few curls to drape over her shoulders, and as a last touch, added two silver pins into the coiffure. Alaina's blue eyes seemed even darker next to the dress, and her fair hair created a lovely contrast to her glowing skin.

"You're a dream, my dear." Her aunt helped her into her cloak. "An absolute dream. Now, let's be off before your uncle decides to leave without us."

The carriage ride to the ball lasted a short time, for which Alaina was grateful. She pushed aside the cloth covering the carriage window to see that much of society had ventured into the country for this event. A footman opened the carriage door and assisted Alaina down from the conveyance. The cool evening air welcomed Alaina. *I wonder if anyone would notice were I not to stay inside for long?*

The ballroom glittered from every angle and the sweet scent of honeysuckle wafted in from the open balcony doors. With no end of people gathering into one room, even one as spacious as the Hillcrest ballroom, Alaina longed to step back outside. After her aunt introduced her to the marquis and his wife, Alaina found herself pulled into the ballroom where the new arrivals stood to meet with new and old acquaintances before moving to the dance floor or refreshment tables.

Alaina allowed her aunt a bit of leeway, if only to give herself time to figure out how to escape her aunt's unnecessarily watchful eyes and endless social introductions.

"Lord Croxley, allow me to introduce you to my niece, Lady Alaina Claiborne."

"Lady Alaina, it is a pleasure to meet you." Alaina found herself facing a handsome man who appeared to be nearly twenty years her senior.

"Lord Croxley." She offered a slight nod. "And from where do you venture this evening?"

"From London, though I've been in the country since yesterday. I have a small hunting cottage that I escape to as often as business permits."

"I understand the need for seclusion, which is why I live my life at Claiborne Manor rather than venture to the city myself."

"Do you find the city distasteful?" Croxley seemed to study her as though dissecting every word she spoke.

"Not on principle." Alaina glanced around the ballroom in search of someone—or something—more interesting than the lord, who attempted to hold her attention. She listened with little interest as he said something about hunting foxes. Her gaze swept the ballroom and then abruptly came to a stop when she saw him. Lord Sheffield stood at the entrance, speaking with the host, and he must have sensed her gaze on him because he met her eyes and returned her glance with a warm smile. Alaina was once again interrupted by Croxley, who attempted to regain her attention, but when Alaina turned back to look where Tristan had been a moment before, he was gone.

"Lady Alaina?"

Alaina turned back toward the lord and her aunt, and the conversation to which she obviously was not listening.

"Yes, Lord Croxley?"

He appeared annoyed, but Alaina did not care and went back to searching for Tristan.

"The hunt tomorrow. Would you allow me to be your hunting companion?"

"I do not hunt, my lord." She left him with nothing more to say. "It was lovely meeting you, my lord, but if you'll excuse me." She began to move away but he reached out and gripped her arm.

Alaina looked at her aunt and saw that Charlotte noticed the impropriety of the action. Grateful that her aunt preferred to avoid scenes, Alaina did not argue when Charlotte firmly clasped Alaina's other arm with a polite dismissal. Croxley ignored the subtle hint and kept his attention on Alaina, glancing only once at the older woman.

"Might we take a walk, my lady? Some fresh air perhaps?"

Alaina couldn't believe the audacity of the man, and something in his eyes brought back dark emotions buried deep.

A vague recollection of memories triggered in the back of her mind, and it was suddenly imperative for her to leave his company.

"You forget yourself, sir. Now please remove your hand."

"My lady, I meant no offense. I simply wanted to escort you around the ballroom, or perhaps you would care for some punch instead?" He still had not released her. She twisted her body away until his hand dropped, and not wishing to cause a scene, Alaina spoke as cordially as possible.

"I thank you for your offer, sir, but I am not thirsty. Now if you would excuse us." She disengaged her arm from her aunt's grasp, took hold of her arm, and gently pulled the older woman in the direction of their hostess and the small group of ladies she was entertaining. She wondered where her uncle was, until she caught sight of him at a table in an anteroom. *He is likely winning another horse off an unfortunate fellow.* She noticed her aunt wanted to say something, but Alaina stopped any conversation with a sharp look. Her aunt started a conversation with the other ladies and let the matter drop.

Too bored to stay and listen to the mundane gossip of London society, but wary of running into Lord Croxley again, Alaina looked around in search of the punch table, because regardless of what she had said, she needed refreshment. Alaina excused herself from the group of women, and found her way through the crowd to the service table. She took the offered glass from the servant, enjoying the cool drink as she glanced around for someone she might recognize. As well liked as she was, Alaina realized she did not know many people beyond mere acquaintances, due to her self-seclusion from society.

"Enjoying yourself, Lady Alaina?"

Recognizing the voice from behind, Alaina turned to find Tristan Sheffield, looking both annoyed and charming.

"I should be grateful you aren't familiar with my given name while my family is near. What is the scowl for, my lord?" Alaina was almost amused with his annoyance until she heard his answer.

"Do you often allow strange men to handle you in public?"

"If you had looked more closely, sir, you would have noticed it was not something I invited."

"In that case, the old chap needs a lesson in manners." Tristan turned as though he was going to go off and find the offensive lord when Alaina put a gentle hand on his arm. He quirked a brow up at her feeble attempt to stop him.

"Trying to save the old chap from a bloody nose, my lady?"

"Hardly," she replied honestly. "However it wouldn't do to make a scene over something so trivial." Her hand still rested on his arm, almost tensely now.

"Did he bother you in any other way?"

"Actually, no." Alaina paused a moment. "Although there was something disturbingly familiar about him—I just can't recall, though my aunt seemed to know him."

"Will you dance with me?"

"Excuse me?"

"Dance with me." He took the hand still resting on his arm and placed it in his own.

"I don't dance, my lord." She tried to remove herself from his hold. It felt a little too good there.

"By choice or fault?"

"By choice."

"Then why come to a ball?"

"The punch, of course." She managed to bring a smile to both of their faces, but the smile quickly left when he began leading her to the dance floor. Looking down at the dance card she had kept carefully guarded thus far, she drew her gaze back up to the now unsmiling man who wasn't paying her any attention at all. She turned in an attempt to discover the reason for the scowl forming on his face, and when that failed, she said, "Tristan?"

Tristan heard her and tore his gaze from the object of his present discord and focused on Alaina.

"Your pardon, my lady, I fear I was momentarily distracted. Shall we dance now?"

Not fooled by his sudden change in mood but more interested at keeping him away from the dance floor, she questioned him. "What left you wearing such a fierce scowl a moment ago?"

"I do not scowl."

"Yes, you do. Your eyes looked fierce and unknown toward someone or something just now. Who was it?"

"I believe your question is about to be answered." Saying no more, Tristan moved to half block Alaina from view of someone walking toward them. Growing impatient with the man, yet unsure of what brought on this sudden display of protectiveness, she stayed at his side for the time being.

"Lord Sheffield, what a surprise to see you in the country."

"Not as surprised as I am to see you here tonight."

Alaina was shocked at the venom behind the words and looked over Tristan's shoulder to see who bore his dislike. She wished she had not.

"Lady Alaina, once again a pleasure."

"Lord Croxley." She acknowledged him tersely and took another sip of her punch, not noticing the pleased look on Tristan's face when she stepped closer to him. Alaina was surprised her aunt had not yet made an appearance to pull her away from a situation that an unmarried young lady would do best to avoid.

"Is there something I can do for you, Croxley?"

"No. I am here to seek out the lady's hand for the next dance."

Alaina turned and was about to offer an excuse when Tristan came to her rescue.

"The lady is already spoken for the next dance." Tristan locked eyes with Croxley and the latter glared back. With one last perusal of Alaina, Croxley excused himself and disappeared into the crowd.

"What was that all about?"

"What?" Tristan watched the crowd into which the other man disappeared.

"I know why I wanted to avoid him, but you . . . there's no mistaking your hatred for the man."

"That goes without saying."

Tristan obviously was not willing to offer up any more

information, but she remained persistent. "You seem to know Lord Croxley well."

Tristan continued to stare at the crowd.

"Have you been acquainted with him long?" she tried again, this time with some result.

Tristan focused on her bright blue eyes for a moment before responding. "Alaina, do not concern yourself with Croxley, and avoid his company whenever possible."

"Why the concern, Tristan?"

He smiled at the ease with which she now used his name. "Croxley is a man with one purpose and that being an unsavory one to discuss in your company. Please, just keep a good distance from him." Tristan looked intently at the woman beside him, but he was not oblivious to the crowd around him, nor was he surprised when Alaina's aunt joined them. He made it a habit to know his neighbors, though seeing her now in close proximity, it appeared the years had been kind to Lady Winston.

"My dear, I have been looking all over for you," Charlotte said.

Alaina wondered if her aunt realized she'd been within sight the entire time. "I'm sorry, Aunt Charlotte, but as you can see, I am perfectly safe." She heard her aunt mumble something and then watched her eyes focus on Tristan.

"Aunt Charlotte, please allow me to introduce a friend. The Duke of Sheffield, Lady Winston. The Duke is our new neighbor."

"A pleasure, madam." Tristan bowed his head slightly and offered Lady Winston a warm smile.

"Indeed, young man, but my niece said 'neighbor.' Why the only neighbors our estate has ever had were Lord Melbourne and his son."

"I have purchased the Melbourne estate, but I was unaware he had a living son with him." Tristan turned to look at both Alaina and her aunt but moved his eyes quickly back to Alaina when he saw her beautiful rosy complexion slowly vanish.

"Alaina, are you all right?" Tristan asked.

Charlotte realized her mistake in mentioning Braden. It took

Alaina a minute to realize they were speaking to her.

"Yes, I'm fine. Would you please excuse me?" She skirted her way through the crowd as quickly as possible until she reached the ladies' retiring room. Tristan and her aunt both followed her from the ballroom but stopped near the entrance.

"Perhaps I should go in after her." Charlotte moved toward the hallway.

"Wait." Tristan stopped her. "What happened in there?"

Charlotte looked first to Tristan, then to the closed door, and then back to Tristan. Charlotte was torn between keeping her silence and using this man to her advantage. Tristan waited patiently for an answer, but by the look of him, Charlotte doubted he possessed the quality in abundance.

"It was the mention of Lord Melbourne's son." He said nothing, and she continued. "His name was Braden. He died when Lady Alaina was ten and he no more than fifteen years old. They were the best of friends."

Tristan knew this much. What bothered him was the way Alaina had reacted. He had only etchings of information about her parents' death and the death of the young boy, but because no one was caught, and at the time Alaina had not been forthcoming with information, the authorities had only a sketchy view of what really happened. Tristan planned to change that.

"How did he die?"

Charlotte knew if she told him anything more, she would be risking her niece's trust and a plan ten years in the making. She thought it was a risk worth taking, since her efforts to match Alaina with Lord Croxley appeared to have failed.

"He was murdered, I'm afraid."

This should have shocked Tristan, but this much he had also known. What he did not understand is why Alaina reacted so severely. He needed to know that—he needed to know everything. *How in the hell had a ten-year-old girl managed to escape with nothing more than a few scratches and bruises?*

Seven

Charlotte motioned for Tristan to follow her into an open sitting room and sit on the settee next to her. Almost everyone had deserted the anterooms for socializing in the ballroom, which left them nearly alone.

"Lord Sheffield, it is not my place to tell you the things I am about to say, but my instincts tell me you could be of assistance to my niece, and therefore I will trust you with this much. I will warn you, however, if you use this information to harm her in any way, you will regret the day you moved into Melbourne Manor."

Somewhat amused and curious by the threat coming from such a dainty lady twice his age, he smiled slightly, not doubting for a minute she would follow through with her threat.

"My lady, I assure you I will do everything in my power to see that no harm comes to your niece."

"We shall see. Alaina has never completely recovered after what happened to her parents or Braden, and I fear its haunting has prevented her from finding her own peace and happiness in life." Charlotte told him what she knew of that night and to his dismay, it was nothing more than what he already knew.

"Why was Alaina not in the carriage with them?"

"Well, she was."

"How then was she not harmed?"

"I don't know much except that somehow Alaina was thrown from the carriage when it rolled down a hill, and she landed in some bushes. That is what she told the authorities at the time, and she refuses to speak of it anymore."

"Then how is it she was there and yet you have no idea what

happened? It's been ten years." Tristan wanted her to tell him something new.

"She doesn't remember, and if she does, she's trying not to."

He had suspected Alaina's resistance to recalling past events and now knew the only way to get answers would be from Alaina herself. A noise drew Tristan's attention away from Charlotte. Both occupants of the room turned to see the object of their discussion standing in the doorway. Alaina did not appear pleased.

"I'm sorry, Aunt Charlotte, but when I couldn't locate you in the ballroom, I began searching these rooms." She studied the pair suspiciously. "Is everything all right?"

"Quite all right, dear. I didn't mean to be gone so long. How are you feeling? Do we need to return home?"

Alaina looked to her aunt and the man beside her. "I'm fine now, thank you, but yes, I wish to return home."

"Oh, well, of course, just let me say farewell to our hosts and we'll depart posthaste." Charlotte moved to the door when Alaina spoke again. "There is no reason for you to leave at this time. Uncle Sebastian is still trying to talk poor Lord Wallace out of his new mare. I will have the driver take me home and then return for you and Uncle Sebastian."

"Darling, it is late, and I will not allow you to go home unescorted."

Alaina's frustration began to show. "I am hardly in need of an escort. The driver is perfectly capable of providing necessary protection though I do not foresee the need on such a short ride. Please, stay and enjoy your evening."

"I can hardly allow such a thing, Alaina. There are too many dreadful people on the country roads at night."

Alaina saw that her aunt regretted the words the moment she said them.

"Might I offer a suggestion?"

Both women looked to the man who had been silent until this point.

"I had intended to depart early this evening as well, and since we are neighbors, might I offer my carriage and myself as escort?"

Charlotte nearly refused on the part of impropriety, but never having been one to pass on opportunity, she consented.

"That is a wonderful idea, Lord Sheffield. Thank you for your generous offer."

"Generous though hardly necessary." *And inappropriate. What is Aunt Charlotte doing?"*

"I insist, my lady."

"Very well. Good night and please give my apologies to our hosts." Alaina bent to kiss her aunt's cheek and waited to speak until Tristan left the room, saying he would get their coats.

"It won't work."

"What won't work, darling?"

Now she turned to her aunt. "I am aware of what you're doing, and I will tell you now it will not work."

"I have no idea what you are speaking of. Now have a pleasant ride home and I will see you tomorrow." She escorted the younger woman out of the room to wait for Tristan. He already waited at the door with the coats and helped Alaina into her black velvet cloak as the driver pulled the carriage in front of the house.

"Shall we go?" Tristan held out his arm for Alaina.

"Look after my niece, Lord Sheffield."

Tristan glanced at the woman on his arm, who presently ignored both of them. "I will. Good-night, Lady Winston."

Tristan helped Alaina into the waiting carriage and followed in behind her. He hesitated a moment before he sat in the seat opposite his companion and tapped on the roof, signaling the driver to start their journey. It was a quiet ride and the moon hid behind dark clouds, cloaking what little light it offered and leaving the interior of the carriage and its passengers in darkness.

"Tristan?"

"Yes?"

"What were you and my aunt speaking of before I walked into the room?"

"About the night your parents died."

The honest reply surprised Alaina. "She doesn't know much,

and it's hardly your business."

"As she said, and I apologize if you feel I overstepped."

"I don't know much either."

"I don't recall asking."

Silence.

"Thank you for your honesty. People still speak of that night, but they often lie about their curiosity."

"You're welcome." Tristan's eyes rested on the woman in the seat across from him, able to better view some of her features now that his eyes had adjusted to the darkness. He thought it best not to ask or reveal anything too soon. She would reveal her secrets when the time was right. Of that, he was now certain. Whatever held her back, whatever she feared, he vowed to break down the barrier.

Nothing more was said the remainder of the ride home, but the silence was comfortable and they soon pulled up in front of the manor. Tristan stepped down from the carriage first to help Alaina down and then walked her up the stairs to see her safely inside, the driver looking on from the carriage.

"Thank you, Tristan. Your kindness is appreciated. I did not wish for my aunt to miss the remainder of the ball, and as much as I try at times, I fear I do not enjoy society's pleasures as much as others."

"I confess I, too, find greater pleasure in the country life and avoid London until duty demands my presence there."

"Lord Croxley seemed surprised you were rusticating."

"Croxley doesn't know me."

She was sorry she mentioned the other man. "A duke uninterested in society. An interesting notion."

"I don't believe I mentioned being a duke, and our hosts are aware of my preference for going unannounced."

"You may refer to yourself as a mere lord, or even a mere mister, but young ladies, when away from the prying eyes and ears of their mothers, will speak at will. Although it was Henry who corrected me when he heard me call you Lord Sheffield. Don't worry, you are still Tristan to me until you say otherwise. You must have your reasons. I will admit my surprise that Aunt

Charlotte and Uncle Sebastian did not realize who you really are.

"Your butler knew the truth?"

"There's very little Henry does not notice. Why is it you never mentioned your title?"

"My title is not who I am. It is just something with which I have to live." He brought her hand up and pressed his lips to her soft skin. "Good evening, my lady."

Alaina watched from the open doorway and wondered at the peculiar situation in which she now found herself.

Eight

The morning brought a bone-chilling rain and the promise of continuing inclement weather. The spring air was icy and it took Alaina longer than usual to rouse herself from sleep—a dreamless sleep. Exhaustion won her over the previous night, and when she had laid her head on the feather pillow, nothing existed, save for the peace and darkness of sweet slumber. Groggily and without haste, Alaina left the bed and went to warm herself by the burning hearth. Sitting down in her favorite chair and covering herself with a shawl to ward off the morning chill, Alaina's mind wandered until she heard a light rap on the door.

"Enter."

"Good morning, my lady. Glad I am to see you up. I've brought your breakfast." Daphne entered the room with a cheerful demeanor and a tray heavy with food. "Your aunt wished me to inform you that she and Lord Winston departed this morning for London."

The news surprised Alaina. "London? But they did not return home from the ball until this morning, and they weren't supposed to leave until next week."

"They arrived home late last night, my lady, and there was a message waiting for Lord Winston requesting his presence in London. Your aunt decided to accompany him, and they did not wish to disturb you." Daphne went about straightening Alaina's bed sheets.

"How long ago did they leave?"

"A little over an hour ago, my lady."

A lord of no great inheritance, Uncle Sebastian had practiced law for fifteen years before he retired to breed horses, but his expertise was often sought for difficult government cases. Alaina was curious but focused her attention on breaking her morning fast with the toast and marmalade on her tray. Then she remembered something. "Daphne, have you met the new housemaid?"

"Yes, we've met, my lady. Has she done something wrong?"

"No, nothing like that, though I'm usually notified of the hiring of new staff, and when I nearly ran into her the other day, she seemed rather skittish."

"She is a mite shy. Her name is Bridgette, my lady."

"Do you know anything of her?" Alaina was not one to gossip with servants, but she counted on Daphne to know what she did not about the household servants. Something about the maid nagged at Alaina, despite the brief conversation with her aunt.

"Permission to speak freely, my lady?"

"You're going to say whatever you want anyway, so say it."

"Quite right. As you said, she is skittish, always dropping something, listening to conversations. She was even sweet on Timmy her first day here."

"Being sweet on the stable boy is hardly a crime."

"Yes, my lady, but I'll be watching her." Daphne was about to leave once more when Alaina again stopped her.

"Why was I not informed of her hiring?"

"If you remember, Samantha grew ill a couple of weeks ago. When she found out she was with child and she might be ill a while longer, your aunt thought to hire a temporary girl to help out until Samantha was back on her feet. Lady Winston must have forgotten, seeing as how the new girl is only temporary. Will there be anything else, my lady?"

"No, thank you."

With a silent nod, Daphne walked into the adjoining room while Alaina sat back to finish her chocolate and mull over the information. Alaina did not believe they needed a replacement, temporary or otherwise, and made a mental note to speak with her aunt.

Ten minutes later, Daphne entered from the dressing room,

where she had prepared Alaina's bath, and picked up the empty breakfast tray.

"I'm going for a ride this morning. Please have the stables ready Noble." Alaina walked into the dressing room with Daphne following behind her.

"It's raining, my lady, and it will only grow worse this afternoon."

"I'm aware of both the current and impending weather, but I'd like to visit Samantha in the village to see how she is coming along." When Daphne didn't say anything, Alaina turned to the other woman and conceded her position. "I will take the carriage."

"Very good. I'll see to having Cook prepare a basket of vittles to take with you." Daphne left the room.

Thirty minutes later, Alaina entered the kitchen, a habit her aunt found inappropriate, to check on the progress of the basket of food and was pleased to see it was packed and ready to go. The butler took the basket out to the foyer and passed it to the footman while Daphne helped Alaina into her cloak.

"I will return in a few hours if the weather permits. Otherwise I will stay in the village until it clears up."

The rain began to pound harder after the short distance to the village, and the driver had a difficult time finding a spot that would not place his mistress directly in a mud hole. He was at last able to help her from the carriage and escort her inside the small cottage. He then went out to pull the horses to shelter.

Alaina spent the next few hours with Samantha Porter and her husband since the weather did not allow him to cut timber. Their other child, no more than a year old, cried when Alaina picked him up, but she was soon able to coax a gurgle out of the young girl, and regretted having to give her up when it was time to leave. Before she departed, Alaina asked Samantha, "Do you have knowledge of a young woman called Bridgette who lives in the village?"

"I don't, my lady."

"There aren't many young women our age here, correct?"

"No, my lady, very few, in fact." Samantha softly rocked her baby. "Is everything all right, my lady?"

"Yes, of course it is. Thank you for your time, Samantha." Alaina smiled. "And take care of yourself."

Upon departing from the Porters' cottage, Alaina noticed a man standing a few doors down in an open doorway. She wouldn't have thought much of it except that his coat and boots were of exceptionally fine materials and couldn't belong to someone in the village. She ignored the prickling sensation in her spine as her driver helped her into her carriage and started for home.

The road had become muddy and difficult to drive during the time she had spent with Samantha, and the journey home promised to take twice as long. The carriage picked up speed and Alaina pulled back the curtain on the small window, noticing she was nearly a mile from home. The rain came down in torrents. She couldn't imagine why her driver chose to speed up now, especially in this weather. Alaina was about to poke her head out to yell up to the driver until the discomforting tingle came to her once again and sent her entire body into shivers. Her mind raced back to the only other time she had been in a speeding carriage, and she became numb with fear. The fear increased tenfold when she heard a shot muffled by the rain and then the shaking began. Alaina tried to remain in control, telling herself they were close to the manor and the driver would not stop if he could help it.

The reassurance gave her little comfort as another shot resounded, this one dangerously close to the carriage. She threw herself to the floor between the two seats and wrapped herself in a ball. It was a few minutes later when she realized the carriage had stopped, but she couldn't lift her body from its huddled form to find out what happened. The door opened and though she saw Tristan standing there, she remained stiff.

"Alaina! What happened?" Tristan carefully helped her up from the floor and on to one of the seats. "Alaina, answer me." He smoothed the hair off her brow as he looked at her ghostly pale face and tried to get some kind of response from her. "Alaina, please say something."

"I'm all right."

She managed to lift her head up, but her color had not returned and Tristan feared something deeper affected her.

"Alaina, you're safe now. Everything is going to be all right. I promise. We need to get you inside. Do you think you can walk?"

She barely nodded, and Tristan stepped from the carriage to help her down. She still had not left the seat. He reached in and lifted her out to carry her inside.

"Oh my goodness, Alaina!" Daphne ran down the steps past the butler. "What happened, Your Grace?" The frantic maid followed as her mistress was carried inside.

Tristan paused in his thoughts long enough to wonder how the maid knew who he was when he had only introduced himself as Lord Sheffield on his first visit. Setting that aside for now, he continued up the stairs.

"I fear there was trouble, but she is unharmed. Where are her rooms?"

Daphne began to protest.

"I'll find them myself." Tristan was unapologetic for snapping at the maid.

Daphne obviously thought better of her position and preceded him upstairs, opening the door for Tristan as he walked over to the four-poster bed and tenderly laid Alaina on the feather mattress.

"Alaina, can you hear me?" He held her, rubbing her hands together in an attempt to bring warmth to her quaking limbs. He noticed the slight nod, and Tristan held out some hope she would be all right. He noticed her lips move and leaned down to hear the words.

"Don't leave me. Please don't leave me."

"I won't. I'm right here." Tristan gingerly smoothed a knuckle over her cheek.

"Please, you must leave the room now." Daphne scooted around Tristan to lay a warm compress on her lady's forehead. "I must get her out of these clothes and into a hot bath."

"Put up a screen, madam, because I am not leaving this room."

"I will not allow this." Daphne sounded and behaved more

like a mother than a maid.

Tristan understood her reasons, but he was not leaving.

"I will step into the hall until she is back in bed, and then I will wait in that chair," he indicated the one by the hearth that Alaina had occupied that morning, "until your mistress is able to talk."

Daphne nodded tersely and looked pointedly from Tristan to the door.

He leaned over Alaina and spoke to her softly. "I will be right outside your door should you need me."

She nodded her acknowledgment and Tristan left the room. True to his word, he waited in the hall until Daphne stepped out some time later.

"How is she?"

"She is better, Your Grace, and said she wishes to speak with you now." Daphne hesitated a moment.

"What is it?"

"What happened? I haven't seen my lady in such a condition for many years and it frightens me." Daphne's distress over her mistress's current state seemed genuine, but Tristan refused to reveal anything to anyone until he found answers and until he discovered who in the manor wished to harm Alaina.

"That remains to be seen. Now I will speak with your mistress, and there are to be no disturbances."

"You do not belong in there."

"Yes, actually I do. No disturbances." He left no room for argument, and after he entered the room, he closed the door behind him.

"Alaina, are you still awake?" he asked quietly and walked over to the bed. He settled down on the quilts beside her and lifted her hand in his. She sat upright with her back against the pillows, and her color had returned to normal, as had her composure.

"How are you feeling?"

"I am better, thank you. I owe you a debt of gratitude for saving my life."

Tristan nodded, and lifting her other hand, he focused

intently on slender fingers as he absently rubbed her delicate skin.

"My concern was not just over your being chased—those men were run off easily enough. I am concerned over the condition in which I found you. Anyone would have been frightened, and you had every right to be, but when I found you on the carriage floor, you were barely breathing." He paused a moment. "It was as though you weren't really there."

"I don't remember exactly what happened after I heard the gunshots. I do remember seeing you in the carriage, and then I woke in my own bed." She stopped a moment to study their entwined hands, wondering why she had not pulled away. She looked up. "What happened today?"

"I heard a gunshot from my stables. When I went to investigate, I saw two men on horseback, chasing your carriage. I fired on them and raced to catch up with you. I fired once more and the men left. I then followed until your driver had you safely back home."

"I've never known highwaymen to attack this close to properties and homes, especially in daylight."

That is what worried Tristan the most. He did not believe they had just been highwaymen. He needed to get in touch with his contacts in London and inform them things were moving along faster than originally expected.

"I think you should probably rest now," he said, deftly changing the subject.

Alaina noticed but made no comment. The pounding in her head returned. "Will you stay for a while . . . just until I fall asleep?"

"I'm not going anywhere. Sleep now, my lady."

Tristan watched her eyes close and her body relax, although she never released his hand.

Nine

The moon shone brightly through the clouds of the dark night, and fatigue soon encouraged Alaina to fall into a deep slumber to the rocking motion of the carriage. She felt safe in his embrace and nothing seemed to disturb her. Her senses became aware of his strong arms, wrapping a little tighter around her. The carriage bounced as they hit a rut in the road, but she enjoyed his comforting warmth too much to let it disturb her. Then she became cold and her eyes opened, watching as her body rolled down a hill. No sound escaped her though she frantically sought a way to breathe. Strong arms pushed her toward the broken door as the carriage continued to roll. Somehow she landed on earth, coldness seeping through her clothes. Her head ached, but the source of the other pain remained elusive.

A bush. She had landed in a bush and the branches hurt but not as much as the pain inside of her. *What's happening?* She fought her way to the ground and then stopped moving. Silence shrouded the night.

Mama, Papa, Braden! What happened? She wanted to cry out from the pain, but instead, she covered her mouth with a scratched palm. She heard the subtle clinking of horses' reins and men talking quietly, but her body refused to move. Cold fear raced through her when she heard laughter, and finding a hole in the bush, she saw what had happened. The carriage lay on its side and she saw her papa lifting her mama out. She waited a moment longer, but Braden didn't come out with them. He must already be on the ground too. A man on one of the horses moved closer and she couldn't see her parents anymore, but when the man spoke, she could hear him. The light of the moon shadowed his face but his voice frightened her. Her parents came back into view and she saw her mother.

"Mama!"

"Alaina, wake up. Wake up, Alaina!" Tristan tried to hold her still as she thrashed out and called for her mother. "Alaina!"

This time the voice registered, and it took her a moment to remember where she was and what happened. She looked around her, trying to find solace in her surroundings. Then the tears came and those strong capable arms wrapped around her shaking body, and the soothing voice spoke softly in her ear as he rocked her back and forth. He held her until the tears became nothing more than slow breaths and finally a quiet sigh.

"Alaina?"

"I'm all right." She pulled herself away from those safe arms and looked up at the man who had somehow triggered the memories she had spent years trying to forget.

"Do you remember anything?"

"I'm beginning to remember too much."

"What do you mean?"

"The nightmares. They're back. I had been able to forget, but now they're back."

"Look at me." Tristan gently tucked a finger under her chin and brought her face around to meet his eyes. He placed his hands on her shoulders and waited until he had her attention. "What have you been able to forget? Your parents?"

She nodded. "I had the nightmares after I came home from Ireland, but the doctors gave me medicine and I forgot them. Now they're back and it's worse than before."

"Calm down." His soothing words helped her to relax, and she lay against her propped-up pillows.

"What happened? Why is it worse?"

She took a couple of deep breaths before speaking. "I only had the nightmares for a short time before I was given the medicine to help rid my sleep of them, but I never saw so much at one time. Tristan, I remembered his voice."

"Whose voice?"

"The man who killed my parents. I heard his voice, but I couldn't see him."

Tristan exhaled deeply. "Neither your aunt nor Daphne said you heard or saw what happened that night."

"They don't know because I didn't remember, or I didn't want to. It was the medicine, but I remember now. They gave me something to ease the pain, and I forgot, but since I met you, it has all come back. I don't know why."

Tristan processed the information carefully. It was possible she had unintentionally suppressed the memories and only now something triggered a reoccurrence. It was also possible for her to remember a voice, but something in her limited memory concerned him.

"You keep saying you were given medicine to make the nightmares go away." He gently took her hand in his own.

"Yes. I remember the doctor visiting, and he gave a bottle to Daphne from which I had to drink a little bit each night before bed. After a while I stopped having the nightmares."

Tristan had his suspicions about what was in the medicine, but now he wanted to understand what triggered this sudden onslaught of her nightmares.

"When did you start having the nightmares again?"

"The night we met. Only they were more like dreams or small pictures at first."

Tristan was somewhat taken aback by this, for he had only been with her a few moments that day by the pond.

"Did anything unusual happen that day?"

"I met you."

"I don't see how meeting a stranger could trigger these memories. Are you sure you did not see something or maybe someone said something to you? Try to remember."

"I do remember—very clearly—and it was a perfectly normal day, except my encounter with you." Then she stopped to think a moment.

"What is it?"

"That was the day you told me you had bought the Melbourne estate. I started thinking about Braden and rushed home."

"Melbourne's son."

"Yes." The constriction in her throat caused the word to come out choked.

Tristan felt a tightening in his chest at the thought of her in the arms of another man, no matter how young. "You must have been close."

She nodded. "He was my best friend. We played together, told stories, and shared lessons—he was a brilliant young man. He was with us that night, but I never saw him leave the carriage."

A sickening suspicion crept up on him. "Did you see your parents killed?"

She nodded again, but the expected tears never came. "I saw my mother fall and then my father was crying and then he, too, was silent."

A knock at the door sounded and without waiting for an answer, Daphne walked into the room, carrying a tea tray.

"It's time for His Grace to leave now, my lady."

Knowing the maid was right, and that he had already compromised Alaina in some way by forcing the staff to give him time alone with her in her bed chambers, he took Alaina's hand in his. "I must return home briefly to deal with some business, but I will return soon."

"Thank you. Will you come tomorrow then?"

"I will come sooner if you like."

"This evening perhaps, for dinner?"

"Until then, my lady." He leaned in to whisper to her when Daphne went to draw her mistress another bath. "I think it best if you didn't tell anyone what you have told me today."

"But, Tristan, I should tell Daphne—"

"No one. Please trust me on this."

"I trust you."

He smiled, kissed her soft hand, and left the room.

"Here, mistress, this will calm you while your bath is being drawn." Daphne handed Alaina her a delicate cup, steam rising from the tea. "Your aunt and uncle will be distressed when they hear of this."

"Oh, don't send anyone to London, Daphne. There is no reason to bring them home after they only just arrived." Alaina took a healthy drink of tea from the fine china.

"Very well, my lady. Your bath is ready when you are. I will be back later with your dress." Daphne left the room, and closed the door softly behind her.

"WOULD YOU CARE FOR a brandy in the parlor, Tristan?"

"A wonderful idea."

The pair left the dining room for the comfort of the parlor, where the fire blazed and the cushioned sofas invited relaxation. The butler poured a glass of brandy from the sideboard and handed it to Tristan while the maid brought in a tea service and then quietly departed.

"You don't care for brandy?"

"I fear spirits and I don't mix well. I simply cannot hold my liquor." She was enjoying the evening with Tristan and felt surprisingly refreshed. Tristan watched her smile and thought he had never seen a more beautiful smile. She didn't smile often enough. He had no wish to ruin the peaceful atmosphere, but they needed to continue their earlier discussion.

"Alaina, I'd like to ask you a little more about your nightmares, if you don't mind."

"Nightmares?"

"Yes, like the one you had this afternoon. About the night your parents died."

"I don't recall having a nightmare."

He was definitely confused now and couldn't understand what kind of game she was playing.

"I was here. You woke up screaming and then told me about the nightmares you've been having since the day we met." *How does she not remember?* She appeared genuinely confused and before Tristan managed to say anything else, the maid who brought the tea service reappeared in the doorway.

"Will there be anything else tonight, my lady?"

Alaina turned to the door.

"Not tonight, thank you, Bridgette."

"Might I bring you another cup of tea or perhaps another brandy for His Grace?"

"No, thank you, Bridgette." *The maid never says two words and suddenly she is eager to serve.* Alaina's patience wore thin when the maid continued to stand in the doorway. "Was there something else you needed?"

Tristan had moved closer to Alaina, a bit bewildered by the maid's behavior and perhaps a bit wary. He couldn't definitively say why, but she seemed oddly familiar.

"Oh, no, my lady, nothing."

"That will be all." Alaina's voice was stern.

"Yes, my lady." The maid turned and quickly existed the room.

"Odd. Has she worked here long?"

"No, she's only temporary while one of our servants recovers from her pregnancy. I'm not certain why my aunt hired another maid. We certainly don't need the help."

Tristan mentally filed away the young maid's name and turned to Alaina. "Back to the nightmare. How can you not remember what happened only a few hours ago?"

"All I remember is you left, Daphne brought me my tea, and then I went back to sleep."

Tristan raised a brow.

"I didn't realize you were still so tired."

"Neither did I, and I don't recall sleeping for long because when I awakened, the sun was just setting and my bath water still warm. This is most odd." Alaina confusion grew to frustration at her inability to recall details of the afternoon.

"I don't know what happened."

"Don't worry about it tonight. It's time I was on my way." *Before his contact left his estate.* "I have to ride to London tomorrow, but I will return in two days and we'll speak of this further. There are things other than your nightmares that I wish to discuss with you." Tristan bent and kissed her hand and made to leave the room.

"Wait."

He turned and waited while Alaina stood and walked over to him. "I'm not whole yet. A part of me is still broken, and I am uncertain of how to fix it. We have known each other such a short time, but you are the only one who understands my frustration enough to be of any help. The memories returned the day I met you, that much I do recall, and I don't know why they are suddenly gone again, but I need your help."

He saw a vulnerable young girl warring with a grown woman, each one watching her parents and friend killed as though it happened only moments ago.

"I will do everything in my power to help you, Alaina, and whatever has suddenly caused you to forget what happened today we'll resolve that as well." He cupped her face in his palms and rubbed his thumb against the smooth skin. "I need you, too, and I'm not going to lose you."

"I'm afraid I can't be who you need right now. I have nothing to offer and the past—"

"Do not worry about the past." He silenced her with a gentle press of his finger to her lips. "That will work itself out." Tristan's body reacted to the smoothness of her skin beneath his wandering hands, and he wanted to show her how he felt. However, it was neither the time nor the circumstances. Regardless of what he said about not losing her, he feared bringing his own tainted past into her life. *Has she not been through enough?*

"Alaina." He spoke her name softly and gently guided her face forward.

"Tristan."

He barely heard her as he lowered his mouth to hers in a gentle caress. She tasted sweet, and he caught the faint scent of violets on her. He pressed for entry into her mouth, gently tracing her lips with his mouth over and over until she opened her own and welcomed him in to continue his exploration.

Alaina was timid at first with this being her first kiss, but she soon found the rhythm of his lips and participated in the dance, allowing him to draw her inward. She allowed the exquisite pleasure to overtake her, losing control of nearly all her senses. She pressed herself up against Tristan and felt the eagerness of his body when he pulled her against him even harder. Running his hand over her back, he deepened the kiss.

A small moan escaped Alaina's lips, and Tristan knew it would take little encouragement to pull her over to the chaise and make love to her. She wouldn't object, but he imagined their first time differently. He slowed the kiss and lightly nibbled on her lower lip.

"Alaina."

"Mmm?"

"Alaina."

This time she came out of her daze and looked up at Tristan. As though she realized what almost happened, she blushed and stepped back.

"Tonight is not the right time for this lesson."

Her flushed cheeks, tousled hair, and dark, heavy-lidded eyes betrayed a woman ready to give herself. It was imperative that he leave before he changed his mind. She would have him in her life after all, and he vowed to spend every moment making up for his past misdeeds.

"What lesson?"

"You will see, my lady. For now, I must depart." He bent down to kiss her nose. "Will you do something for me?"

"Of course."

"Don't leave the manor alone. Take Timmy with you."

"What about Daphne?"

"No, I think it best if you take Timmy. Will you do this for me?"

"Yes, but I don't like this. I won't allow some person to take away my freedom nor will I be confined to my own home."

Alaina struggled, but he knew she would heed his request.

"I won't be long. Just two days."

"Very well."

"Good-night, my lady."

"Good-night, Tristan."

He left under the cover of darkness on his magnificent steed. From her place by the parlor window, she watched him ride off and remembered being in his arms just a moment before. She wished he had remained there to lend his strength. Alaina turned at a sound from the hallway, but no one stood by the door. Not wanting to stay in the room alone any longer, she took the lantern and went up to her rooms, and for the first time in her memory, she locked the door.

Ten

"Enter." Alaina called out to whoever knocked, and she looked up from the household accounts.

"I beg your pardon, my lady, but a messenger arrived with this." Daphne held out a small envelope as she walked over to the cherry wood desk and handed the missive to Alaina.

"Thank you." The maid nodded and excused herself from the room.

Alaina set her quill aside and opened the envelope to read a short, nondescript message from her aunt.

Alaina,

An old acquaintance delayed your uncle, and we extended our time in London. We will return in a fortnight.

Aunt Charlotte

How unlike them, but there is plenty to keep me busy while they are away, she thought as she looked back at the books she had promised herself to work through.

Later that evening, Alaina took her meal in the study as she continued to work over the household accounts. Charlotte had been seeing to the chore of late, insisting that Alaina not worry over trivial things. Alaina hardly considered the management of one's household trivial, but her aunt seemed to believe it was her contribution, and Alaina had conceded.

Now that her aunt and uncle were gone for a short time, she decided to catch up on a few neglected tasks. She had been trying to figure out her aunt's method of calculating, and it had taken all afternoon to decipher what should have been simple household accounts. She checked and rechecked every column. It was frustrating that the columns failed to add up the way they should. Alaina had always been proficient in mathematics, and she knew there was more money spent than was necessary to run their household.

Finally deciding to complete the task tomorrow and ask her aunt about the books when she returned, Alaina set aside her quill and stood to blow out the lanterns around the room. Since darkness had descended while Alaina had been lost in her work, she left the room with the remaining lantern, closing the door behind her. Cool air caressed her face and a chill crept slowly up her spine.

Am I imagining things? Alaina turned around quickly, the lantern held high. "Is someone there?"

She wasn't prone to fantasies, nor did little sounds tend to bother her, but she always trusted her instincts, and right now the faint prickles coursing up her spine made her pause. Alaina felt a strange tightness in the pit of her stomach—an unpleasant tightness. The butler usually left a few candles lit in the halls whenever Alaina remained downstairs late, but darkness cloaked everything save for the single lantern she held.

Not wanting to remain downstairs alone, she quickly climbed the stairs and went to her chambers. The lights had been extinguished in there as well, and only a few embers remained in the fireplace.

"This is all too odd." Walking to the hearth, she placed a few more logs inside and stoked the fire, bringing a soft glow to the room. Shrugging away the suspicion that she was not alone, she moved to her bureau and pulled out her nightclothes, which Daphne had neglected to lay out for her. The maid never forgot to do anything. Not bothering with the dressing screen, Alaina went to the bed and laid out her nightgown while she undressed. When she finished, she stoked the fire a bit more, set the lantern on the small table next to her bed, and pulled down the covers. It had been a long day. *Perhaps exhaustion is causing my mind to play tricks on me.* Her eyes closed in an attempt to hurry sleep.

Someone is in this room.

Alaina turned the words over and over in her mind.

Keeping her eyes closed so she wouldn't startle whoever might be with her, Alaina steadied her breathing and prayed for the person to leave. The sound of someone losing their footing and bracing their fall on a bedpost escalated her fears. Opening her eyes a fraction, she saw the culprit had lit a candle and the soft glow of the light moved slowly toward the side of the bed. The light barely broke through the darkness, but the shadows the light cast appeared feminine.

Thinking perhaps Daphne had forgotten something earlier and was trying not to wake her mistress, Alaina opened her eyes just as the person reached the side of her bed. She now saw the person's face as they placed the candle on the bedside table. Alaina experienced momentary relief when she recognized the individual, and then gasped in shock as strong arms pushed her onto the mattress.

"What are you do—?" Alaina cried, but her protest was cut off by the damp cloth pressed onto her mouth, and she struggled for only a moment. Then there was only blackness.

TRISTAN STOOD AT the front door of Claiborne Manor waiting for someone to answer his rap at the door. When no one came to the door, he knocked again and took another glance at the nondescript carriage in the drive. The door opened behind him, and he turned to find a rather glum-looking butler standing before him.

"Good day, Henry, I'm here to see Lady Alaina." Tristan entered the house and handed his coat to the butler.

Tristan took a closer look at the butler. "Whatever is the

matter, old man? Are you well?"

"Quite well, Your Grace. It's Lady Alaina."

"What about her?"

The butler didn't say anything at first, and Tristan's instincts told him that something was seriously wrong. *What possibly could have happened in two days?* He moved to shake the butler into speaking, but a loud voice from behind halted his steps.

"Who are you, sir, and what business do you have here?"

Tristan turned to see Daphne and a familiar man standing in the doorway of the study. His panic grew tenfold, but he was able to hold it in check. The man recognized him and walked over to where he stood in the foyer.

"My apologies, Your Grace. You are not who I expected to come through those doors." He shook Tristan's hand.

"What is going on, Sergeant Dunby? Where is Lady Alaina?" He looked to first Dunby, then Daphne, who still stood in front of the study, fidgeting with the edge of her apron.

"She's missing," replied a grim Dunby.

"When? How?" Tristan couldn't decide if his anger stemmed from everyone's incompetence or his own decision for leaving her alone.

"The maid found her gone this morning," offered Dunby, indicating Daphne. "She told me she went to deliver the lady's breakfast but found her gone. From the look of things, she had been sleeping, and the only sign of struggle were some mussed up blankets."

"Her blankets?"

"They were thrown everywhere, but I found no blood and nothing was broken. Other than a few clothes lying on the chair, the room appeared normal according to the maid."

Tristan processed this information and his anger grew as he played every possible scenario in his mind. He ignored Dunby for a moment and turned to the butler. "How did this happen, Henry? Did you hear nothing?" He then turned to the maid. "Daphne, you retire after Alaina. Was there nothing you heard?"

Both the butler and maid looked apologetically to Tristan, but it was the butler who spoke.

"I heard nothing. I should have done something. Lady Alaina sometimes remains in the study late at night. I lit the lanterns in the halls and we all retired for the evening. I should have stayed down there with her." Henry shook his head in pain. "My deepest apologies, Your Grace."

Tristan merely nodded to the older man, wishing everyone would stop "your gracing" him.

"It is not your fault, Henry. We will find her and bring her home."

"Yes, Your Grace." The butler's worry was apparent, as he turned and walked toward the back of the house.

"Sergeant, will you please join me in the study?"

Dunby followed Tristan into the room, barely glancing at Daphne on the way, and closed the door behind him. Tristan looked around where Alaina had been working late into the night.

"When did they call on you, Dunby?"

"They sent the stableboy around this morning." Dunby stepped up to the large desk, his eyes briefly glancing over the papers he had skimmed during his initial inspection of the study. "Members of the staff have informed me that you have spent some time in the lady's company recently. Is this true?"

"Yes. However, business took me away to London for a couple of days." Tristan paced. "What I don't understand is why her aunt and uncle are absent. She had been expecting them the day after I left, which is why I felt comfortable enough leaving."

"Yes, well, her maid informed me that on the day they were to arrive, a messenger brought a letter for Lady Alaina, informing her they planned to stay in London for a fortnight. I couldn't find any such note during my search of the study or the bedroom, but the staff seems to have been aware of the change in schedule."

"Have you found anything else?" Tristan circled the desk.

"Not yet, but I wasn't through questioning the maid when you arrived."

"I'd like to join you if you don't mind." Tristan moved back behind the desk, his eyes on the stacks of paper and open ledger.

What am I not seeing? "Did you open the ledger or was it lying open like this when you arrived?"

"It was open."

Odd.

"I'd better get to that interview. I am not going to throw jurisdiction at you on this one. You're likely to find out what's going on more quickly than I, since you are acquainted with the lady."

Tristan looked over at Dunby. He had known the man for more than fifteen years, being just a young boy when his father introduced them at a horse race. They had been helpful to one another over the past few years, and Tristan knew he could trust Dunby to keep his confidences.

"I appreciate that, but right now I just want her found, and I'll use every resource available, including the locals."

Dunby nodded and stood up to find Daphne, who waited in the hall. Daphne was motioned into the room, and she closed the door behind her. Tristan waited for her to take a seat at the sergeant's invitation, while Tristan remained behind the desk and Dunby stood by the window.

"I have just a few more questions, ma'am," promised Dunby. "You said that you didn't hear anything out of the ordinary. Is this correct?"

The maid nodded, glancing at Tristan and then back to the sergeant. "As Henry mentioned, we had retired to our rooms before the mistress."

"Isn't that a bit unusual for no one to be awake when she was downstairs?"

"No, sir, Lady Alaina sometimes remains downstairs late in the library, even when her aunt and uncle are home. It didn't seem unusual for her to be in here so late. She gave us leave to retire." Daphne nervously tucked her hands into her pockets, and Tristan noticed her skirt bunched up where she kept grabbing the cloth.

"What time was that?" asked Dunby.

"We remained downstairs until approximately ten o'clock. Henry lit the lanterns and then we retired."

"Was there anyone else in the manor that night?"

"The cook, but she left about half past eight for the village to visit her daughter, and the two upstairs maids live in the village and left at eight." Daphne stopped her twitching, but she still appeared distressed. "Then there's Bridgette, but I assume she left at eight o'clock with the other girls."

"Who is Bridgette?"

"The temporary downstairs maid Lady Charlotte hired a short time back, sir. She also lives in the village."

"Is she here so we might speak with her?"

"No, sir, she sent word her brother was sick, and she required leave for a few days."

Tristan thought back to the other night when the skittish maid had come into the parlor, remembering her strange behavior and now her absence. It was all too coincidental. Tristan didn't believe in coincidences. He stood when the sergeant excused Daphne. Dunby looked down at his notes for a moment and then turned his attention to Tristan.

"What do you think?"

Tristan hadn't spoken throughout the entire interview, but Dunby knew he was thinking. Tristan was just like his father had been—always one step ahead of everyone else.

"I'd like to find this Bridgette, and then find out where Lord and Lady Winston are."

"The maid said they were still in London."

"I'd like to confirm that. Besides, they need to be notified." Tristan looked thoughtful for a moment. "Sergeant, if you wouldn't mind sending men out to search—" Tristan held his hand up when Dunby was about to interrupt. "I'm sure you've already done that, but I want it done again." Dunby knew the authority the young man wielded, and friend or not, Tristan was better at this than he.

"I'll be on my way, and I'll inform you if anything turns up."

Tristan nodded and shook the man's hand, showing him to the door.

Henry and Daphne had disappeared for the moment, but when he found Henry, he asked the butler to make the staff available in the event he needed to question anyone. Tristan then took the opportunity to do some investigating of his own. First, he asked the butler to call in a stableboy to deliver some correspondence for him. Tristan could have sent them from home, but he was unwilling to leave Claiborne Manor until he searched the entire house. He needed information, and no one was better at wheedling out unwanted information than Charles Blackwood, an old chum from Eaton and Oxford. He sent a message requesting another friend, Devon, to come posthaste. With their help, Tristan knew he could uncover the people responsible for all the wrongdoings and find Alaina.

Once the letters were sent, he began his search of the house, beginning in Alaina's chambers and working his way down the halls, catching only a quick glimpse of either the maid or the butler. They kept to themselves, not questioning what he was still doing there. The house appeared to be the same as when he left a couple days ago, except, of course, Alaina's room. The blankets were in the condition Dunby mentioned, but nothing else had been touched. He suspected the messy blankets had been caused in part by Alaina's fighting whoever had taken her, and by the kidnappers trying to find one to cover her.

It was well into the evening when Tristan concluded the first part of his search and left for his own home, instructing Henry that no one should be permitted into the manor, and to notify him if anything out of the ordinary happened. If Henry thought it odd that Tristan gave orders, he said nothing. Servants were not in the habit of questioning a duke.

The following morning Tristan returned to Claiborne Manor to find things exactly as they had been the previous evening. He shrugged away Henry's assistance, thanking the man, but he wished to go through everything himself. Daphne told him that Alaina had been in her study late into the evening, and Tristan wanted to find out what kept her attention.

Three hours later, he finished reading through the papers and documents in half of the desk drawers. He wished her aunt and uncle would answer his summons and return home. He needed their help in looking around the house, and he needed some answers. Bent over the contents of yet another drawer, Tristan was lost in his own thoughts and didn't hear the two men enter the room behind the butler.

"Your Grace," Henry interrupted.

Tristan looked up but kept his expression bland. "Thank you, Henry."

The butler left and Tristan rose to greet his guests with a hug and a slap on the back.

"Charles, Devon. It's good to see you both." He stepped back and tried to smile for his friends, but it lacked honesty. "Thank you for coming."

"Your message said 'urgent,'" replied Charles, "and we were close."

"Give him a chance to explain, Charles." Devon turned a circle to look at the room. "Then perhaps he might tell us why we are here."

Tristan looked at his longtime friends. "The secrecy was necessary, and I need your help finding someone."

"Intriguing," said Devon. "Who might this someone be?"

"Lady Alaina Claiborne. She went missing two nights ago. Dunby has been here, but there are too many gaps for my liking, and no one seems to know anything."

"Where is her family?" asked Charles.

"She has an aunt and uncle who I hope are on the train from London. I sent a telegram yesterday to inform them of her disappearance." Tristan dragged a hand through his hair in frustration.

"Claiborne? The name sounds familiar," said Devon. "This wouldn't be Christopher and Clara's daughter?"

"Yes, it would."

Charles leaned against the edge of the desk. "I didn't realize you were going to be in such close contact with her during your . . . ah . . . investigation."

"Plans change." Tristan offered nothing more.

"What do you want us to do?"

It didn't matter who asked. Tristan looked at both men and smiled. The three of them had been through much together over the years, and their friendship had never wavered.

Thirty minutes later, the two men were out the door, and Tristan resumed the task of going through the papers on the desk. With thoughts of Alaina going through his mind, he closed the last drawer and picked up what looked like the estate account books. Tristan couldn't help but wonder why her relatives had not, at least, answered his telegram.

Eleven

The offensive odor roused Alaina from her delirium. Soft pattering reached her ears, followed by a low grunting. Her hands reached out to touch the stiff fabric of whatever she lay on, and she immediately pulled them back. The aching in her head became worse when she attempted to open her eyes, but she managed to adjust her sight to the dimly lit room.

Where am I?

Alaina slowly sat up and scooted off the edge of the hard cot, then sat back down and lifted her feet up. Peering down, she watched a small rat scurry across the floor. Taking in deep breaths, she checked the floor for any other surprises and stood up. It took her a moment to find her balance.

Bridgette! Alaina remembered. *But why?*

She walked carefully across the dirt floor to the narrow door and pounded. "Someone's out there. Bridgette? Answer me!"

Alaina continued to hammer her fist against the door, ignoring the throbbing in both her hand and head. "Open—"

The force of the door opening hurled her backward, and her foot stepped on something soft that squealed.

"Shut your mouth!"

Alaina scrambled to rise and found herself face to face with a grotesque man. "Who are you? I demand to be released."

"You shut your mouth, I said!" The brute stepped toward her, but Alaina held her footing.

He's likely to kill me anyway. "I don't care what you said. Do you know who I am?"

He took another step forward and laughed, revealing yellow

and black teeth.

Oh heavens, that breath! Please kill me first. She wanted to close her eyes, but she refused to give him that advantage.

"You're my reward once they're done with you."

"When who is done?"

He hefted his large shoulders. "They paid me to watch you, so I'm going to watch you—then I'll have you."

Alaina took a couple of deep breaths to stop the bile from rising in her throat, but the only air in the small room was tainted with stench. "I won't fight you. Please, tell me why I'm here."

He paused a minute and then smiled. "Don't suppose it matters if you know or don't know." He laughed. "But I don't know why. The rich man said to keep you here, and I'll keep you here."

Rich man? "The woman who brought me—is she here?"

"I wanted her, too, but she went away. She wasn't pretty like you." He reached out as though to touch her. Alaina finally stepped back.

"You won't fight me now." The man laughed and stepped toward her again.

Stupid brute with no brains. Alaina slapped his hand away and dropped to the dirt, groping around for anything she could use as a weapon. Her body wanted to gag, but instead she grabbed the rat as it brushed against her hand.

The brute lifted her off the floor, but when he turned her around Alaina threw the squirming rodent and ran.

"Bloomin'—"

Alaina cut off his words with the slamming of the door. She fumbled around for the lock and latched it. The door nearly vibrated from the hammering of his fists.

Please don't let there be anyone else. She ran down a small corridor and into another door. *Not locked.* The cool night welcomed her. Her feet landed upon dirt, rocks, and twigs that dug into the soles of her bare feet but still she ran. Holding her skirts up, Alaina splashed through a small stream and continued to run. Her breathing quickened until it became too difficult for her legs to move through the field. The cold earth welcomed her body when she stumbled over a rock. She lay there, waiting, until her mind went black.

"IS SHE DEAD?"

"Not yet." The woman knelt down and pushed aside the golden hair. "Take her back to Claiborne Manor."

"We can't, Bridgette" The younger man pulled Bridgette up. "We weren't even supposed to stay here. We were told—"

"I don't care anymore, Sidney." Bridgette lowered her voice. "We can't do this to her. Mama would turn in her grave if she knew what we'd done."

"You know what he'll do to you," Sidney said. "He didn't give you a choice."

"I had a choice, and I chose wrong." Bridgette grabbed his arms. "I tried, Sidney, I did, but I can't do this. They said they only wanted to ransom her, but that man we left her with . . . she can't go back to that place."

Sidney shook his head. "If he finds out—"

"We don't matter to them, and no amount of money is worth our souls." Bridgette embraced her brother. "Please take her home."

"What do I tell them?"

"That a man—a lord—told you to return her, and then return the carriage to the pub in the village."

"I don't like this."

"Please. You have to know this is wrong."

"I know."

"Help me." Bridgette saw the lights go on in the ramshackle house across the fields. "Hurry." She lifted Alaina's legs while Sidney raised her limp body. Together they carried her out of the field and lifted her into the waiting carriage.

"Why doesn't she wake up?"

"She must have hit her head on something when she fell." Bridgette turned to her brother and embraced him once more. "Wait. I am coming with you. She will need help and it is two days journey to the manor. You can't stop and care for her on your own."

"They know who you are. If she wakes up—"

"I have belladonna that I can give to her." She watched Sidney's eyes grow wide. "I'll be careful with it, I promise. You may stop in the village, just before the manor, and I'll wait there for you."

She climbed into the carriage and positioned herself so that Alaina rested against her.

"WHAT IS THE MEANING of this? What is going on here?"

Five days had passed and still no new information had surfaced. Tristan had been home only once to gather clothes and speak with his butler. He had fallen asleep in Alaina's study more than once, and the dark circles under his eyes attested to the poor sleep and lack of appetite. Devon and Charles had arrived two hours ago without news and had been talking with Tristan when the angry voiced interrupted their conversation. They stood as an older couple entered the room.

Tristan stepped forward. "I trust you are Alaina's uncle?"

"Of course I am. Now tell me what you are all doing in my house, and where is my niece?"

"Your Grace, what are you doing here?" Charlotte repeated her husband's question in a gentler tone.

"You know this man, Charlotte?"

"Yes, Sebastian, this is the Duke of Wadebrooke, though Alaina introduced him as Lord Sheffield. I apologize for not knowing who you were sooner. This is my husband, Lord Winston. As you can see, my husband and I are confused by this situation. Please tell us what is going on here." Charlotte appeared too calm for someone who had just arrived to find a strange man taking up residence in her house.

"Lord Winston, my lady, I surmise you did not receive my telegram, or you would not be surprised by my presence in your home. I had expected you days ago. Your niece is missing." Tristan no sooner said these words, when Lord Winston had to hold up his wife who had fainted—he looked peaked himself.

Sebastian glanced up at the three men, but his anger remained focused on the man standing behind the desk.

"I received no telegram, and it's not your concern, but my wife wished to remain over in London for a house party. Now, you have no right to be here. You are trespassing and must vacate this property before I call the sergeant, duke or not."

Alaina's uncle didn't stand much taller than his wife, putting him a head shorter than Tristan's six feet. Despite his lack of height, he was a man who had obviously spent many hours outdoors, attested to by his tanned skin and barrel chest. His hair might have been graying at the temple, but he would likely prove a formidable opponent—for someone else.

"Lord Winston, I apologize for the circumstances under which we have met, and for the situation we now find ourselves in, but your niece is missing and that is of greater import than calling Sergeant Dunby who is at this time searching for your niece." Tristan watched the emotions play over Lord Winston's face. He still held his wife, who appeared to be coming out of her faint. He left her in the maid's care to walk over to the desk, still ignoring the other men in the room, who seemed content to remain ignored.

"Please excuse me. I fear the shock of your news caused me to lose my temper." Sebastian held out a hand. "Perhaps you may tell me how this happened."

Alaina's uncle slumped down into a chair. Tristan sat across from him and told him everything he knew from the moment he had arrived, including his conversations with Dunby and the servants, and the arrival of Devon and Charles. Lady Winston returned halfway through the briefing.

"It appears my wife is acquainted with you on some level, but I wonder, why is it you concern yourself with my niece?"

Tristan studied the man for a moment before he answered. "I have recently acquired the Melbourne estate and had the pleasure of meeting your niece shortly afterward. We became friends, and I am concerned for her welfare." Tristan said nothing more for he did not want to jeopardize everything they had worked for up until now. He watched as Sebastian took his turn studying him carefully.

"I appreciate what you are doing to help find my niece. I do not know what I would do if anything happened to her."

Sebastian was clearly a strong man and managed to quell his emotions, but Tristan knew he suffered. Lady Winston remained silent throughout the conversation, doing little more than touch her husband's hand and hold a kerchief to her nose.

Sebastian continued. "I have connections through London, and I will notify them immediately to help in any way they can."

Tristan thought this over for a moment, knowing he did not want outsiders involved but wishing not to draw suspicions. Tristan merely nodded in agreement, left the couple in the study, and escorted his friends out. When they reached the front door, Devon turned to him with a solemn expression.

"I have to return to London in the morning and will check in with the detectives you hired there." He looked over Tristan's shoulder toward the study door and then back to his friend. "Do you trust them?"

Tristan wasn't surprised by Devon's question because he had asked himself the same thing. Their extended absence was still a matter to be resolved, but he didn't believe Alaina's uncle had anything to do with her kidnapping.

"For now, but I have more questions for them. I don't want to raise suspicions at this point. In fact, I need to ask you both if you would be willing to—what the hell?"

All three men now turned their attention to the long drive where a carriage raced toward the house, the driver barely able to control the team. Two grooms ran from the stables, having spied the runaway carriage, and reached the drive in time to see the team head straight for them.

Tristan bounded down the front steps with Devon and Charles right behind him just as the driver managed to skid the carriage to a halt. The horses reared back, and it took both grooms to settle them.

"What in the bloody hell were you doing, man?" Tristan yelled up to the frightened driver. "You could have killed someone."

"I'm sorry." The driver's voice and body shook. "I only did what I was told."

Tristan stopped in his tracks, as he was about to throttle the man, and looked up at the driver. "What do you mean? Who told you to come here?"

"He didn't tell me his name. I was only supposed to make the delivery. I don't know anything more. I swear." The driver was shaking and Tristan knew real fear when he saw it.

Devon called out, "Tristan, you'd better come over here."

Tristan moved over to the side of the carriage where Devon held open the door while Charles stood behind him. The latter moved toward the open door, but Tristan was quicker.

"What the devil? Alaina, can you hear me?" Tristan carefully stroked her hair. Her eyelids fluttered open for a moment and then closed again. She breathed steadily.

Holding her in the carriage, Tristan attempted to wake her while Charles waited outside to help him when the time came to lift Alaina down. Devon questioned the driver who still claimed he knew nothing. A man paid him a large sum to make the delivery and that was all he knew.

When Alaina finally showed signs of consciousness, and Tristan found no visible injuries, except for a few bruises, he handed her to Charles and then took her back in his arms. He carried Alaina inside, passing her aunt and uncle, and ignored Sebastian's attempts to reach his side. Tristan did not stop as he climbed the stairs quickly to reach Alaina's chambers. Charles passed from behind to push open the bedroom door, and Tristan rushed in, depositing Alaina gently on the bed.

Daphne ran into the room behind them, took one look at her mistress, and thought to intervene. "Your Grace, please leave me alone to care for her. I'll call for you once she wakes."

Nearly two hours later, Tristan returned to the room to sit beside Alaina while Charles occupied Lord Winston and his wife downstairs. Devon had volunteered as chaperone after Sebastian insisted the duke not be alone with Alaina. Alaina's eyelids fluttered again, and Tristan spoke her name as he continued to stroke her hair.

"Tristan?" Her raspy voice sounded painful, and Tristan looked over at his friend who poured a glass of water from the tray Daphne had left behind. He handed the glass to Tristan and then moved back over to the hearth.

"I'm here, Alaina. Drink this." He carefully lifted the back of her head as he placed the glass to her lips, urging her to drink.

She coughed a few times, the pain in her throat unbearable, but she had to speak with Tristan. Alaina urged the fuzziness in her mind to go away and tried to ignore the pain of her body as she attempted to sit up.

"Careful, Alaina, stay down."

"Tristan," she began. It hurt too much to clear her throat but she continued, ignoring the pain. "I saw who it was."

"Who did you see?"

"I saw the maid, Bridgette. I never asked my aunt about her." Those few words had been torture for her to speak.

Tristan eased her farther into the pillows. "We'll speak more later. Rest now."

The doctor arrived and immediately went to work.

"You'll both have to wait downstairs. Send in one of the maids."

Tristan hesitated, but when the doctor crossed his arms as though to delay treatment until he left, Tristan followed Devon downstairs. When the pair entered the parlor, Charlotte jumped up in outrage.

"I demand to know why I have not been allowed to see my niece. This is our home, and you have no right to keep her from us by locking us out."

"Charlotte, sit down and calm yourself." Her husband looked at the men as though wondering the same thing.

"I wanted to be certain she remembered what happened to her. The doctor is now with her and will allow her visitors later." Tristan's words failed to pacify the couple, but they kept quiet. He said nothing more to them for the moment and walked into the hallway with Devon.

"If it would help, I can delay my departure," Devon whispered to his friend.

"No, you've been delayed long enough. And I'd still like to know if our men in London have found anything. We have Alaina back, but we still have no answers. Charles is here for now, so we'll make do until you return."

Devon watched his friend. "What are you thinking?"

"I'm not certain if we can trust them." Tristan kept his back to the study door. "Do you remember hearing about the details of the Claibornes' murder?"

Devon nodded. "It was before our time, but agents still speak of it. Why?"

"Something about the stories from then, and the stories I'm hearing now don't add up."

"Do they ever?" Devon put a hand on his friend's shoulder. "We'll find out what happened. I know what this case means to you, and what it meant to your father. We'll find them."

Tristan nodded but remained silent.

"I'll see myself out," Devon said to his friend and left the manor.

There were still too many unanswered questions, and Tristan wanted this resolved. It was no longer their investigation alone— these men had changed that when they added a kidnapping charge to their list, and Tristan had no doubts the same people responsible for the kidnapping were the ones he sought. He still had not figured out the connection, but he believed it had something to do with the death of the Claibornes, the Melbourne boy, and Tristan's own dark past.

Shortly after Devon left, the doctor came downstairs to report his findings. Alaina bore some bruises and a few cuts but nothing too serious. She had been severely dehydrated and malnourished during her absence, and the doctor recommended she try not to speak for a few days until her throat had a chance to heal. She slept now and was not to be disturbed until morning. The doctor left a few more instructions for her care until he returned in a few days to check on her. He collected his fee— paid by Tristan—and departed.

Tristan did not want to leave without speaking with Alaina, but he knew she needed her sleep and he desperately needed some of his own. Besides, it was not likely that her aunt and uncle would grant him and Charles hospitality for the night. He informed the couple of his intention to return in the morning, and after pulling the butler aside, telling the man to send someone to him if anything happened, Tristan and Charles left the manor.

They were a half a mile away from Tristan's stables when he spied something to the right of his vision. He looked more closely and noticed someone sneak away from his stables and hurry toward the trees. Tristan urged his stallion into a run. He was closing in when the man leaped on the back of a horse and ventured deeper into the trees. Tristan knew from his exploration of the property that a stream ran on the other side of those trees. He wanted to catch up to the man before he reached the water.

Charles had also seen the man, and when Tristan had gone after him, he rode to the stables to check for anyone else.

The culprit turned around to see Tristan closing in on him and lowered his head closer to the horse, urging the animal to move faster. A shot fired out and Tristan fell from his horse while the other rider broke through the trees and crossed to the other side of the stream. Tristan hit the ground, a jarring pain shooting through his arm and side. He landed on a patch of grass—small blessing though it was—and grabbed his arm. He pulled his hand away to reveal blood slowly seeping through his coat. The bullet had gone completely through the flesh on the underside of his arm, just barely missing his chest. Swearing at the pain as he tried to stand up, Tristan whistled for his horse, but he lacked the strength in his arm to pull himself up easily. After many failed attempts, he managed to gain leverage by using his good arm and slumping over in the saddle. He saw Charles coming through the trees, and Tristan looked at his friend wearily.

"The bastard got away, but there had to be another one who took that shot." Tristan gingerly held his arm against him.

"There was. I found him a few hundred yards away from here, and he's tied up in the stables now. Billy's watching him,"

Charles said, referring to his friend's stableboy. They made their way back to the stables only to find no one around.

"Where did you leave them?"

His friend pointed toward the door. "Right over there, by the haystacks."

"Billy?"

Silence.

"Bloody hell." Tristan painfully slid from his horse with another jarring thud, and led the stallion into the stables, handing the horse's reins to Charles.

"Billy, Jacob?" He called for both the groom and his driver. *What the hell is going on around here?* He then heard a thud coming from one of the stalls.

"Billy, is that you?"

The noise grew louder, and he and Charles approached the stall. When Tristan pushed the door open, he found both men on the ground, hands and feet tied together. Charles pulled a knife from his boot and cut through the ropes, setting the men free.

Once free, Jacob pulled the cloth from his mouth. "Your Grace, those blokes surprised us and when we came to, the man was gone and we were trussed up like turkeys."

"How many were there?" The throbbing in Tristan's arm and side increased.

"Two of them, but they were all covered up in black—we couldn't see their faces." It was then Jacob noticed Tristan's shoulder. "Blooming hell, look at your arm. We'd best see to that. Billy, you see to the horses there for Lord Blackwood and report to the house."

Tristan allowed Jacob to issue the orders, Charles looking on in amusement, until he too noticed the color on Tristan's face. He handed both horses over to Billy and followed the other two men into the house.

"I should call for the doctor." Jacob attempted to dress the wound, and though there was not a bullet, Tristan had two holes in his arm and a cut across his side.

"I don't need a doctor. Just patch it up." The pain eased

slightly after drinking the brandy Charles thrust at him. Tristan mumbled something about wasting good brandy and took a sip. The sip turned to a healthy portion when Jacob stuck the needle through his flesh. When the servant finished the stitching and padded the arm, Tristan lay back in the chair and turned to his friend.

"Obviously my little stream jumper turned back and brought a friend with him."

"Or two more waited in the shadows in case things fouled up," countered Charles, his friend only nodding at the possibility.

Tristan stood up and walked from the room into the library. He lay down on the long sofa while Charles and Jacob stood behind him.

"Wake me if anything happens," he said as his head hit the cushion.

"You wouldn't hear the house fall down."

"I heard that, Jacob. Charles, you know what to do," Tristan said, not waiting for or needing a reply.

Twelve

ristan arrived the following day as promised. Jacob complained that Tristan would pull his stitches if he rode and refused to saddle the stallion. They finally compromised and Tristan took the carriage. He did not fully believe himself capable of sitting a horse yet.

Since Charles left the previous evening for London to meet up with Devon, Tristan traveled alone. Tristan entered Claiborne Manor only to find Alaina sleeping. The doctor had given her a sedative to help her rest, and she wasn't expected to wake anytime soon. Frustrated, Tristan returned home and then sent Billy with a message to an investigator to meet him there. He arrived three hours later.

"I'd like you to look into another matter. My man found this last night when he followed the culprit who shot at me." Tristan handed him a gold chain with a small ruby pendant.

The investigator raised a brow in question.

"The necklace belongs to Lady Alaina Claiborne. I harbor no doubt that her kidnapping, and the incidents on my property last evening are directly related, and I want to know how and why."

"I will get back to you as soon as I discover anything." The man lifted something from his pocket. "As to the other item of business . . ." He set an envelope on Tristan's desk and left.

The single sheet of paper contained a date, a time, and a location, but nothing else. His thoughts drifted toward the night of Alaina's kidnapping. The maid and butler said she stayed in her study late into the evening, and Tristan remembered finding papers and account books spread out on the desk. Then there was the driver who claimed he knew nothing. When they asked where he was supposed to return the carriage, he gave them the address of a pub in the village where the remainder of his payment waited. They searched the carriage and did not find a sign as to whom it might belong to or where it had come from. Alaina had told him she saw Bridgette come to her room that night, but the maid was nowhere to be found at the moment.

Tristan paced the study while his frustration mounted. They looked everywhere and the only one with the information they required was Alaina. He must see her, even if he had to force his way through. Tristan also wanted to speak with Charlotte Winston about her choice to hire Bridgette, and he thought now a good time to ask them about the note they sent Alaina about their extended stay in London. London was a short ride from here and a courier could make the trip in a few hours riding at a good pace. His reply should have been received and responded to the following day. Tristan had spoken to the man he had sent the message with, confirming the success of his trip. The messenger located the Winstons' London home without difficulty, but the couple behaved as though they had never received the message.

He stood back up and paced until someone knocked and opened the door without waiting for a response.

"Your Grace?"

"Hello, Henry. How is everything?"

"Grim."

"How so?"

Lord Winston entered the front hall, halting their conversation.

"Sheffield, what can we do for you today?"

"I'm here to see Alaina."

"I'm sorry, but she isn't allowed visitors." The older man stood his ground and though he seemed to mean well, Tristan wasn't going anywhere.

"On the contrary, sir, I will see Alaina. It is imperative I speak with her. She has information about who came to her room that night, and I want to confirm a few things." Both men turned as a loud crash sounded behind them. Charlotte had collided with the maid who was about to climb the stairs, and the tray of dishes now lay broken and scattered on the floor.

"I'm sorry, mum," said the maid as she knelt down to pick up the broken pieces of glass. Henry went over to help her, and another maid who had heard the ruckus entered the room with a small broom. Both men still focused on the scene, but rather than looking at the mess, their attention focused on Charlotte.

"Is everything all right, my dear?"

"Of course. Just a clumsy maid."

The accused one scowled and finished cleaning up the glass, then returned to the kitchen and the other two servants followed her.

Tristan filed the incident away as was his habit, then turned his attention back to Alaina's uncle.

"I insist on seeing Alaina. She is the only one who can give us any answers to finding her kidnappers."

"She isn't well, and must not be disturbed." This came from Charlotte who had moved to stand by her husband. "Nor do I understand what authority you believe you have here."

"I insist, madam. Either she speaks with me, or I call upon the sergeant for an arrest, seeing as how you are impeding my inquiries. She is the only witness in a criminal investigation—an investigation in which Sergeant Dunby gave me leave to offer assistance." Tristan told the partial truth easily.

Charlotte bristled under the threat and turned to her husband for support, but he had turned thoughtful eyes on the duke and nodded.

"What is your business with official matters? This is something for the police to handle, not an outsider."

"I assure you, madam, it is in my power to see that you and your husband are removed from this house, and if that does not work, I will take Alaina with me."

Charlotte paled and Tristan silently dared them both to call him on the matter. They thought better of the situation and backed down. Authority or not, a duke in his position wielded great influence.

"I prefer you question her, Sheffield. There is no need to call the police at this time. Daphne told us Alaina has asked for you." Sebastian stepped aside, pulling his wife along with him.

Tristan nodded, without offering thanks, and left the couple in the front hall as he climbed the stairs to Alaina's chambers. His arm throbbed with each step. Ignoring the pain, he stepped onto the landing.

The upper floor was quiet except for the slight movements of the staff. He looked around and then quietly inched the door open to Alaina's room, cloaking himself in warm light from the dim candles on the mantel and nightstand. Daphne stepped away from Alaina when Tristan walked inside.

"Alaina, how are you?"

"Tristan?"

"Yes, it's me." He moved to her side and sat on the bed after Daphne moved over to the other side of the room. Alaina appeared tired but more alert, and her voice seemed stronger than when they had last spoken.

"I can't wait to leave this bed. I miss my garden and my horses. I'm going rather insane in here all day."

Tristan smiled at the frustrated look on her face and pushed an errant lock from her forehead.

He heard Daphne clear her throat and ignored her.

"You're supposed to be resting."

"I don't want to rest anymore. I want to find the people who did this to me and get back to living my life." She accepted the cup of tea Daphne offered. Tristan declined the same offer.

"I will speak with Alaina, now—alone."

"I am not to leave her side, Your Grace."

Tristan turned around and looked at the woman.

His probing expression clearly told her what would happen to her if she failed to obey. Daphne nodded and took her leave.

"There are those daggers again." Alaina brought Tristan's attention and smile back to her.

"They come in handy from time to time. You've already been

through a great deal, but I need to know what happened. You said you saw Bridgette in your room that night, but you were tired and I wanted to confirm."

"Yes, it was Bridgette. I never got around to asking Aunt Charlotte about her, but I also remember other voices. They blindfolded me, but she wasn't alone—another woman and a man, I think."

"Bridgette has disappeared." He tried reassuring her when he saw the disappointment etched across her face. "I have men out looking for her, but thus far they've found nothing. We will find the people who did this, I promise. Do you think you could recognize the voices?"

"Perhaps the man's voice, but the woman always spoke too quietly. I only recognized it was a woman because of her scent. She smelled of lavender."

"Anything helps."

"It's a common scent for a woman, Tristan. My own aunt wears it, as does the reverend's wife."

"We'll catch them."

The determination in his voice almost made her believe it was true. "I'm grateful to be home, but I still don't know why I was returned, or taken for that matter."

"Neither do I . . . yet." That very thing had been on Tristan's mind ever since his heart stopped racing when he found her in the carriage. There had been no ransom, and according to the frightened man who had driven her, he was only supposed to make the delivery—no demands. *Perhaps they were trying to scare her, but to what end? What could anyone possibly want with her, and what could she possibly know?* He ruminated for a moment and then looked down at Alaina.

"You should sleep. You don't have your full strength yet."

"I'm tired of this bed and this room, but I'll sleep if you promise to return soon."

Her request pleased him more than he expected it to, and he smiled at her, caught up in the moment.

"What will you do first thing when you get out of bed?"

"Ride Serendipity."

"Is Serendipity your horse?"

"Yes. Crown Glory, my father's horse, sired him. My father loved that stallion, and when Serendipity was born, he gave him to me. He's coming along in years, but he's still faster than most."

Tristan held Alaina's hand and the smile disappeared from her lips.

"Why did you put forth such effort to find me, Tristan?"

"I didn't find you. You came to me. It turns out I was rendered useless during the search. Your captors were rather clever."

"That's not what I meant. You expended great energy into the search and hired those men. Why? Daphne told me you stayed confined to the study downstairs during my absence."

Her question was direct and honest, and Tristan believed it time to give her a few answers. She had trusted him, and now he needed to trust her. She waited patiently for him to respond. He released a breath and laid his other hand over their joined ones.

"The first day we met at the pond, you were the picture of fire and stubbornness. I will admit the only women who speak to me in such a manner are related to me. I admired your spirit, and then when you showed me your gardens, I felt . . . close to you somehow. When you went missing, I panicked. I feared losing your companionship."

"You wanted to find me so you would have someone to take afternoon tea with?" She teased, but Tristan was serious.

"I didn't want to lose a friend." His voice remained steady but lowered as he finished. "I didn't want to lose you." He spared a glance at her and found her smiling.

"I didn't want to lose you either."

A rush of relief washed over Tristan, and he held her hand a little tighter.

"There's more, Tristan." She no longer smiled.

"Yes there is, and it's time I tell you the full truth, or at least what I know. I carry the title of duke, but I work as a government official of sorts. I investigate crimes against the British government. I came here originally because of one of those investigations. We thought perhaps you were indirectly involved because of your parents' involvement. Then I met you, and things became complicated."

"You knew who I was when you saw me that day at the lake." It wasn't a question. She then added, "Devon and Charles. They also work for the government."

This too wasn't a question but he gave her a nod anyway.

"What became complicated?" No accusations, no lectures, no anger—just the one question he feared more than her anger.

"You and me—us. I never meant for this to happen, but it has, and by God, I won't lose it or you." He wanted to lighten the conversation, but she looked worried.

"What is it?" Anxious that he had scared her in some way, his heart began to twist and then unwind again when she spoke.

"I want to find who did this to me and to you." She indicated the arm he favored. "I don't know why, but I sense as though whoever took me knew me from before."

"Before what?"

"Before my parents died."

Not surprised by this, Tristan wondered how much she truly remembered from the night of her parents' accident. He considered that perhaps the two incidents were related before, but the same question kept coming back into his mind: Why kidnap her only to return her?

"I wanted to ask you earlier, but you were still too weak. Do you recall the night they took you, beforehand, when you worked in your study?"

She nodded her head, wondering where he was going with this.

"Do you remember why you were there at the late hour?"

Alaina turned her head slightly, as if trying to recall the exact details of the night. Her mind remained cloudy from whatever she had been given, until she recalled the long hours she had toiled over the household accounts.

"I spent most of the day going over the estate ledgers. I had forgotten about it because it seemed trivial at the time, but I remember spending all of that time trying to balance them—one ledger contradicted the other."

"Do you not keep track of the books?"

"Not normally. I gave the task over to my aunt some time back, and the estate manager meets with us once a quarter. Aunt Charlotte said she wanted something to keep her occupied. I had been working on them since I was seventeen, and when she offered, I had no idea she wasn't skilled enough for the task."

"How long exactly has she been handling them?"

"Eight months. I have always been good with numbers, but her methods escape me. I plan to ask her about them, but is that important right now?"

"Perhaps." Her aunt's reactions to certain events since she returned had caused Tristan to question the older woman's loyalty to her niece. He knew Alaina would not yet accept this idea, and kept the thought to himself for now.

A light rap on the door followed by Daphne and a tray of tea and sandwiches halted their conversation, and they watched as the maid set her burden down on the small table by the hearth, then turned and shook her head at the pair.

"You'd best get downstairs, Your Grace. If I have to listen to one more complaint from my lady's aunt about how you've already compromised her niece beyond repair, I'll have to resort to slipping sleeping agents in her tea." Alaina let a giggle escape while Tristan looked uneasily at the maid, and then back to Alaina.

"That's my cue to leave, and we should probably keep our meetings to the parlor."

"You don't like the bedroom, Tristan?"

His stomach tightened, and he wished Daphne was not in the room. His voice sounded a little strangled when he spoke. "The parlor, Alaina."

She grinned at him, delighted she had been able to throw him off his bearings. Alaina wasn't sure when she had decided that she cared for him but she did. That he cared for her in return pleased her greatly. Despite Daphne's being in the room, Tristan bent over to kiss Alaina's forehead, barely restraining himself from following a trail to her mouth. He stood to leave and closed the door quietly behind him.

"Don't look at me that way, Daphne. I have not felt this comfortable or at peace around anyone since . . . well . . . for a long time, and I like knowing I have someone I can talk with and trust. My parents would have loved Tristan." Alaina smiled to herself, remembering the affection her parents had always shown for each other.

"Your parents weren't careful enough around you, but I will tell you that your mother was the most proper lady I had ever known, though she purposely forgot many rules when it suited her. I suppose you are like her in many ways."

Alaina choked up, but there were no tears to betray her feelings. She couldn't remember the last time anyone in the house had spoken that much about her parents. It wasn't until Tristan that she began to remember how good it felt to remember and how painful.

"Thank you, Daphne." Unspoken thoughts passed between them, and Daphne dismissed herself. Pulling a cloth from her apron and holding it to her face, she left the room and closed the door behind her, leaving Alaina alone with years of memories and unshed tears.

ALAINA WOKE THE NEXT morning refreshed and eager for the new day. It had been four days since she had arrived home in the unmarked carriage with no memory of where she had been or why she had been taken. Her clothes covered a few lingering bruises and a small cut on her collarbone, but she felt renewed. After the continual bed rest, she was in desperate need of a walk through her gardens and a visit to the stables.

Tristan found her in the gardens when he arrived an hour later. The vast Claiborne gardens were truly a marvel. It took him a few minutes, with the aid of a gardener pointing him in the right direction, before he found her. She was in the greenhouse, perched on the stone bench in the midst of her rose garden where they had sat the first time she had brought him here. He watched as she gently rubbed the petals of a dark pink rose and then brought the bloom close to drink in its scent. She painted a beautiful picture of health and vitality, and it was difficult to believe that just a few days ago he had feared for her life.

Alaina looked up at the sound of footsteps on the cobblestone and smiled as Tristan approached her.

"I'm pleased to see you're well, though I had expected to find you indoors." Tristan sat beside her on the bench.

"I'm perfectly fit to be outside, and tired of being confined to the manor." Alaina twirled the bloom between her fingers.

"Have you spoken with your aunt and uncle about the maid and their note?"

"Not yet. They've gone back to London, and they didn't make much of an effort to see me over the past few days."

A sudden uneasiness coursed through Tristan's body. "Why did they return to London with everything that is going on here? Did they say why or how long they would be gone?"

Alaina shook her head. "They were gone when I woke up. I found a note in the study when I came downstairs but nothing else."

She did not look pleased, and Tristan understood the sentiment, but he had to set that aside for a task more pressing.

"Charles returned from London with the news that they have found Bridgette. She tried to hide but finally surfaced to look for work. Apparently, her new employer is acquainted with Devon. He questioned her, but she offered no names. Devon turned her over to our men for further questioning. He didn't want to say what little she had revealed until he had more information, but he told me he had to go to Ireland and would return here as soon as he was through."

"What's in Ireland?" Alaina absorbed everything he said.

"Devon isn't certain, but he believes that's where the trail is leading him. Apparently, Bridgette became flustered when he angered her, and she said something about a place called Willow's Way. He recalled hearing about it—a cottage of sorts in the country." Tristan stopped when he saw Alaina turn pale. "What is it?" Worried, he grabbed her hand and lifted her chin to look at her eyes.

"Willow's Way."

"Correct."

"My mother, oh my mother . . ." she whispered. "Willow's Way was the name of her cottage in Ireland. I haven't been there since that holiday. I never went back."

She didn't cry or shake, but she met Tristan's gaze, and he realized what she might think.

"They didn't take you there. It's too far away, and you weren't gone long enough for them to have made that trip." He pulled her closer to him. "Listen to me. What do you remember about the cottage?"

She shook her head. "I don't remember. I wasn't there long before the ball, but I remember a large tree. It rained a lot, and then it was dark when we went to the Benbrooks'. The ballroom was beautiful, and I danced with my father."

Tristan realized she was in another place right now, recalling moments from her past. He let her continue without interruption.

"People filled the ballroom, and Braden looked so handsome. He didn't want to build a tree house because we already had one at home. He told me about his father. Oh my, I had forgotten about his father. He said Lord Melbourne beat him, but I don't remember why." Alaina stopped speaking, shaking her head rapidly to clear the unwanted thoughts. Tristan circled his arms around her, and she sank into the safety of his embrace, unaware of the subtle changes in him. However, she was aware of the sudden changes in herself and pulled back enough to look at him, abruptly changing the subject to cover her embarrassment.

"While in London, my aunt accepted a few invitations for the season and has insisted I go along."

"And you don't want to go."

"It's not just that I don't want to go, since I'm not one for balls and frills, but I also fear that in the midst of all those people, whoever it was who took me, may manage to blend easily among such a large gathering."

Tristan agreed but wondered how much safer she was here. Bridgette may have been in the room when Alaina was abducted, but she would have required help to carry Alaina outside, down the stairs, and into a carriage. Henry was the only servant living in the house who would have had the strength to accomplish this, but he was also the only one Tristan currently trusted. The stableboys and groomsmen lived above the stables or in the village, and Tristan suspected her aunt and uncle more than them. *No, whoever the co-conspirator was didn't have to have intimate knowledge of the manor. Bridgette was their inside source and their pawn.* What mattered at this point was Alaina's safety, and Tristan believed she was in no more danger in London than at Claiborne Manor. In London, he had more people he trusted to watch over her and those around her.

"Tristan?"

"What? Oh yes, sorry." Tristan turned his attention to her. "I believe you should go to London for the season. Or at least part of it."

"Why?"

"I know it's a lot to expect, but will you go because I ask? I believe it will be safe, for now."

"Very well, I'll go."

"That's it? No argument?"

"I trust your judgment, and right now I need someone to trust." Alaina pulled away from Tristan. "And if your government people can help better in London, than I should be there." Alaina moved over to a bush of deep gray roses she had spent the previous summer cultivating. She had been able to create the long stemmed flowers exactly how she had envisioned them, but they lacked any real scent, which she decided was worth the sacrifice for something so beautiful.

"Alaina." Tristan stood behind her.

She had been aware of him moving toward her, heard his steady footsteps, but more than that, she had sensed his closeness and felt when he was near.

Alaina didn't turn around when he laid a gentle hand on her shoulder. He did not say anything at first, and they stood there. Breath by breath, the minutes passed until Tristan removed his hand from her shoulder and gently turned her around.

"I need to leave now while I can. I will return to escort you to London."

"Where will you be?"

"Just across the road. You know the way." He smiled. "I ask only one favor. Send a man over when your aunt and uncle return or when you hear from them."

She did not question him, but her expression told him she was uncertain.

He continued. "I would come by tomorrow, but there is much to set in order before I go on the extended trip to London."

"I will send word if and when I hear from Uncle Sebastian and Aunt Charlotte, but for now I too must set things in order before London." Alaina moved away and walked toward the door, but Tristan's voice prompted her to stop.

"Will Daphne and Henry accompany you?"

"Well, yes. The London house is minimally staffed. Why do you ask?"

"Who will be staying here?"

"Only Eldon and Timmy. They live in the village but look after the horses. They'll remain at the manor while we're gone. The other maids will come in during the day." Alaina waited for him to answer her previous question.

"I'll return soon." Tristan left, leaving her baffled and without answers.

Muttering something about men and their inability to communicate, Alaina exited the greenhouse and walked through her gardens, wanting to be certain they hadn't been neglected during her absence. Her attention was drawn away from another hybrid bush by a glitter in the trees. She walked a little farther along the path toward the trees, thinking it was probably just the afternoon sunlight, but then the sun disappeared and there was the glitter again—like a mirror reflecting light.

"How odd." She started walking more quickly when she heard shouting behind her. Turning around, she saw one of the stable hands coming toward her in a gait resembling a half-walk, half-run, which Alaina couldn't help but find humorous.

"Eldon? Whatever has you in such a rush?" Alaina walked

back toward him, trying to relieve him of any further panting.

"A messenger, my lady, came by only a few moments ago and said you were to have this straight away." Eldon held out a sealed envelope, inviting her to take it. "He told me no one else was to see it."

"Did you recognize him, Eldon?" Alaina felt an uncomfortable prickling sensation in the pit of her stomach and knew it was more than hunger.

"No, my lady, but he was riding a mighty fine steed—too fine for him."

"Why do you say that?"

"Because the bloke didn't speak any better than a gutter rat, and his clothes smelled like he'd been living with those rats. But the horse . . ." Eldon let out a low whistle. "Mighty fine steed— 'bout as nice as some of the beasts you have here."

Alaina stared at the envelope she still held but decided she should be alone when she read it, fearing that it was going to be unpleasant. Good news rarely came with urgency, and the events of the past couple of weeks had brought out her cautious side.

"Eldon, please ride toward the old Melbourne manor and tell the duke exactly what you have just told me. You should be able to catch up with him on the forest trail."

He nodded even as he rushed back toward the stables.

"Please hurry." Clutching the envelope against her, she walked back to the greenhouse, forgetting about the glimmer in the trees. She slipped a finger under the edge of the paper, breaking the wax seal. She pulled one corner away from the other, and her eyes scanned the carefully penned words.

"ALAINA." TRISTAN PULLED ON the reins of his horse, bringing the animal to an abrupt halt.

Alaina didn't have a chance to climb down from Serendipity's back before Tristan reached her and pulled her down from the animal. He held her close until her feet set down on the well-traveled path.

"Eldon told me about the messenger, saying you needed me

to return. I didn't expect to find you coming to me." Tristan ran his hands lightly over her arms, shoulders, and gently up her face, as though checking for an injury. "You're shaking. What's happened?"

"The letter. I read it after Eldon left and . . ."

Alaina and Tristan turned at the sound of a horse and rider coming toward them. A moment later Eldon reached them.

"My apologies for leaving you behind back there, Eldon," Tristan said to the man.

"Quite all right, Your Grace." Eldon glanced down at Alaina and prepared to dismount.

"I'm all right," Alaina assured him. "Thank you for riding out for Tristan, but you may return to the manor."

"My lady—"

"I'll look after her, good man." This time Tristan walked over to stand next to the horse. He extended his hand up and surprised by the gesture, Eldon shook the duke's hand. Eldon nodded to the pair and set his horse into a brisk walk back to Claiborne Manor.

Once out of hearing distance, Tristan turned to Alaina. "We're closer to your home, but if you're willing, I'd prefer we discuss this mysterious note at Melbourne."

She said unexpectedly, "You really should change the name."

He blinked and managed a smile. "Will Sheffield House suffice?"

"Thank you." She wiped a tear from beneath her eye. "I know it's silly after all this time."

"It will never be silly." He slid his arm around her waist and guided her back to her horse, helping her onto Serendipity's back. Gaining his own mount, he rode by her side the short distance to Sheffield House.

"THE TEA WILL BE along shortly." Tristan walked into his study where Alaina waited for him. She stepped away from the window and without saying anything, handed him an envelope.

"Your mysterious note. What did it say?" She didn't answer

but just motioned to the envelope he held. Tristan took out the single sheet of paper and read the few neatly scrawled lines.

Ten years ago you got away.

Your kidnapping was a preview of what is to come.

They will come for you soon enough.

Tristan looked up from the note to glance at Alaina, who had moved back over to the window. She was looking out, her back to him, stiff and unyielding.

"Is this from the same man who rode to the manor?"

"How much did Eldon tell you?"

"Only what little he knew about the messenger. I wasn't far out of the trees when Eldon caught up to me." He studied her a moment and then added, "Apparently you were just behind him."

"I didn't know what to do when I read it. I reacted, and riding to you seemed the only right thing to do. You see, I had a horrible feeling when he handed me the note."

"What caused you worry?"

"I saw something in the trees. Perhaps it was nothing, but there was a light where there shouldn't have been."

"Someone was watching you?"

"I am not certain." Alaina crossed her arms as though embracing herself. "There's little I'm certain of these days—I could have imagined it."

Tristan doubted that. It was more likely someone had been watching her from the forest. He drew her attention back to the paper he held. "Have you ever received a message like this before?

"Never. The note may be threatening, but why warn me? Would it not be more effective to surprise me?"

"I don't think you want to know what I think." Tristan led her to a settee and sat down next to her.

"Yes, I do." Before he refused, she said, "I need to know."

"I believe whoever sent this to you is watching you closely, enough to know your aunt and uncle weren't home. I do not believe you imagined what you saw in the trees."

Alaina looked at Tristan strangely. "You don't think my family had anything to do with this?"

Tristan took her hand in his and held on when she tried to pull away. Her body tensed, but he knew it was time for her to hear the words he dreaded saying to her.

"I cannot offer proof at this time, but yes, I do believe they had something to do with this. At least your aunt has raised suspicions." He held onto her hand. "I know this isn't what you want to hear, but before you go to London, you need to understand that you may be living with someone who played a part in your kidnapping."

Alaina didn't look at him, but she couldn't move away either because he still had a firm grip on her hand.

"Alaina?"

Her focus was on the landscape outside of his window. *If only I could be out there riding across the land. If only this moment had not happened. If only history could be undone. If only . . .*

"Alaina."

"I just can't believe that my own family, the people who I've been living with for the past ten years, had anything to do with my kidnapping. It just doesn't make sense."

"No, it doesn't, but my men have been investigating—"

"What do you mean 'investigating'?" Alaina turned her alert blue eyes on Tristan.

Alaina waited for him to answer but then threw out another question. "Did you not say that whoever took me had something to do with my parents?" Alaina saw the answer on his face before he responded and managed to wrench her hand free before standing.

Tristan stood next to her. "Wait."

"No. Don't say anything. In fact, don't speak to me again until you're ready to share the complete truth and leave nothing out." Alaina moved passed the butler in the hallway, not waiting for him to open the door. Her horse waited, tethered to an iron post in front of the house under the watchful eye of a groom, and in no time, she was on the animal and racing off the property.

Tristan watched from the doorway, not bothering to stop her and knowing he would have to expedite his plans when they reached London. He had hoped for stronger proof, but now it was time to ensnare the guilty parties. He turned and went back into the house, motioning for his butler to follow him into the study.

"Andrew, it's time for us to move things up a bit. Here's what I need you to do." The other man moved behind the desk with Tristan to look over papers he had pulled out of the desk drawer. The two men spent the next few hours in the study, pausing only when Devon and Charles showed up, and then again when the same men complained that their host was starving them. Andrew left to fetch refreshments from the kitchen since most of the staff had already retired. It was late into the night when they finally formulated the last of their plan. Charles and Devon left the manor and Henry retired to his room, leaving Tristan alone in the noiseless study. Surrounded by the peaceful night, his thoughts drifted to the mistress of Claiborne Manor.

ACROSS THE ACRES, DARKNESS enveloped Alaina, her surroundings illuminated by the flickering flame of a lamp. She moved around in the attic, searching through trunks of the items that had come from her mother's cottage in Ireland. It was difficult to replay the many memories that reminded her of her parents, but she also found it calmed her. She had avoided these things since they had been delivered years ago, but now her fears became secondary. She hoped something from her parents' past might shed light on what was happening in the present. Alaina rummaged through a trunk of some of her mother's clothes, pulling them out and smelling them, hoping for a faint whiff of the soft rose scent her mother used to wear. There was something lingering around the old clothes, and it took Alaina back to a time when she was a little girl. Nevertheless, the memory ended there. She paused for a moment, as if the scent reminded her of something else besides her mother. She subsequently released the memory when she saw the bottom of the trunk was not as deep as it should have been. She pulled out the remaining dress and ran her fingers along the bottom and edges. She next looked on the outside of the trunk. Nearly six inches of extra space remained near the bottom on the inside.

Alaina moved her fingers along the inside edges and became excited when she found a gap. Slowly reaching her fingers into the hole, she simultaneously pushed down on the other edge for leverage and surprised herself when the bottom tilted to reveal the extra space beneath. Removing the thin board, she set it aside and gasped when she turned back to the trunk.

"Oh, Mama. What did you do?"

Thirteen

"*Alaina? Where are you?*"

"*I'm right here, silly.*" *Alaina stepped from the shadows.*

"*Your parents are looking for you,*" *he said, scolding her.* "*You know you shouldn't be out here alone.*" *Braden tried to be gruff with her, but he wore a smile.* "*Are you going to tell me what's bothering you?*"

"*I miss Claiborne Manor and Serendipity. I miss my gardens and the peace I found there.*" *She walked over to Braden and took his hand.* "*I miss home, Braden, I want to go back.*"

"*It's not time to go back yet.*"

"*We should go back now—leave here and go home now. We don't have to wait for the ball to be over.*" *Alaina's tears threatened to fall.*

"*Yes we do. Your parents aren't going to leave right now. It would be rude,*" *he said.* "*Besides, aren't you having a wonderful time?*"

"*I was when I danced with you and Papa and was drinking punch and eating cookies, but I don't like it here anymore. It feels scary.*" *Braden brought her hand up to his lips and gently pressed against them.*

"*You never need to be scared with me around, Alaina. I will always watch over you. You know that, don't you?*"

"*Yes, I do.*"

"*I love you, Alaina.*"

"*I love you too, Braden.*"

Alaina welcomed the sweet warmth washing over her as she

found herself drifting deeper into the dark oblivion of dreams. Except the thrashing began and she found herself sinking.

The carriage wouldn't stop. It just kept rolling over and over. She couldn't focus on her mother and father. She still held Braden or perhaps he held onto her. She saw the opening where the door had been and then saw her father try to reach for her as they kept rolling. He was also holding onto her mother. Braden had a tight grip on the seat, and they weren't moving as much, but she felt someone pushing her away and turned to look at Braden. The words refused to come and she panicked.

What was he doing? Alaina gripped him tighter until she saw his face and looked in the direction of the opening as it appeared again. It was all happening too fast. She shook her head rapidly, knowing what was happening but unable to stop it. Braden pushed her again when the opening became visible, and he took that one moment of opportunity, releasing the seat and using both hands to push her up and through the doorway. Alaina still couldn't scream when she hit the ground and rolled down the hill into some bushes that tore at her clothing and her skin. Her arms and legs hurt, but she did not move, didn't think she wanted to.

Panic ripped through her when her focus returned, and she saw in her mind what Braden had done: he had let go of the seat and pushed her to safety.

What happened to them? Alaina tried to feel her body and will it to move to go after her family. There were noises coming from above and below her. She realized the carriage had stopped near her. She had rolled down the hill until the bushes stopped her. Her body slowly obeyed her despite the pain. The inside pain was hurting her more. What had happened to her family? She tried rising to her knees, but the bushes surrounded her. She couldn't move much and then didn't want to when she heard voices she didn't recognize.

Her eyes darted from the top of the hill to the bottom where she saw the carriage turned over on its side, but she couldn't see anyone until a few men slowly made their way down the hill, some riding horses. One of the men on the horses ordered another to look inside the carriage. The other man climbed up on top of the carriage, and then spoke to the one on the horse.

Her parents were alive and coming out of the carriage! First she saw her father and then her mother. Where was Braden?

Her parents went to the other side of the carriage and one of the wheels blocked them from view. She heard her father speaking to the man.

"The boy is dead."

Braden? No, it is not possible. Alaina willed the tears back though she knew they were going to come. She kept her eyes on her parents and the tall man on the horse who was ordering everyone else around. The moon's shadow hid most of his face. He wouldn't move, but she knew the voice, or thought she knew the voice. Then he moved into the moonlight, and she saw his face. She didn't recognize him.. Her eyes stayed focused on what was happening, the haze of tears fighting their way through.

Her father shouted at the man and so did her mother, but then a gun fired, and she saw her mother fall down. Her father was crying and screaming at the man on the horse. Her father held her mother close to him, but she wouldn't move. Her father knelt in front of the man and another gun fired. Her father fell to the ground. She didn't make any noise—couldn't make any sound. A man went back into the carriage and came out holding something. It seemed like a box, but she was unsure. She glanced back at her parents. She wanted to turn away, but she stayed, unmoving, until the man on the horse spoke again. She thought he had seen her because he seemed to look directly at her, but he spoke and everyone left. Alaina sat quietly where she was, her eyes never leaving the hill where the men disappeared since she was afraid they might come back. She waited for what seemed like a long time, but she heard nothing else.

The bushes still poked her, but she found the opening where she had fallen through and tried moving back out the same way. There were more scratches now, but she was free from the thorns. Her legs ached with simple movement, and the rest of her body was still in pain, but she somehow found the strength to walk on her injured legs to the carriage. Her parents were lying there, but she couldn't go over to them. She walked around to the other side of the carriage where there was a window on the back and looked in.

He didn't move when she said his name. He had been close to the window yet unable to escape. Alaina reached her hand inside and touched his cheek. The tears she had fought earlier fell, and she grabbed him.

"Alaina?" It didn't register for a moment that someone spoke to her from behind, but then she looked over her shoulder and back at the hand she held. She must be dreaming.

"Braden?"

"Yes."

"But how?" she asked, looking back at the body inside.

"I wish there was another way."

"What do you mean?"

"I brought you back here."

Confusion gripped her.

"I brought you back here to show you the truth."

"You're not real, are you?"

"Not in the way you mean. I wanted you to see so you could find the answers you need."

"What answers?"

"The answers to your parents' death, to what's happening now."

Confusion marred her angelic face for a moment. "I haven't been kidnapped? I'm only . . ." she paused as she realized what was happening. "I'm not really this young girl anymore, am I?"

"No, you're not."

"Then why do you make me remember the pain?"

"This was the only time I knew you, but I've watched you over the years and wanted to be with you."

"I wanted you with me too. I am unsure of what to do."

"Yes, you do, and you know who can help you."

"Tristan?"

"Yes."

"How do you know about him?"

"I told you I've been with you. I always will be, Alaina, but not in the way I wanted. There is someone else in your life now who can take care of you."

"Why now? Why wait all of these years?"

"It was time. You needed him in your life before I could give you this."

"I don't think I understand."

"You will."

"Braden, I miss you so much. I miss Mama and Papa."
"They miss you too, Alaina, and we all love you so much."
"I'll find the man who did this to us."
"That is what I fear most, but it must be done. Just remember to not let go."
"Let go of what?"
"Never let go of him. He is yours now. Forever."
"Not forever, Braden."
"Open yourself to him. We want you to find peace."
"I don't know how."
"You will. He will help you, and you will help him."
"Don't go."
"It's time for you to hold on to another. I will always love you."

Alaina woke to a cold room because the fire had never been lit, but her hand wiped away the sweat on her forehead. Sometime in the night, she had thrown the covers off. Breathing deeply, she sat on the edge of the bed. She wiped a light sheen of moisture from her brow. The tears she had accumulated over the years fell down her cheeks. She let them come until they lulled her into a deep and peaceful sleep, muttering aloud, "I will always love you."

"ALAINA DEAR, ARE YOU ready?" Charlotte stood in the doorway of her niece's bedroom.

"Yes, Aunt Charlotte, I'll be right down." Alaina faced her dressing table, barely glancing at her aunt.

Charlotte simply nodded and left the room. Displeased with her aunt and uncle, Alaina took a long look at the spot her aunt had occupied seconds before. They had arrived at Claiborne Manor the day before, saying they planned to leave for London the following morning. They weren't forthcoming about what they had done or why they had left, then after what Alaina found in her mother's trunks the week before, she wasn't certain she wanted to discover more.

Her relationship with her aunt and uncle was now forever

altered. She had trusted them, all of her life, and losing that trust pained her. Alaina had yet to tell Tristan of her findings, but she sent word to him, informing him that they would be leaving for London. He sent a reply, asking her to wait until he arrived the following morning.

Alaina waited for him right now and delayed their departure for as long as possible. Her aunt and uncle hadn't said anything when she told them Tristan would be accompanying them, nor had they expressed a desire to accommodate him by waiting. She was ready to find another gown to change into when a knock came at her door.

"Enter."

"My lady." Daphne stepped inside. "The Duke of Wadebrooke has arrived and is waiting for you downstairs. I must say your aunt and uncle are growing a trifle impatient."

"Thank you. You may tell them all that I will be right down."

"Yes, my lady."

A short time later, the foursome sat in the carriage, the spare horses tethered behind them. The sporadic conversation during the first twenty minutes of the drive entailed her aunt and uncle responding to Tristan's polite inquiries in monosyllabic answers. It wasn't until Alaina mentioned going through her mother's old trunks that everyone's curiosities were piqued.

"What did you find?" asked Charlotte.

"Old clothes, mementos, and photographs. I had hoped to find something that might have shed some light on what has happened." She left the thought without further explanation. Sebastian seemed disinterested, Charlotte shifted in her seat, and Tristan looked at her as though trying to figure out the game in which she seemed such a confident participant.

Fourteen

"It's the safest way for Alaina to be out in public." Tristan stood beside Alaina, careful not to show too much familiarity in her uncle's presence. "People will be less likely to bother her."

"Pretending to be engaged is not the only way to keep Alaina safe."

Tristan didn't blame Sebastian for not supporting the idea, but he wouldn't relent. "Nevertheless, it's the only way I can be close to her without drawing unwanted attention."

"Did anyone ever stop to think about what I thought of all of this?" Alaina sat on the settee in the drawing room, content to let Tristan speak, but she had finally grown tired of the arguing.

"Alaina, this is the best course, and is most likely to keep you out of harm's path. No one thinks anything of a husband escorting his wife everywhere."

"I never said I disagreed with you, Tristan. In fact, I think the idea logical, and it may be the best way to keep me safe." Alaina didn't mention his background because she wasn't sure how much everyone else knew. "However, I do have one concern."

"Which is?"

"Because of who you are, the culprit may be less likely to try something and then in turn, wouldn't that make it more difficult for you to catch him?"

"She's brings up a good point." Sebastian did not miss the baleful look Tristan sent his way.

"Yes, she does. However, I believe that is the least of our worries. I want to catch the miscreants, but more importantly, I wish to prevent more harm to her."

"How will she find a husband if everyone is already to believe she is engaged?" Charlotte finally spoke up, drawing everyone's attention to her.

"Aunt Charlotte, I've already told you. I am not interested in searching for a husband. My parents didn't meet during the season, and I don't plan on meeting my future husband while skirting around a ballroom." Alaina stood and moved to sit beside her aunt. "All I want is to catch these people and then return home to Claiborne Manor and my own life."

Charlotte fussed with her kerchief and refused to meet Alaina's eyes. "It seems as though you've already made your decision about this, so I am going to bed, but let it be known I am vehemently against this plan."

"It is my decision to make."

"Of course it is, child." Charlotte stood, turned away from her niece, and left the room.

"This has been difficult for her."

"With respect, my lord, it's Alaina whose life is in danger, not that of your wife."

The older man looked at the young duke. "I hope you realize that if anything happened to Alaina, it would devastate us."

"It's Alaina I'm concerned for, and I will protect her." Tristan stood face to face with the other man, who then turned to his niece.

"You are of age, and I cannot tell you what to do. I pray only for your safety, but keep others in mind when you go ahead with this plan of yours." Sebastian turned and departed, following in his wife's footsteps.

Tristan walked over to the settee to sit next to Alaina. "Are you sure this is something you're willing to do?"

"I hadn't realized you were giving me a choice." To his credit, Tristan cringed. "I understand why you're doing this, but do you really believe the measure will help catch these people?"

Words failed Tristan at this point. In one regard, if he told her the truth in its entirety, he risked losing her cooperation or worse, her confidence. On the other hand, he could continue to lead her blindly down this path and hope for her continued trust. Neither sounded like a good choice, so he did what he always did in the end and chose the best of the worst options.

"Alaina, I think I've discovered who two of them are." He placed a finger gently over her lips when she started to protest. "It's important for you to listen to me right now because after I'm done, you may change your thinking and choose to return to one of your estates, never to see me again."

She stared into his eyes a moment and nodded her head, letting him understand she would listen. Tristan reluctantly removed his finger from her soft lips.

"You are already aware of Bridgette's involvement with your kidnapping, but you also need to accept that your aunt was somehow involved." He paused to gauge her reaction, but she remained still and silent. "I realize this is difficult for you to believe, but I need you to know what I've learned if this is going to work. We have evidence. As I have mentioned, I work for the British government, but what I failed to disclose was my role. My men and I work on special assignments that search out and locate enemies of the government, and we're sent in to deal with them."

"Deal with them how?" Alaina regretted asking the moment she spoke the words.

"In whatever way necessary. There's more I haven't told you, much more, and I need you to think about what I'm about to say. My father worked in a similar capacity for the government, which is how I fell into this line of work. A few years ago, I was handed an old case of his, one that had been left unsolved because the same men he was investigating, murdered him."

Alaina wanted to say something but felt he needed to finish what he was trying to tell her. She gently laid a hand on his and encouraged him to continue.

"My father requested your parents' case, in part, because they had worked together, but also because they were friends."

"Are you trying to convince me that my parents were agents?"

"Not exactly. They did work for the government but not in the same capacity as my father. They passed information to my father on various cases, most of which my father was able to solve because of the material they had shared."

"You're saying they were spies."

"In his papers, my father always referred to them as associates—nothing else."

"What else did you learn from your father's papers?"

"Alaina, you are too calm. I expected something more from you—to at least be angry with me or to deny everything about your parents I have told you thus far."

"Do you prefer I shout and accuse you of lying?"

"No, never that."

"Perhaps I am calm because I believe you, or at least part of my conscious believes you."

Surprised, Tristan watched as she stood and walked over to the bookshelves and moved aside a collection of Emerson's work. She pulled out a small stack of folded papers and then walked back, handing him the documents. "Whether I like it or not, my parents were involved with something, and I believe now that is why they were killed."

Tristan took the papers from her outstretched hand and unfolded them, careful not to damage the worn documents. He read the first two paragraphs and then skimmed through the rest of the parchments.

"Where did you find these?"

"Under a false bottom in one of my mother's trunks in the attic. There are more, but this is all I risked bringing with me to London."

"Have you looked through all of these and the others?"

"Yes, but most of it was written in the same form as the documents you're holding. It's English but it doesn't make sense. Although, by the look on your face as you read, you understand every word."

"Yes, it's a code developed by my father and yours in case these papers were ever found. My father had made a note in one of his journals about missing papers in a safe house. I'm assuming now the papers you found were the ones he wrote of." Tristan stood and paced the room, speaking aloud but not really to Alaina. "It's possible the trip to Ireland was to include a meeting with my father. His journals indicated he was there at the same time. He was supposed to meet someone the day after your parents died, so it made sense they wanted to return home. However, it does not make sense to meet with two children underfoot in a small cottage when they could have met at the ball. Or perhaps they scheduled to meet the following day at the country house, but something happened to make them decide to leave the ball."

"Tristan?" She waited.

"Tristan."

He turned abruptly. "Did your parents say why they had wanted to leave the ball rather than stay over into the next day?"

"I don't remember."

"Yes, you do." He walked over to her, grabbed her shoulders, and gave her a slight shake. "Yes, you do remember. You just don't want to, but I need you to remember."

"I promised to tell you anything I could, but this I just don't know." Her voice cracked, but she held her shoulders stiff beneath his hands, her back straight, and her head held high.

Tristan hoped that pressing her wouldn't push her so far away that she'd be unwilling to come back, but he had to risk it, for her sake as much as for his.

"The same men who killed your parents killed my father. He only investigated crimes to the government, which means these same men are still wanted and dangerous. My father got too close, and now he is dead. Someone knew what he was doing, which makes me believe someone on the inside was involved. I don't want this to be true anymore than you do, but it happened and now your life is in danger. I need you to remember what happened . . . please." Tristan knew that somewhere in her memory, the pictures of a cold and frightening night waited for release. The nightmares were the key to unlocking those memories. He never desired to cause her pain, but she was now the only one with the answers, and he needed her to be strong.

"I've spent every waking moment since that night trying to bury the memories, to forget everything. When the nightmares returned, I knew it was time to release my hold on the past. I recall glimpses, and I hate the unknowing because the pictures are unbearable. I realize how important the truth is, and I can trust you, but I don't know who else to trust anymore."

"You mean your aunt and her reaction to you going through your mother's things?"

"No wonder you're good at your line of work." She stood and paced the room. "Regardless. You are right. My uncle did not appear to care, but Aunt Charlotte seemed uncomfortable and wouldn't look at me after that. Then you tell me she is involved. I don't want to believe this about her, and as much as I wish to prove you wrong, I fear the truth will prove you right."

Tristan gently lowered her back down onto the settee. He looked up to the door when he heard noises in the hall. Her aunt and uncle had gone to bed. The noise went away, but Tristan remained alert.

"What's wrong?"

Tristan turned his attention back to Alaina and couldn't, or wouldn't, stop himself from gently stroking her hair.

"I heard something. Likely one of the servants."

"I didn't see either Daphne or Henry return from the market, but they should have retired for the evening." Alaina and Tristan both stood, but he stopped her before she moved far.

"Just let me go out there first. I'll come back in and tell you when everything is clear."

"Tristan, I'm sure it's nothing . . ."

"Humor me." His words didn't stop her, but the look he sent her way over his shoulder did—for the moment.

Tristan walked out into the hall, closing the door behind him. Some of the lights in the hall had been turned down, and the few lanterns still lit were drowned by the moonlight, pouring in through the window. If Henry or any other servant had been there, the drapes would not be fluttering from the open window.

Hearing nothing, Tristan walked through the hall to the back of the house, checking the rooms as he went along. Finding no one on the lower level, he slowly followed his path back toward the front staircase and pulled the knife from his boot when he saw a shadow against the wall.

"Tristan?"

Tristan swore under his breath and moved down the hall.

"I told you to stay in the study."

"You were taking too long. Besides, I know this house better than you, and I'm more likely to notice if something is wrong."

He didn't doubt his capability to search the house without her, but he preferred not to argue the point.

"Stay behind me and please stay quiet." He once again moved to the staircase with Alaina close behind him. They made their way slowly up the stairs, and upon reaching the top of the landing, Tristan pushed Alaina up against the wall causing her to gasp.

"What was that for?" she whispered harshly, only to be stopped by a hand over her mouth and a voice at her ear.

"There is someone up here." He removed his hand, hoping she understood that she needed to remain silent. Tristan moved down the hall, keeping close to the wall, opening and closing doors as he went. He stopped when he heard a noise from inside the door he was about to open and felt something press his body. He heard a faint grunt from behind. Tristan turned to find Alaina pushed up against him, and he wished the darkness did not prevent her from seeing the look he sent her way.

"Keep quiet." He inched the door open, his senses acutely aware of her soft form, her delicate scent, and the way she innocently brushed against him, yet he tried to ignore the way her body felt so wonderful against his back. Tristan looked inside the room, realizing his mistake when he saw someone sitting up in the large four poster.

"Who's there?"

"It's me, Uncle Sebastian." Alaina moved out from behind Tristan, skirting his arm as he tried to stop her from going into the room. He followed her into the darkness, closing the door behind him.

"Where's your wife?"

Sebastian looked to the other side of the bed and shook his head.

"I'm not sure."

Alaina sat at the edge of the bed beside her uncle, watching him look around the room.

"She must have gone down to the kitchen for a late snack. She does that sometimes." Sebastian got out of bed, surprising Tristan and Alaina by being fully clothed. He noticed the direction of their eyes and explained.

"When Charlotte dragged me up here, I planned to return downstairs after she went to sleep, but when we finished enjoying our nightcaps, I was exhausted and must have fallen asleep."

Tristan glanced around until he found the glasses and walked over to the small table by the fireplace. He picked up both glasses and sniffed the contents, finding nothing amiss.

"What's going on here?" Sebastian laid a hand on Alaina's shoulder, the weight bothering her. She was beginning to dislike the gesture. She stood and walked to Tristan.

"Uncle Sebastian, we heard something downstairs near the study and Tristan thought perhaps there was someone else in the house. Henry and Daphne have not returned, and most of the lights are banked. We saw no servants downstairs, and when we came upstairs, we heard something in the hallway. Now Aunt Charlotte is missing—"

"Alaina."

She stopped speaking and looked over at Tristan, who still held the knife.

"What of that isn't true?" she demanded of Tristan.

"Alaina, I think you should stay here with your uncle, and I'll finish looking through the house."

"Now wait a minute." Sebastian slipped his feet into house shoes. "My wife is somewhere in this house, and it was likely you heard her. I won't have you wielding a knife in her presence."

Tristan sheathed the knife. "That doesn't explain the absence of the servants."

"I'm not staying here."

Tristan turned his attention back to Alaina and then to Sebastian. *There are far too many Claibornes under this roof.*

"Find your wife. Alaina and I will keep looking around up here."

"You can't order us around in our own home, duke or not. This is private property." Sebastian walked toward the door. "I think you've overstepped your bounds, Sheffield, and if it wasn't at my niece's insistence, you wouldn't be here."

"Uncle Sebastian." Alaina placed a hand on her uncle's arm to stop him from leaving. "Tristan is here to help us, and I trust him to find who is behind all of this."

"Very well, then let him find out. I'm going to find your aunt." Sebastian walked quickly and stiffly out of the room, leaving Tristan staring at Alaina in surprise.

"You believe everything I've told you?"

"After what I have found and all that has happened, I have no choice but to believe you. I'm not fond of these nightmares, and they've been the same for the past week, but if I can remember what happened the night of my parents' death, then perhaps I can live the rest of my life in peace." Alaina kept her eyes focused on Tristan.

His fingers slowly entwined with hers. A light fluttering started in her stomach, and then it quickly escalated to an uncomfortable, yet not unpleasant, hammering.

"Alaina, I don't want you staying here. It's not safe."

"I have no other options right now. I think this is the safest place for me in London. I haven't spent more than a few weeks here over the years, and people wouldn't expect me to be here."

"They'll learn soon enough that you're in residence. You can stay at my home. It's just down the road."

Alaina shook her head in disbelief. "I may not care how society perceives me, but they are aware of who I am, and I would disgrace myself and my family if I stayed in your home."

"Not if we married."

Alaina stared, shocked and uncertain, wondering if he meant it. Perhaps he was joking, but she found nothing funny about the look in his eyes. *This man is completely serious.*

"Tristan . . ."

"We're already pretending engagement, so why not marriage? It would give me even more freedom to protect you because you would be under my roof."

"No one will believe such a thing."

"Then we'll make it real, and it can be annulled after we solve the case. I cannot protect you the way I need to if we are not together. I realize you don't want to do this, but I'm asking you to consider it."

She kept her eyes focused on him, allowing the seriousness of the situation to settle in. The problem was not in pretending to marry him, she realized. *A part of me truly wants marriage to this man.* Alaina turned away from him, focusing her eyes on the first thing she found. He read her well, and she did not want him to guess the thoughts floating around in her mind.

"Alaina?"

She controlled her body language, or so she hoped, and turned to look at him again. She was about to speak when her aunt and uncle walked into the room.

"Still here? Well, as you can see, there was no cause for worry. Your aunt was fixing a late snack in the kitchen, as you suspected, Alaina." Sebastian didn't mention that he found her with her snack on the opposite side of the house. He looked uncomfortable as his wife walked back to the bed.

"I don't know what all of the fuss is about." Charlotte sat on the edge of the bed, a half-filled teacup in hand. "And I think it's time for the duke to leave and return tomorrow."

"We're to be married." Everyone turned eyes to Alaina in surprise, including Tristan.

Charlotte rose and dropped her tea. "What do you mean 'married'?"

"I mean we are to be married."

"Absolutely not, Alaina." Sebastian rushed forward and planted a finger on Tristan's chest. "If this is some hero game, Sheffield, I promise I'll have your head."

"I don't play games, Lord Winston. I need to be with Alaina at all times, and I can't do that unless we're married."

"You wish to risk her reputation and her heart by marrying her for a short time, and then leaving her to find another?"

Before Tristan could further defend his plan, Alaina stepped between the two men, while Charlotte stared on. "Tristan, Uncle Sebastian, perhaps you are interested in hearing what I have to say about all of this?" Both men turned to her, but neither offered any encouragement.

"Alaina—"

She held up her hand, not allowing Tristan finish.

"Now I want both of you to listen well. This is my decision, and I'm agreeing to marriage because I believe it is the best way to keep out of harm." Her stomach roiled. "Even I can't pretend something like this, so we will have a legal ceremony. I am certain that with Tristan's title and connections, it won't be a problem for him to obtain the necessary licenses without the usual postings and delays. The sooner we accomplish the deed, the faster we find out who is behind all of this, and then I can return home."

"I have already obtained the necessary licenses."

Alaina looked over to him with surprise. He crossed his arms.

"We won't allow this, will we, Sebastian?" Charlotte now stood beside her husband.

"It's my choice, Aunt Charlotte. Neither of you has any legal say in what I do, but I had hoped you wanted to keep me as safe as possible, and I do hope for your blessing."

"You can't mean to do this without our consent?"

"Regrettably, yes, Aunt Charlotte, but I would like your support. Since Tristan has already obtained what we need," she sent a pointed look his way, "we will find someone to perform the ceremony as soon as possible. Unless of course that has also been seen to?" She looked over at him again. This time he had the decency to blush, and she shook her head, wishing all of this surprised her more.

"We can't allow this, Sebastian." Charlotte clung desperately to her husband now, but he looked down at his wife and then over at Alaina and Tristan.

"They've made their choice, and she doesn't need our

consent." He turned and escorted his wife back to the bed.

Alaina wished to say something more to them but knew there was nothing reassuring to offer. Tristan laid a hand on her shoulder, and she left the room with him. She watched him close the door and then allowed him to lead her down the hall to her own room.

"I'll wait for you to get your things."

"What?"

"I think it is best you come with me tonight. We will be married tomorrow, and no one will question why you are staying with me. No one will be aware that you are at my home this evening, and I promise you will be safe."

Alaina hesitated.

"I have a small staff at the manor, and two of my friends and associates are staying as well." Tristan wished there was something to make this better for her, but what he possessed in skills, he lacked in eloquence when dealing with women. He studied her, wishing he could give her a wedding day filled with family and smiles in a big garden with bright flowers everywhere—her garden, next to her fountains. He knew neither of them would say the truth aloud, but she should be marrying for love, able to look forward to a lifetime with her husband and children. This temporary marriage would alter things for both of them.

Alaina nodded her head and went to gather her things for the night. Tristan would send someone tomorrow to get the rest. Daphne and Henry were still absent, which worried her greatly, but right now there was nothing to do but go with Tristan.

Alaina glanced around her room before stepping into the hall. Closing the door behind her, she took Tristan's hand. She needed the connection, needed to receive comfort.

Tristan felt the same need. His eyes found their joined hands. Then he lifted the bag from her and smiled. She smiled back. They walked down the corridor, down the stairs, and out the door where the carriage waited. The rain poured upon them and forced a quick dash to the carriage.

"Do you still believe someone was in the house?"

He paused briefly before answering. "Someone was outside the study."

Alaina didn't point out that he hadn't answered her question, but she let the matter rest and packed what she could on her own. She did not wish to wake a maid only to have gossip spread through London.

The brief drive continued in silence and only necessary communication flowed between them once they arrived at his London house. Tristan had to call upon one of the maids to help Alaina upstairs. Alaina vaguely recalled meeting Tristan's two friends before she was escorted to the upper level and shown into a lovely room—quite lovely for a bachelor's residence. It was simple but elegant. A large four-poster bed occupied the center of the room, looking out through floor-to-ceiling windows, and a fireplace covered a portion of the wall across from the bed. White lace linens adorned the bed, the tables, and the windows, and Alaina wondered what female had slept here in the past. Too weary to worry over something trivial, Alaina let the maid unpack her small bag and help her into her nightgown. After she dismissed the other woman, Alaina climbed into bed and drifted to sleep where she was no longer safe from the nightmares.

Downstairs, Tristan sat in his study with Charles and Devon, swirling amber liquid in his glass, while his mind remained focused on the woman upstairs.

Devon looked to Tristan and then to Charles with a smile on his face. The other man had also noticed that Tristan's mind had not been on the conversation.

Devon grinned. "She's a beautiful creature."

"Yes, she is." Tristan stared at the fireplace.

"It will be difficult to marry her and still not have any . . . ah . . . privileges," Charles said.

"What?" Tristan looked up at both men, realizing he had been caught daydreaming over a woman.

"Now, isn't this interesting, Devon? Our fearless leader is in love."

Devon nodded his head, a slight smile on his face.

"What are you talking about?" Tristan swallowed the rest of his whiskey. "I'm concerned for her and wish to keep her safe, nothing more." He knew, of course, that neither of them believed him. "I assure you I am here for the case and will do whatever it takes to solve it."

"Are you trying to convince us or yourself?" asked Charles.

Tristan couldn't answer the question. These men were his closest friends and knew him better than he knew himself half of the time. They had been there when he lost his father, and they understood how important it was for him to find the people responsible for his father's death. Right now, it annoyed him that they knew exactly what was going through his mind, and it annoyed him even more because they were right.

"I'm going to bed. I trust you two can find the way to your old rooms."

He left them both, sitting in the chairs, smiling at each other. They raised their glasses at Tristan's departing back and drank.

"What do you think he'll do about it?" asked Devon.

"You mean if he doesn't convince himself he's not in love with her?"

"Yes, that."

"Well, Tristan does always get what he wants."

"That he does, my friend, but I wonder if this time isn't different."

"Oh, how so?" asked Charles.

"In the past, he's never let anything interfere with his work."

"True."

"He's never lost before," Devon said.

"True again."

"He's never been in love before."

"Very true. What's your point?" asked Charles.

"What if she doesn't love him back?"

Both men knew that when Tristan did something, he put his whole self into it, and they didn't doubt it would be the same with loving a woman. If that woman did not love him back, the pain would likely turn him into a bitter and angry man. They refused to let that happen.

"I suppose we should do something about this," said Charles.

"Suppose so." Devon finished the brandy in his glass.

Fifteen

Alaina Sheffield, Duchess of Wadebrooke was married to Tristan Sheffield, Fifth Duke of Wadebrooke and Earl of Edenton.

Shouldn't this be the happiest day of my life?

The forms were signed, the only witnesses being Devon and Charles. Her aunt and uncle refused to come. Her wedding gown was the nicest dress she had packed for London—a pretty, sapphire green, boasting a daringly low bodice. Although lovely, it was not what she had imagined wearing on her wedding day. A wedding night with her husband did not await her. She wouldn't be decorating a nursery in his home or making plans for their future.

Her wedding night consisted of returning home with Tristan and his friends. The servants managed to prepare an incomparable meal, and the company of friends was welcome, but when the meal ended, Alaina excused herself and went upstairs to the room she had occupied the night before. Alone.

Tristan stared after Alaina's retreating back. His wife. But he didn't feel like the lucky bridegroom. He still thought it was the safest thing for Alaina, but now he had to wonder, *Is she any safer with me?*

"Congratulations are in order, my friend." Charles tipped up his glass.

Tristan wondered how long it would take to kill a man with a look.

"All I'm saying is you've made your bed, and now you have to sleep in it. Well, maybe not the bed you want . . ."

Tristan sent his killing look to Devon now, wondering how

he had gotten himself into this. His life was about a combination of careful planning and impulses, but his impulses had never led him to marriage.

"I appreciate your support, gents," Tristan said dryly. "Really, I do, but if you don't mind, I'd rather save the congratulations for another day."

"Assuming there is going to be another day for congratulations," said Devon.

"The day we break this case and catch these bastards." Tristan stood and left the room, his friends staring after him.

"The poor chap has no idea, does he?"

"Oh, he's aware, but that's his problem." Devon turned to Charles with a glass half raised. "So old friend, shall we take the celebratory bottle of champagne and retreat to the study? I don't think it will be used elsewhere tonight."

"After you, old chap."

HE HEARD A SOFT sound coming from the other side of Alaina's door. Tristan stopped, wanting to open the barrier and comfort Alaina, but he knew he had no right. He was her husband now, but he made her no promises. Everything had been a pretense and they both knew it. Still, he couldn't blame her for the misery she now felt. He supposed it was only fair that he was as miserable as she did, but that didn't give him the right to go in there and hold her, not unless he was willing to make those promises to her on a permanent basis.

He was unable to offer that kind of life to anyone, not with his line of work. He had sworn after his father's death never to allow anyone to affect him to such an extent again. He had, though, and it had happened without his knowing, without planning. *Hell, I don't know when it happened because right now I cannot recall not being in love with her.* As much as he loathed to admit that his friends were right, he was definitely not sleeping in the bed he wanted to be in. Cursing himself, he walked to his room, threw his jacket on the bed, and looked around. It was quiet and lonely. Not bothering to change, and having instructed the staff to retire early, he lay down on a bed meant for two and tumbled into a disturbing sleep.

Alaina heard him stop at the door. He made no sound, but she knew he stood there, waiting. She longed for him to come inside. She could not ask of him what he was not willing to give, and if she opened the door and her heart to him, she would be forcing him to make a commitment. It mattered not if she loved him. She was still unsure how she felt about the discovery. Many years had passed without letting anyone into her intimate circles, blocking off unrealized feelings. Her aunt and uncle did not receive the fullness of her love because she thought she had lost the depth and ability when her parents and Braden died. Now she had to live knowing that she never lost the love she had dreamed of, but it was still out of reach.

Alaina then heard him walk down the hall to his bedroom, the bedroom they should have shared that night, the bed where they should have talked of hopes and dreams and children. *Damn him and damn all men and damn herself. Good grief, even my thoughts are vulgar.* She was weary and did not feel up to continuing an argument with herself. Alaina had turned away the maid, who was temporarily taking Daphne's place since she and Henry seemed to be on a permanent holiday. It worried her, thinking the worst had happened to them. Tristan had sent men to look for them, and there really wasn't anything else to be done.

Alaina lacked the energy to do more than remove her dress and skirts. She didn't bother with a nightgown and fell asleep hoping answers would come.

"I wanted you with me too. I am unsure of what to do."

"Yes, you do, and you know who can help you."

"Tristan?"

"Yes."

"Why now? Why wait all of these years?"

"It was time. You needed him in your life before I could give you this."

"I don't think I understand."

"You will."

WITH THE MORNING LIGHT shining dimly through the clouds, Alaina longed to return to her dream and to see her parents once again. She stared out her bedroom window as she pulled the silver-handled brush through her long hair. Across the lawns and gardens stood the greenhouse and farther still were the stables. When she needed to work through a problem, or to stop her tears from flowing, she sought solace with her horses. *Now I am married.* Setting the brush on her dressing table, Alaina secured the mass of hair with a ribbon and left the room to find her husband.

"Tristan?" Alaina stepped inside the room where the three men huddled around the large oak desk. They all looked up when she entered, and Tristan came around to her when he saw the brightness of her eyes.

"Are you all right?"

The worry in his voice calmed her somehow. He would keep her safe and protect her. Whether or not he held onto her remained to be seen.

"I remember everything now."

"Everything?"

"I saw the man who killed my parents."

Tristan grabbed her shoulders and leveled his eyes at her.

"When? How?"

"I'll explain the 'how' later—in private." She glanced over his shoulder at his friends. "It's a private matter. Right now, I can tell all of you everything I remember about that night."

Tristan followed her to a chair and helped her into it while Devon and Charles took seats of their own. She told them every detail, of how her parents died, and of finding Braden in the carriage. She told them of the man on the horse, describing his voice and his face. She had forgotten the face before, but now everything seemed clear. When she finished, they were silent for a moment, and then the questions began.

"You said there was a box?" asked Charles.

"Yes, the man went back into the carriage and he came out holding a box."

"Do you remember a box of any kind being in the carriage?"

asked Devon.

"No. I tried to think of it last night, but I just don't remember seeing one. I remember one of the seats lifted up, but my father usually kept an extra blanket and a gun under there." Alaina shrugged her shoulders, wishing she recalled more.

"You did well, Alaina." Tristan had held her hand the entire time and had yet to let go.

"We need to find these people, Tristan." She looked down at their joined hands and then up at him.

"We will." He brought her hand up to his lips. "We will."

"This man," Devon began. "If you saw him again, would you remember him?"

Alaina nodded. "Yes, but it's strange. I don't recall ever having seen him, but I remembered his voice. I knew his voice from somewhere."

"I promise you both. These people will get what they deserve." Charles addressed them as a unit.

It brought both hope and sorrow to Alaina as she looked at her husband. "Yes, they will."

Sixteen

"Will you be all right tonight?"

"I think the worst of the dreams are over."

"You always called them nightmares before."

Tristan stood in the doorway to her bedroom, watching her move efficiently about the room. Every day, he had warred with himself about what he had dragged her into, and he felt even worse because if he had to do it over again, he would not change anything. It wasn't his right to keep her for his own, but watching her now, Tristan knew he would never let another man have her.

"They were, but last night it was different." She slowly turned her attention back to him. "Tristan, please come in. I want to speak with you."

She sat at the end of the bed and motioned him to join her. Wary of trusting himself, Tristan hesitantly closed the door and walked over to sit beside Alaina, careful to put sufficient distance between them. Unfortunately, he didn't think there was enough space to keep him from wanting her.

"Last night, I dreamt of more than what I had told you and the others downstairs." She took a deep breath. "I had the same dream once before, but had forgotten about it, and what I didn't forget, I tried to block from my thoughts. I dreamt Braden was with me. I was ten years old again and we were at the ball in Ireland. I wanted to leave early, but he kept telling me it wasn't time yet, that no one was ready for me to leave. I didn't understand it, at first, because we were talking about the ball, but then we weren't at the ball. He told me it was time for me to remember and he loved me."

Alaina stopped long enough to glance at Tristan, but his face remained passive, and he only nodded for her to continue. "I saw everything from that night, everything I had told you about, but I didn't want to block it out because I knew Braden was there with me, reliving it with me. I wanted to see everything, but when it was over, he told me there was someone else to look after me now. However, he would always love me and be there to watch over me."

Alaina took Tristan's hand, and he focused on her eyes. He remained passive and patient, but his eyes told her something troubled him. "Tristan, I understand our marriage is a facade, but you would do anything to protect me. Braden knew about you, or it was my subconscious, but I do not believe it's that simple. He knew you would always take care of me."

"What did you tell Braden when he said he loved you?"

Surprised, Alaina took a second to answer. "I told him I loved him."

Tristan stood, walking over to the window.

"Tristan?"

"I shouldn't be jealous of a young man who died ten years ago, but a part of me is embarrassed to admit I am."

"Why are you jealous of Braden?" Alaina stood and joined him by the window.

"Because you loved him."

Understanding dawned and she stood in front of Tristan, drawing his attention.

"Tristan, I enjoyed the love of a ten-year-old girl. Braden was my best friend, and we swore to marry one day. However, that was a long time ago, and though a part of me will always love him, it will forever be the love of one child to another. He was part of my family."

Tristan looked down at her, seeing her sweet and tender smile. He didn't care what events had brought them this far, but he knew one thing for sure—he wasn't going to lose her.

"I love you, Alaina."

"I love you too, Tristan." She took his hands in hers. "What happens now?"

"That depends. Do you wish to remain married?"

"For the case or for you?"

"The case will end someday."

"We won't."

"Then I suppose there's only one thing to guarantee you can't get an annulment."

"What did you have in mind?" She smiled, and he slowly walked her back to the bed.

"Alaina, there are no certainties on the outcome of this case, but I want a life with you and I want a family with you. There's a good deal about me and my past I have not told you."

"I don't care what happened in your past," Alaina promised. "I care about your future and my place in it."

"You are my future."

"That's all I needed to hear. Now show me."

ALAINA WOKE SLOWLY, BUT her smile quickly spread. She felt refreshed and whole, and for the first time since her parents' death, she welcomed true happiness into her life and her heart. The deep-rooted, lingering fear that something bad happened every time she found happiness had disappeared. Nothing was going to ruin this new gift. Stretching and turning, Alaina reached out to the other side of the bed and found her husband. Her smile grew. "Hello, darling."

"Hello, beautiful." Tristan stroked a finger down her cheek.

"Wait." Alaina cleared her eyes and looked at Tristan, who lay on the bed fully clothed without his shoes.

"Where have you been?" she asked, disappointed he had left her after last night.

"I'm sorry, darling. I hated to leave, but Devon and Charles found something and needed to speak with me."

Alert now, Alaina sat up in bed. "Is everything all right?"

Tristan had wanted to wait until they were both with Devon and Charles, but he thought, *Better to prepare her for what lay ahead.*

"Alaina, Daphne was found late last night. The police discovered her and came over to tell us early this morning. Henry is still missing."

Alaina stared off into the room as Tristan pulled her gently toward him.

"She was with us for many years, Tristan. She was like a mother to me when mine died." Alaina turned her head into Tristan's shoulder, but the expected tears did not come. She feared the years of suppressing her feelings regarding her parents and Braden's death had hardened her.

"If you don't want to go down, that's all right, but I wanted to tell you before someone else did."

"No, I want to go down. I just need a minute, and I don't want a maid up here today. Will you fasten my dress?"

"Well, I seem to have the unfastening part down, so the opposite shouldn't be too difficult." He watched the small smile form on her soft lips. If he did only that, it just might be enough to get her through what was to come. Tristan kissed her brow gently and then moved to her lips. On a second thought, he pulled away.

"Darling, if we start this now, it will be hours before I get you tucked into any clothing."

Alaina pushed past the sorrow and smiled at her husband. She left the bed to sponge off at the washbasin and then moved to find a dress in the trunk Tristan had brought over. Pausing a moment, she turned to look at her husband.

"I love you, Tristan. Thank you for showing me it was possible." Quickly she took out her dress and went into the adjoining washroom to clean up, leaving Tristan smiling and humbled.

Thank you. She said those words as though he had bestowed her with a gift. If that was the case, he would spend his life showering her with gifts. Alaina came back into the room, and he fastened her dress—with a few delays—and then they made their way downstairs to speak with Devon and Charles. Devon had just finished relaying the story given by the man who had informed them of Daphne's demise.

"Was it painful?"

They all knew what she asked but did not know how to

respond.

Tristan spoke up. "Our man said it appeared to be done quickly. He found no other cuts or bruises. I don't think she suffered."

Nodding her head, Alaina held tightly to Tristan's hand. "And what of Henry?"

"We're not sure at this time, but all evidence indicates he is still alive."

"Why kill Daphne and not Henry? It makes more sense to dispose . . ." she choked out the word, "the greatest threat. Henry may have been older, but he was much stronger than Daphne and he knew how to fight."

All three men looked at Alaina in surprise.

"She's right. It would have made more sense to have kept Daphne alive," said Devon.

"Unless she had given them a reason not to," said Charles.

"Did anyone see anything?" asked Tristan

Devon shook his head. "They haven't found witnesses yet, but they're speaking to everyone they can find in the building across from the docks where she was found."

"All right, in the meantime, I think we should draw these men out in the open."

"What did you have in mind, Tristan?" asked Alaina.

"There's a ball tomorrow night. Your aunt had accepted the invitation, and I think we should go." Tristan was speaking to the other two occupants of the room, but he was looking at her.

Touched by his consideration, she squeezed his hand and smiled. "I'll do whatever needs to be done."

"We'll be back tomorrow night and ride to the ball with you," said Charles, as he and Devon stood to leave.

"No ladies to join you, gentlemen?" asked Alaina.

Devon just grinned. "Not while we're working, Duchess." With that said, both men left.

"Tristan. How are they doing?"

"Your aunt and uncle?"

"Yes."

"Devon went over to see them this morning to tell them

about Daphne, but they denied him access through the front door." He paused, and then with her encouragement, he continued. "They had a message for you. They told Devon to tell you that if you continued in this marriage, they would no longer be a part of your life." Even as he told her, he regretted it and wanted nothing more than to take the words back when he noticed the pain on Alaina's face. She said nothing for a long time but stood and moved to the other side of the room.

"I'm not leaving you or this marriage. If they love me so little as to make an ultimatum, then it is their choice. We're going to this ball and we're going to find these people. I am certain I will recognize this man if I see him. I believe he is a member of the gentry, and perhaps I already know him."

"Why do you think that?"

"I cannot be certain—but remember when I said his voice was familiar? He sounded cultured and well-spoken, as though he had been educated, and I recall my parents recognized him. I assume he moves around in society without anyone suspecting him." Alaina watched as Tristan paced the room for a few minutes, speaking short sentences as though he were going over notes in his head.

"Do you remember if this man was young or old?"

"I really wasn't a good judge of age back then, but I am positive he knew my parents. He must have been closer to their age or older perhaps." Alaina looked up for a moment, trying to recall what they had said that night.

"You remember something else?" Tristan moved closer to her.

"Yes, it was as if they had history with each other from long before, a deeper connection perhaps. I'll recognize him when I see him, I'm certain of it."

Tristan realized what he was about to do would never be sanctioned by his agency. Then again, he and the others weren't ones for following all of the rules, much like his own father had been.

"Well then, let's lure him out."

THE CLEAR SKIES AND crisp air enhanced the beautiful night. The music wafted through the rooms of the mansion, mingling with the sounds of conversation and laughter. The ballroom glistened with candlelight and mirrors. Overhead the chandeliers shimmered and vibrated from the sounds of the band playing a waltz. The sideboards were piled with food and drink, the servants diligently handing out punch and hors d'oeuvres. It was apparent everyone was having a wonderful time. Even Alaina found herself smiling but that was because of the man beside her.

Someone announced them upon their arrival, and because their marriage had been one of secret and surprise, it became the talk of the ball. Tristan and Alaina conversed with an earl and his new bride, but as kind as they were, Alaina found herself losing interest, and she scanned the ballroom.

"See anything?" Tristan leaned over to whisper in her ear.

"Not yet, but it is still early." Her eyes went back to their search.

Noticing her lack of concentration on the current conversation, Tristan excused them and moved her out to the dance floor.

"Talk to me."

Alaina allowed her body to move with the music. The sensation of Tristan brushing up against her brought back delicious memories of the other night and a blush crept into her cheeks.

"Should I be flattered?"

Alaina smiled.

"Before, I imagined how I would react to seeing this man again. He killed my parents, and all I can think about is seeing him fall to the same fate."

"That doesn't make you a bad person."

"I want to believe you, but I still feel as though there is some other way. Then I stop myself and realize perhaps there isn't."

"That's not all, is it?"

She watched the other couples as Tristan guided her around

the ballroom. "I want to learn more about my parents because ever since I discovered those papers, I realize they were strangers to me in many ways."

"They weren't. You knew the most important part about them—their love for you and for each other, as well as their dedication and devotion to family. They would have done anything for the people they had loved. They were good and honest people who tried to do good for others. Those are the things you knew and the only things that mattered." He kept her swaying against him, ignoring the people looking on and whispering. Tristan knew she didn't want this kind of attention and did his best to keep her mind on other things.

"You always say the right words. Thank you." She reached up to kiss him lightly, drawing away with a smile on her lips.

"Not always, but I do my best." He returned the kiss.

A sound at the entrance of the ballroom drew their attention. They both turned around with everyone else when someone announced the arrival of the Duke of Rothschild and Lord Melbourne. The last name gained Alaina's attention immediately, while the arrival of both had Tristan moving them slowly toward the front of the room. It took some careful navigating through the crowd when they were stopped every few steps by someone else congratulating them or wanting a look at the new duchess. It took them a few minutes, but they managed to reach the outer circles of the room, where debutantes and their hopeful mothers looked on while gossiping with the elder members of the gentry.

"Do you see him yet?" asked Alaina, and Tristan realized she spoke of Melbourne, not knowing who the other man was.

"Yes, they're coming this way."

"You have met the duke?"

"Yes. He's in the business."

Understanding dawned on her. "Is he helping you on your case?"

"No, he worked with my father and he's an old friend." Alaina nodded and waited for the men to reach them.

"Good evening, Sheffield," said Rothschild. "You are well, I trust?"

"Quite well, Rothschild."

"I should think so. Heard you found yourself a bride." Rothschild trailed his eyes up and down Alaina. Tristan wondered at the look he saw in the man's eyes and studied him more carefully.

"I did. Anthony Rothschild, my wife Alaina Sheffield, formerly Claiborne," supplied Tristan and turned to the other man. "Lord Melbourne, I believe you and my wife are already acquainted."

"But of course." The earl bowed. "You are well, Duchess?"

"Quite, thank you, Lord Melbourne."

Melbourne merely nodded, but the Rothschild spoke. "I knew your parents. You have a remarkable likeness to your mother."

"So I've been told by those who knew her best." Alaina offered no warmth in the reply.

"I was sorry to hear of your loss."

"Thank you."

Again, the words were cold, causing Rothschild to step back and Tristan to take a closer look at his wife. Silence reigned for a few seconds and then Melbourne spoke.

"If you'll excuse us, there are people waiting for our arrival in the billiards room." The lord nodded to Tristan and bowed to Alaina.

"If there is ever anything you need, my dear, please do not hesitate to call upon me." Rothschild lifted her hand and kissed it lightly. It took all of Alaina's willpower not to pull away. Tristan instantly noticed her discomfort and decided to pull away from the pair.

"We won't keep you from your game," Tristan said to the men and guided his wife to the far edge of the ballroom, away from listening ears.

"Alaina, what is it?"

"It was him."

"I agree. Why Rothschild keeps company with Melbourne is beyond understanding."

"No, Tristan," she said with quiet fierceness. "The duke. He was with another man, but it was the duke who I saw that night." She looked up at Tristan. "Rothschild killed my parents."

Tristan pulled her farther away and down the hall until he found an empty room and guided his wife inside, closing the door behind him. It took him a moment to find the candles and light them. When he did, he moved over to the sofa with Alaina and settled down, holding her close to give her comfort.

"Are you sure it was him?"

"The nightmare was quite vivid, and I knew I would never forget his face again. Since he had also been in the business, I may have heard him speaking with my father once before. At times I found myself walking past and listening in for a minute or two."

"He worked with my father," Tristan said, the disappointment clearly showing in his eyes. "I worked with him on my first case and I never suspected . . ." He didn't finish his thought, and Alaina lifted her head from his shoulder to study him.

"You said you believed that the man who killed my parents, killed your father." Tristan nodded his head. Neither one had to say any more as the thoughts tumbled through their minds.

"This isn't going to be easy, Alaina."

"Was it ever?"

He shook his head, willing her to understand.

"It's more than that. Rothschild is a duke and a confidante to Parliament. He is also a high-ranking officer in the government department in which I work. Convincing everyone he is a murderer and thief is not going to be easy."

"But not impossible."

"I don't believe in the impossible." He smiled down at her. "Otherwise I would not have had you." His smile deepened with hers, and he leaned down to kiss her, relishing the feel of her lips. He wished they were home. The sooner this business ended, the sooner he could give her the life she deserved.

He stepped back a moment. "Wait, you said he was with another man."

"Yes, he was. A man I didn't see but heard his voice. My

parents knew him, too. He's the one who spoke to them, but his face was hidden in shadows. He is familiar, but I don't recall from where or how."

"They never said his name?"

She shook her head. "If they did, I don't recall."

"Don't worry, we'll get them all. One way or another," Tristan promised. "I'm sorry to be the one who brought back the memories." He spoke softly against her lips.

She pulled back from him.

"Tristan Sheffield, you have nothing to be sorry about. I pushed everything away, suppressed all of my feelings and my memories for years, too afraid to remember. You showed me I had the courage to release the fear. Never once did you doubt anything I told you, and even now when I accuse your father's friend of murder, you don't doubt, but accept what I say to be true."

She let the anger simmer, and Tristan couldn't help but kiss her brow where it crinkled.

"I am sorry," he said, but continued when she looked like she was going to pounce on him, "that we are not in a more appropriate place for what I would like to do with you." He leaned down to do something wonderful to her neck and a laugh escaped.

"I do love you, Tristan."

"I love you, my duchess. However, the plans invading my thoughts will have to wait until we return home. We must give our excuses and locate Charles and Devon."

They stood and started for the door when it opened and the two in question stepped inside, leaving the door open as though in preparedness for them to leave.

"You found Melbourne with Rothschild?" asked Charles.

Tristan nodded. "It was Rothschild who Alaina saw that night."

Devon slowly nodded, understanding everything the accusation entailed. "What do you want to do about this?"

"We need motive and evidence, neither of which we have on Rothschild. I also want to learn why he and Melbourne are here together." He then turned to his wife while still addressing the two men. "I don't want either one of them within one hundred miles of Alaina, and if they are, I want you to inform me." He turned his attention back to his friends, sending a clear message that they were to help keep them away from Alaina.

"We still have a few men we can trust," said Devon. "They'll be notified immediately."

"You're ready to leave?" asked Charles.

"Yes, we'll make our excuses."

Charles smiled. "Already done. The carriage is out front."

Devon said, "He knows you too well."

"It's a comfort and a nuisance." Tristan smiled at his friend.

"Shall we, my lady?" Tristan tucked Alaina's arm through his and guided her outside, where a servant waited with their coats. They bundled into the carriage, closing the windows to keep out the cold air. Once they arrived at Tristan's home, Tristan and Alaina headed for the house, but Charles and Devon walked toward the stables.

Alaina didn't need to ask what they were doing, though she prayed for their safety.

"I realize the situation is grim, but have I put all of you in too much danger?" Alaina asked.

Tristan stopped on the stone steps leading to the front door. He shook his head at the butler when he opened the door for them. "What makes you believe you're putting anyone in danger? If it will cause you less concern, we would be pursuing this case under any circumstance. Uncovering a traitor is not something the agency won't chase."

"Nevertheless, I can't help but feel responsible for the extent to which you're going. You may have to kill a man."

"It won't be the first time."

Alaina knew he didn't like to speak of his past, the work he had done, and the lives lost as a result of his work. The whisper of fear clouding her emotions was not for her safety, but for his, and he didn't allow her the opportunity to respond.

"Understand this, Alaina, not one ounce of responsibility rests with you." Tristan assured her. "This fight began long ago and none of us could have prevented the outcome. All we can do is finish it."

Seventeen

"**T**ell me again why we do not just kill the bastard." Tristan glanced up from the papers on his desk and glanced at Devon.

"I'm not going to turn myself into a murderer." Tristan kept his voice calm, though it contradicted the anger roiling within.

"Justice isn't murder."

"It is if we do this." Tristan moved around the desk and faced his friend. The man they wanted had killed Alaina's family, Tristan's father, and if that wasn't enough for Devon and Charles to hate him, he used to be one of their own. "My friend, no one wants this man dead more than I for what he has done to us, my father, and most especially to Alaina. If the need arises, I will not hesitate to put a lead ball in his chest, but until that time comes, we find another way to bring him in. There are too many people on his side and we need proof."

"There are just as many people on your side, Tristan, if not more," said Charles.

Tristan considered his other friend, who currently made use of one of the wingback chairs by the fireplace.

"Unfortunately, right now those same men insist on the proof before condemning a duke and a government official." Tristan now spoke to both men directly. "Believe me when I say I want nothing more than to hunt this man down and slit his throat, along with every other man on his payroll, but there is a woman upstairs whom I love more than my own life, and I will do anything to keep her safe. If I go on a manhunt for Rothschild, I put her life in jeopardy. We still haven't discovered who he's working with or how many."

Charles stood and went to Tristan, placing a brotherly arm around his shoulder. "She would not think any less of you as a human being if you killed Rothschild." Charles smiled at the surprised expression on Tristan's face. "We have been friends for many years now and I will support you, whatever your decision. There has never been a moment in those years when you loved someone or something more than your work—until now."

"My family, you, and Devon."

"You know what I mean," said Charles. "I will stand beside you," he repeated.

"As will I, whatever your decision," said Devon, joining them.

Tristan studied one friend and then the other, recognizing their willingness to give their lives for Alaina. That knowledge gave him more comfort than he believed he deserved. Tristan's gaze shifted toward the doorway and saw Alaina standing there, a smile on her face.

She had heard some of what they had said and instantly vowed her devotion to Tristan's friends. She looked at her husband and noticed how tired he seemed. Neither of them had slept well the previous night, and she saw how heavily the responsibility weighed on him. He tried to hide the fear and anger inside, but she saw his pain. She held out her arms to him when he came to her and welcomed the light kiss.

"You should be sleeping," he said to her softly.

"I couldn't stay in bed with all that is going on. I need to help in any way I can. I'm tired of waiting." She then leaned around Tristan to focus on the other two occupants of the room.

"Good day, gentlemen."

"How are you?" asked Devon.

"I'm fairing. I think I can speak for all of us when I say I just want this to be over."

The three men voiced their agreements and they all settled down in the study, where they had been taking most of their meals, much to Andrew's dismay. The conversation stopped long enough to allow a maid to bring in a lunch tray.

"Charles, you had something you wanted to discuss with us," Tristan said after they had all sated their hunger.

Charles contemplated the room's occupants and decided directness was the best approach.

"I think we should invite Rothschild here—for supper."

"You want to bring that bastard into this house?" Devon had to keep from yelling.

Tristan motioned for him to hold back and lent his attention to Charles.

"Why do you want to bring him here?" Tristan held Alaina's hand in his own.

The gesture was not lost on Charles, and he knew Tristan asked why he wanted to bring the threat closer to Alaina.

"Alaina wouldn't be here but back at Claiborne Manor. The supper would be for us and him. A gentlemen's gathering, if you will," said Charles.

"I won't leave her there alone."

"You wouldn't have to. My brothers arrived from Ireland this morning and can stay at Claiborne Manor with Alaina," said Devon.

Tristan thought this over for a moment. He trusted Devon's brothers as much as Devon himself, and he knew Alaina would be safe with them. Still, he didn't want to leave her because as much as he trusted them, he didn't trust them to care for her the way he could.

"No," he said simply. "Besides, something like this could have the opposite effect and ruin our chances if he realizes we suspect him."

"We're running out of time," said Charles, catching Alaina's attention.

"What do you mean?"

Immediately Charles realized his mistake and turned to Tristan apologetically.

Alaina regarded her husband. "What is going on here?"

"Alaina," Tristan said knowing his words could anger her. "We have only a short time left. The men we're after are making a final shipment of goods from the country—munitions and likely classified correspondence."

"Why didn't you tell me this before?"

"I wanted to protect you from this part of my life."

"Is this the reason why my parents were killed?"

"Yes."

Alaina stood and paced the room for a few minutes, then turned back to the men.

"How long?"

"Alaina . . ."

"How long?" she asked again.

"One week."

"I see, and what were you planning on doing? I suppose Charles made the suggestion for me to return to Claiborne Manor to keep me tucked away, and that the dinner is just a cover for what you really had in mind." She looked at each of them accusingly and then focused her attention back on Tristan.

"What were you really planning, Tristan?"

He didn't want her involved in this any more than she had to be. "Alaina, please understand that I want to keep you safe, and this part of the work would only endanger you greatly."

"What were you planning?"

There was no mistaking the quiet plea in her voice. He stood and went to her, drawing her focus to him alone. Like his, her eyes showed every bit of what she felt, and he didn't like what he saw.

"Alaina," he began, but she pushed away from him.

"You may refuse to tell me, but I will not leave you behind to play the hero and get yourself killed. I will not become a widow, now or ever. Do you understand me?" She wanted to yell, not caring about the other two men in the room. They had all lied to her. She glanced once more at each of them and left the room, closing the door roughly in her wake.

"Perhaps we should have told her," said Devon.

"Do you really believe that?" asked Tristan, looking to the door through which Alaina had exited. "She's in enough danger as it is, and if she knew the extent of our plans, she might find a way to persuade me to give up the idea."

"Let her try, Tristan, if it comforts her to try," said Devon.

"I don't think that's what he's worried about, friend," offered Charles.

"All right, what is worrying you?"

Tristan walked to the window and kept his back to them when he answered. "I would do anything for her, no matter what it cost me. If she truly wished to, she could stop me from doing this, simply by asking. Even if it meant giving up all we have worked toward." Tristan turned back to his friends. "We continue as planned. Devon, inform your brothers of our plans—we will need them. Charles, do you know where your man is?"

"Yes. He waits at the building where we found Daphne."

"Good. Keep him there for now. Someone might return."

"You can back out of this, Tristan," said Charles.

Tristan considered it for a moment. He imagined walking away from the work, taking Alaina away from here, and living out their lives together in safety. Yet, he couldn't turn away from the job any more than he could leave his wife. "We continue as planned. Things are already set in motion, so we finish this."

Both men nodded and left the house—Devon to retrieve his brothers and Charles to relay information to another agent. Tristan waited a moment longer, thinking about his part and what he still had to accomplish. Looking over at his desk and then at the clock, he sat down and shuffled a few papers around.

"Bloody hell." He pushed the chair back, left the room and took the stairs two at a time. He walked to the master suite and listened at the door, but he heard nothing that resembled the sounds of someone moving around. Tristan thought about knocking and then swore again. It was his room too, and if she wanted to be stubborn and sequester herself from him, that didn't mean he still couldn't go in. Pushing the door open, Tristan went inside and immediately saw her.

She sat by the window, and he sensed she knew he stood there but ignored him, which didn't help the situation and only increased his guilt. A part of him wanted to keep watching her while the sun shined through her hair, bringing out different shades of gold. He saw how downtrodden she seemed with her knees curled up against her, her head resting against the wall. He sensed she might be lonely too. It tore at him that he had been the cause.

Alaina had stopped being angry the moment she reached the bedroom—well, almost. She understood his reasons for not telling her, but she still felt betrayed and more strongly, she was terrified, which likely accounted for most of her anger.

Anger is easier than fear.

Understanding Tristan's work and the danger he faced didn't help, but he had told her some of what had happened in his past. What he'd been through frightened her. That he had not shared all of his plans with her made her believe what they faced was worse than anything he'd ever done.

"Alaina?"

"Yes?"

Tristan sighed with a small measure of relief. At least she wasn't going to ignore him.

"I don't feel I was wrong by not telling you, but I realize I should have told you that there was something I couldn't tell you."

She finally turned her eyes toward him.

"I must love you a great deal to have understood what you just said."

He tried a smile and was disappointed when she didn't return it with one of her own.

"I'm sorry. I never meant to hurt you. What makes it worse is that if I could go back and change any of it, I wouldn't. I didn't tell you because I couldn't bear the thought of you knowing what I had to do." Tristan waited as Alaina continued to study him.

She stood but kept the distance between them. "Tristan, you telling me this only escalates my fear because I don't know what lies ahead. Not telling me something is worse than keeping the truth from me. I trust you but that doesn't diminish the fear. Share with me. Tell me why you hold back. What has happened to you to make you unsure of people?"

"You want the truth? Every sordid and despicable detail,

every life I've taken, every person I've hurt?" Tristan studied her, his eyes filled with pain. "Do you not realize I would give anything to erase the darker deeds of my career?"

"I'm your wife and I understand your need to protect me. That does not mean protecting me from you, from who you are. I love you, not because of what you've done, but because of who you are now." Alaina stepped closer to him. "What we've been through, what we must go through, will mean nothing if we can't be everything to each other."

"It's not that easy." Tristan closed the distance between them and glided his hands up the length of her arms. "If I held nothing back from you, I would relinquish the piece of me which allows me to do this job."

"Or you could end up with everything you've ever dreamed of having." Alaina lifted his hand from her arm and placed it on her heart.

Tristan's moist eyes gazed into hers. His hand remained where it felt the beating in her chest, and he lowered his lips to meet hers. It wasn't a kiss meant to possess but to release himself from emotional bondage. Her fingers slid up his back, circling, until she held him close, wrapping him completely in her arms. His strength rippled through her and she closed her eyes, allowing her imagination to sweep her into the future.

They walked along the edge of their pond, the summer breeze caressing them, their son showing their daughter how to catch a butterfly. The wind carried their laughter, and the reflection from the pond caught the glimmer of golden hair as the children skipped rocks.

Her eyes opened, and her heart beat in time with his.

"I'm still scared." She did not want to lose the future she had just seen.

"So am I." And for the first time in his life, he could say that and mean it. He never had anything or anyone as precious as she to lose before.

"Tonight, I don't want to be afraid." Alaina studied his face. "I just want to feel you."

"And so you shall." The whisper kissed her ear as his lips

trailed down her neck. The time for words had passed, and tonight they were alone. The world outside of their love did not exist as he carried her to their bed and gently laid her down.

Their movements were slow and tortuous. A gentle sigh and soft moan escaped her lips while his lips found a path down her neckline to the soft swell where her breasts began. Slowly, each one removed the other's clothing, switching off as if in a dance—a beautiful and seductive dance. Both of them wished to extend this union for as long as possible, each taking their time, each discovering parts of the other that they had not known existed.

He covered her with his long body, running his hands gently up and down the length of hers. Lifting his head until his eyes met hers, he saw the shimmer of a tear turn her eyes to a blue, rivaling the brightest of sapphires, and kissed the tear away.

Her hand trailed up his arm and shoulder, then his neck, gently bringing his face back down to her. Their breathing went from feather-soft to laborious. Tristan wished to prolong the moment for as long as possible. He continued the torture on her body until she climaxed again and again. When she couldn't take anymore, and he couldn't hold back any longer, he entered her, filling her while together they reached a shattering peak.

When they had both settled and she shifted under him, he held her in place and smiled softly, whispering, "Stay still, my love, we're making a baby."

The single tear returned to kiss her cheek, but the smile reached her eyes. He held her that way until sleep swept her away.

Sometime later, removing himself from her, he kissed her brow and left the bed, careful not to wake her. He went into the adjoining washroom and soon returned fully dressed. He looked from the window to his wife. Darkness had descended and she slept, her breathing soft and steady. Silently he moved to the door, but his gaze shifted back once more to the sleeping form in the center of the large bed.

"I love you, Alaina. I hope that someday you'll forgive me." He closed the door softly behind him, and keeping silent, he found his way downstairs and into the study.

Several minutes later, Andrew knocked lightly on the door and entered, finding Tristan writing at his desk. "May I bring you anything, sir?"

"No, thank you, Andrew. You may retire for the evening."

"You're certain, sir?"

"Yes. I'll see you in the morning."

"Very good, sir."

Tristan watched the door close behind his butler and leaned into the back of the leather chair. He had discovered early in his career that keeping a detailed journal of his cases helped him learn from past mistakes to avoid future errors. These were not the reports sent to the main office but rather personal thoughts and feelings related to his cases. His eyes skimmed through the previous entries relating to the deaths of the woman and child in Scotland. He closed his eyes, recalling every detail. He and his friends had vowed not to speak of it, but it helped to remember, and he hoped reliving the experience would make him a better agent. Clearing his mind and redirecting his thoughts to Alaina, he smiled and returned to his writing.

Nearly two hours later, Tristan heard horses outside his study window. Tristan walked to the window and watched as Charles, Devon, and Devon's brothers dismounted. He left the study to meet them at the front door, but before he reached them, the door opened and they stood in the entry.

"Should I bother to ask how you made it past the locked door?" Tristan asked the men.

"Just practicing." Devon grinned.

"Your timing has improved." Tristan motioned for them to follow him into his office.

"Is she all right?" asked Charles, when the door closed behind them.

"For tonight." He turned his attention to Devon's brothers. "Thank you for coming, Derek and Zachary. I'm trusting you with her life."

The men nodded, understanding that if anything happened to her, they would meet a far worse fate than anything that might befall her.

"She'll be safe here," Derek promised, "but what do you want us to tell her?"

Tristan raised his eyes to the ceiling as if he saw right through the floors and into their room. "I doubt she will need an explanation. Somehow, I'm certain she's already figured it out."

The men went over their course of action once again until they were satisfied that they all knew their parts. Papers were burned in the large stone fireplace with the men watching until every scrap turned to ash.

Tristan turned to his longtime friends. "It's time," he said, and the men gathered their things and quietly left the room.

Everyone departed the house silently and made their way through the darkness to the stables behind the London house. Derek and Zachary went upstairs to check on Alaina.

Devon had already saddled the horses and left them tethered for the men, thankful that the stable hand was old and half-deaf. When all three men were on their horses and ready to leave, Derek and Zachary came running from the shadows.

"Dash it all men, what's wrong?" asked Tristan.

Derek did not look forward to relaying his discovery. "I went to check on Alaina right after you left. She wasn't in her room. We searched the house, waking up a couple of the servants, but she isn't there."

Tristan paled and a sickness entered his heart. "How is that possible? The doors and windows are locked. We were right there." He jumped down from his horse and turned to the others who had followed suit. "Devon, you carry out your portion of the plan. We need to at least keep an eye on them. Charles, you come with me."

Devon and his horse left the stables at a gallop on the winding road leading into town. He raced his horse until they reached the bridge beyond the outskirts of the village.

Tristan and the others hurried back into the house, and with the help of the new butler and upstairs maid, both of whom had been awakened, they searched every room again, checking every closet and corner before they moved on to the next. She wasn't there. Tristan stood next to the bed he had left her in just a short while ago, cursing himself for leaving her in the first place and not understanding how she could be gone.

There were no signs of struggle, nothing missing except her robe. Charles moved into the room and stood next to Tristan.

"We're continuing with the plan," said Tristan.

Surprised, Charles asked, "The original plan? Your wife is missing."

"I know, just as I know Rothschild is behind it. I swear when I get my hands on him, there won't be anything left for the undertaker to work with." He left the room in a hurry, and Charles and the others followed him to the stable, where they silently saddled two additional horses. Tristan wasn't waiting for them. "Finish here and then catch up. You know what to do."

"Wait," said Charles. "Don't be rash, Tristan, it could get her killed. We have to think this through."

"To hell with that. The bastard has my wife, and I'm not going to think about it while there's even the slightest chance I could get to her before they do something . . ." He didn't finish the sentence but just turned the horse and left.

Charles swore silently and jumped on his horse. "Go to Devon, tell him what's happening, and stay with him." Charles then turned and rode off in the same direction as Tristan.

Derek and Zachary finished with the horses and rode out to the bridge.

"WE THOUGHT YOU were dead."

"Your mistake." His laugh sank any hope Alaina believed she might have.

"I trusted you. My family trusted you. All of these years you spied on us, waiting for what?"

"Why, for just this moment, and the beauty of it is that even your special agent husband and his friends trusted me. A nearly perfect plan from start to finish."

"You began with my kidnapping. How will you finish it, then?"

"Actually, it began with your parents, and it will finish with you in about the same way." She gaped at him in sheer disbelief. "You helped them kill my parents?"

"I'm only a messenger."

He moved over to the small barred cage and watched her pace from side to side. "You may as well make yourself comfortable. It could be a while." She remained standing, and he continued talking. "You were raised better than to ignore others when they're speaking to you."

"Why?" Alaina asked.

"Does it matter?" asked Henry.

"Yes, it does. My family has always treated you well."

"True, but someone offered me more money than I would make in half a lifetime as a butler. Of course your parents saw right through the men who offered me this job."

"What are talking about?"

"No, that's enough for now."

"You won't get away with this."

"Why, my dear, I already have." Laughing, he left the room and closed the basement door behind him.

Alaina steadied herself and surveyed her surroundings. The window above her cell and the one next to her, secured with heavy bars, offered no means of escape. Chains hung on one wall and wooden benches sat along the opposite wall. *No escape.* She berated herself for being such a fool. When Henry had come into her room, she was so surprised, she did nothing more than stare, giving him enough time to subdue her, then carry her silently down the servant's staircase, and bring her out to a waiting carriage. He had taken great delight in telling her exactly how he had done it and gotten away with it, assuring her that if anyone actually found her, she wouldn't be alive to tell them anything.

Alaina glanced down at the single cot in the cell and shrank back, not wanting to think about how many diseases and vermin lurked in the mattress. She remained standing on her bare feet, the cold and dampness seeping through to her blood, and she hoped Tristan would find her. She also hoped he would be safe. Alaina laid a gentle hand on her stomach, her heart longing and filled with hope.

Eighteen

The biting cold and imminent rain forced anyone venturing outside to protect themselves under layers of clothing. The wind blew, whipping trees and howling through alleys. A storm threatened and black clouds shrouded the night sky in complete darkness. Neither the moon nor the stars shone to help light the way, but these looming threats did not pose any obstacles for the agents. Tristan had spent many similar nights rusticating in the countryside with his father, learning the sounds that came out of the shadows. He could tell the difference between an animal and a person moving in the forest or distinguish between the call of a bird or two people communicating under the cover of disguise. But never before had he ever needed to utilize his skills and talents to such a degree.

Charles crouched down beside him. Neither one of them moved as they blended in with the noises of the night. The horses grazed in underbrush not far away, but the wild animals were too silent as if they sensed something in the darkness. Tristan always trusted an animal's instinct over that of a human, and things were too quiet for his comfort.

A flickering of light in the distance drew their attention, and both men froze. A faint whistle echoed to them from the same direction. A door opened, then closed, and the light disappeared into the shadows. They quietly and cautiously moved closer to the clearing, gazing across the way to the massive run-down building. It appeared abandoned, and the light had vanished as though the night had only been playing with their minds. Feeling it safe now to speak, Tristan turned to Charles. "I don't suppose you're of a mind to investigate?"

"Devon wouldn't want to miss this."

Tristan nodded his agreement. "I only hope the plan for the bridge worked—I want those bastards dead."

Charles had never seen this kind of anger in Tristan, at least not since the tragic night in the Highlands two years earlier. Charles recognized that Tristan wasn't thinking like a lawman but like a husband. He also knew Tristan chose to execute violence only when necessary, and he might choose to kill whoever stood in his way tonight.

DEVON AND HIS BROTHERS waited, prepared for whatever or whoever would come their way, but he worried. His instincts warned him of danger. The agents had only ten more minutes before he went after Tristan and Charles. His brothers had informed him of the change in plans, which caused Devon to second-guess the current strategy.

They expected the culprits to be experienced and to practice a measure of stealth. Reports had indicated riders would be coming this way, which meant they should have been there by now. His associates should also have arrived.

Devon and his brothers waited on horseback, the only sound coming from the animals. Then Devon's horse perked up its ears at the sound of hooves clomping on gravel. He glanced at his brothers, knowing he wouldn't have to tell them to be quiet, and they waited. Two minutes later, two riders crested at the hill and halted before the bridge. Devon waited for them to continue on, but they just sat on their horses as if waiting for someone or something. The uneasiness crept further into Devon's stomach, and his long ingrained intuition told him to leave. He didn't know how or why, but they were being set up. They were no longer the hunters in this chase. Devon turned backward to his brothers and with a slight flick of his hand, they followed him quietly and slowly back through the trees until they no longer saw the road, and when they thought they were far enough away, they rode in the opposite direction.

"I'M GOING IN."

Charles put a hand on Tristan's shoulder to stop him.

"You don't know what's in there. It could be suicide."

Tristan glared at his friend, a war raging inside of him.

Charles thought he saw a touch of madness in his friend's eyes and stepped back. Charles glanced back to the house and thought that if he investigated the front, perhaps he would find the culprits first, minimizing the risk of bloodshed.

"I'll take the front," said Charles.

Tristan hesitated but nodded.

Both men crouched low and made their way to either side of the building. Tristan had just reached the back door when the first muffled scream reached his ears.

"DEVON, WAIT A MINUTE." Devon pulled his horse to a stop and turned to look at his brother.

"What is it?"

"Listen."

He didn't hear anything for a minute, and then he heard the sound of a carriage on the road. They weren't near the bridge anymore, but he heard the rolling of wheels on dirt and rock. The three men pulled their horses farther away from the road and out of sight.

A moment later, two riders, followed by a carriage, rounded a curve and headed in their direction. Devon knew by instinct that although they were not the same men from the bridge, they were all acquainted. The riders passed, and the carriage drew closer with the flaps on the windows open to the night air. The dark evening obscured the faces of the passengers, but he heard voices arguing. He recognized at least one of the voices, and the other seemed vaguely familiar.

They allowed the small caravan to pass and waited until they were out of earshot before speaking. "We'll take the back roads and with any luck, we'll come out in front of them—we have to get to Tristan," he urged. Turning to Derek, he said, "Return to the city and inform the captain of the situation. We need men at Claiborne Manor and the London house."

"It will be handled," promised Derek. "Good speed, brothers." He turned and headed back to the city, leaving the other two riding toward unknown dangers.

As HE FRANTICALLY MADE his way through the old house, Tristan ignored the pain in his shoulder from breaking down the back door. The dark and dank building reeked with an unpleasant odor, wafting from the skeleton of every room. It appeared as though someone had been there periodically. An inch of dirt covered the floors except for the well-trodden paths from the kitchen and the back hallways. Tristan heard rats scuffling along the upper floors. The smell of death pervaded and lingered in the air.

He continued his search but discovered nothing out of the ordinary. The muffled screams stopped the moment he had broken through the back door, and he now looked everywhere for a basement door. Charles met him halfway through the search, revealing he, too, had found nothing.

Tristan spotted the latch in the kitchen floorboard first.

Charles placed a hand on Tristan, holding him off, wanting to go first, but Tristan shook him off and pulled up on the heavy door. The corridor leading down was darker than the rest of the house and smelled much worse. Feeling their way along the wall, both men carefully made their way down the steps. A dim light ahead cast shadows and glowed a little brighter with each step they took. Picking up his pace, Tristan moved toward the light and came to another door. This one was bolted shut and on the other side came the moans—barely audible.

"Alaina?" Tristan yelled through the bars in the door. He heard a small moan.

Charles studied the lock for a moment. "We won't be getting through this one easily."

"Like hell we won't," Tristan said and pushed Charles back. Aiming his pistol at the bolt, he sent two clean and easy shots into the lock and swung it open. The room was brighter than the corridor with two lanterns hanging precariously from one wall. Four cells stood side by side, each one no bigger than a small closet. Someone swung out at the men. Tristan received a scrape to the side of his head. It took only a second for Charles to put a bullet through the man's head. Tristan quickly searched the small enclosures for signs of life and panicked when he saw who lay in the last cell. Running over, he grabbed the bars and shook with every ounce of strength his body possessed. Lying on a filthy cot, Alaina was tied up at the wrists and ankles, stripped down to the last of her clothing. Charles moved over beside his friend.

"I didn't find any keys on the guard."

"Alaina?" Tristan inspected his wife from the other side of the bars. She appeared only half-conscious. He took Charles's gun and fired a bullet at the lock on the gate, but it wouldn't budge.

"They certainly knew how to make cells in my day." The voice came from behind them.

Tristan tensed and turned around.

"Now don't look shocked, gentlemen. I hope you don't mind the mess, but my days as a butler are over."

Tristan stepped forward, energy and anger radiating from his body, but Charles held him off. Henry shook his head at them and made a "tsking" sound, mocking them. He held a large gun in one hand and swung a set of keys on the finger of his other hand.

"Now, I suppose you're looking for these, but you must know I'm not going to give them to you. You see, I had hoped to be rid of her and on my way before you or your friends arrived, though it seems we underestimated you."

"Why?"

"Ah, why would I do this? Well, the money of course. You see, someone is paying me a lot of it to get rid of this little problem of theirs." He indicated Alaina. "And seeing as how I was tired of serving her family for all of these years, it seemed like a wise financial decision."

"You sick bastard," Tristan growled out. "You won't walk away from this alive, Henry. I suggest you pass me the keys."

"Oh, I know I will. You must understand that I have made my deal and been offered safe passage from England. I am merely the messenger, not the executioner, and I have nothing to worry about, though I am unable to offer you the same reassurance."

"You weren't hired to kill Alaina?"

Henry studied Tristan for a minute before answering. "In fact I was, though it turns out I don't have the constitution for it—unless absolutely necessary. I suggest you cooperate."

"If you plan to escape, then you'll have to kill us first, and that won't happen." Charles eyes remained focused on the doorway behind Henry.

"There will be someone along shortly to dispose of you and Alaina. Now as for the young mistress over there, or should I say, Her Grace, she has not been the most cooperative of captives. She took it upon herself to injure one of my men when he entered her cell. Pity that she had to be punished. I had hoped hers could be a quick and painless death."

"I'm glad I can't say the same for you." The gleam in Tristan's eye conveyed everything he wanted to do to the man, which brought a moment of fear to Henry.

"What the—?" Henry said nothing more as a bullet found a clean path into his back. He fell forward, a stream of blood flowing from beneath his chest. Tristan lifted the keys from Henry's limp grip and unlocked Alaina's cell.

Charles followed him inside, removing the wristbands, while Tristan unraveled the rope at her ankles. Once he freed her, Tristan wrapped his coat around her and lifted her off the cot. He recognized the shouts coming from the room outside of the cell, and holding her close, he carried her out. Devon knelt beside Henry's body, searching his pockets.

"Is she all right?" asked Devon, motioning to the form in Tristan's arms.

"She will be. Couldn't have asked for better timing, but how did you know we were here?"

"It's a long story. I'll tell you after we return to Claiborne Manor. Once she is tended and comfortable, we have another problem to deal with. Come on. Zachary is outside with the horses." Devon waited for the others to leave and followed behind, tucking a piece of paper in his pocket that he had found in Henry's jacket.

Alaina, only half-conscious, rode back to the country, encompassed in Tristan's arms.

Nineteen

Tristan refused to allow anyone into his room for two days and only came downstairs to eat, not wishing to disturb Alaina with servants walking in and out of the bedroom. His friends understood but still worried for him.

"Where's Tristan?" Devon walked into the dining room, which contained a full breakfast buffet. Charles was reading some papers, barely touching his coffee and toast.

"He's still with Alaina." Charles set the documents on the table and turned to Devon who joined him, holding a plate filled with breakfast meats and poached eggs. "I suppose we do have to eat."

Devon smiled wearily. "I suppose we do," he said, and started in on his eggs.

Charles refreshed his plate and sat back down. He ate his food, barely tasting it. "What do you think he'll do?"

Devon looked up from his plate and studied his friend.

"I don't know. All he's thinking about right now is Alaina, though I can't blame the man. If my family was in danger, nothing would stop me from protecting them."

Charles studied Devon. "I'm trying to recall a time when you've spoken of your family, but I cannot. I don't know anyone beyond your brothers."

Devon paused. "Perhaps because I don't speak of them."

"Any particular reason why?"

"I've nothing important to share."

Charles sensed he should move away from the topic but pressed him with one more question. "Are they alive?"

"Tristan is the only other person to ever ask me that

question." Devon leaned back in the chair and set his utensils alongside the plate. "I don't know."

Charles nodded. "Sometimes that's easier."

"Easier than what Tristan is facing right now?"

"Neither of us can understand what he's feeling regarding Alaina, but we've all lost friends to these traitors. I just hate to think of all of the men who have died, trying to bring these people to justice. They all died in vain."

"They didn't," said Devon. "At least not all of them."

Charles considered him as Devon slipped a small stack of papers across the table. Charles turned them around and skimmed the top pages. He glanced up at Devon. "Where did you find these?"

"Alaina said she had found these papers in her mother's trunk under a false bottom. Last night it kept me awake. I went to the attic to inspect the other trunks and found two more with false bottoms. One contained foreign currency and land deeds. The other trunk held these documents and a few journals."

"What kind of journals?"

"I didn't read them, but from what I could tell, it appeared as though the Claibornes kept meticulous records of every encounter or assignment they took for the government. Most of us keep records, but we don't normally hold onto them after the mission is completed."

"Perhaps therein lies the answer," said Charles.

"What do you mean?"

"We're not spies."

"Yes, we are," argued Devon.

"We act on the information, but we don't spend months or years gathering it. We rely on others to do the initial research and we take things from there." Charles shuffled through the papers, his eyes scanning the lower edges. "I remember seeing a notation on the corner of a packet we received. It was our first case and . . . Yes. Here it is." He passed the single sheet of paper to Devon and pointed to the lower corner.

"C.C." Devon glanced up. "Christopher Claiborne."

"Have you told anyone else about these and the journals yet?"

"No, I hoped to show both Tristan and Alaina this morning," said Devon.

"I see no reason to wait."

"TRISTAN, I'M ALL RIGHT, really."

"I just don't want you to rush anything."

Alaina smiled at her husband. On the morning that they had arrived home, the sun had crested at the horizon, and she had slept all day and through the night. The second day, Tristan refused to let her leave their bed, but today was a new day, and she wasn't going to spend it in their room.

"I'm all right. I can walk, talk, and I am certain I can even run and ride. I can't stay in this bed another moment."

Tristan looked at his wife and brushed a soft golden lock of hair from her brow. "I know. I just keep thinking about what they did to you, and how you were when I found you."

"Don't," she pleaded. "Don't do that to yourself. You saved my life." Her hand caressed his face. "I knew you would come."

"I'll always come for you."

"I know. Now about this bed—" A knock at the door interrupted her.

Gritting his teeth, Tristan got off the bed and went to the door. Alaina watched as he kept it open only enough for him to speak with whoever stood on the other side. After a minute, he turned to her.

"It seems your wish is granted," he said. "Devon found something we need to see."

Alaina pushed aside the covers and scooted off the bed. "It's not over yet, is it?"

Tristan walked over to her and took her in his arms.

"My love, I'm afraid we're not even close."

Alaina lowered her head to his shoulder. "Tristan, has anyone heard anything from my aunt and uncle?"

He regretted not having a chance to speak with her about what Devon saw at the bridge the night they found her, and still he dreaded telling her.

"I think you should dress, and we'll go downstairs to hear

what Devon has to say."

"I read you too well." She stepped back from him. "What aren't you telling me?"

"Your aunt and uncle haven't contacted anyone whom we know of, but Devon did see your aunt the night we left London."

"What do you mean saw her? Where?"

"Well, not exactly saw her—it was too dark. But he recognized her voice. She rode in the carriage with someone else whose voice he hasn't been able to place yet."

Alaina let this sink in. "Did he see in which direction they traveled? Was my uncle with them? Why didn't he stop and speak with them?"

Too many questions, Tristan thought, and he didn't have all of the answers—at least not ones she'd want to hear.

"They were headed away from the city, but the road they traveled on veers off and turns north toward Scotland without much in between. He doesn't recall hearing a third person in the carriage, and he didn't stop them because he believed they were fleeing the city. Devon said he heard arguing. Two riders rode in front, which means they might have been expecting trouble."

Alaina moved away and lowered herself to the edge of the feather mattress. She had to find her uncle if she was to learn the truth.

"Tristan, I want to listen to what Devon and Charles have to say, but then I need a favor."

"Anything."

"I need you to send someone to find my uncle and bring him back here."

"He may not want to come. They haven't tried to contact you."

"I know, but I need to speak with him, and right now I don't want to leave Claiborne Manor."

"I'll send Derek this afternoon."

"Thank you—again." She smiled. "I fear I will be saying that to you often."

"I enjoy hearing those words." He grinned. "Especially after we enjoy—"

"Tristan!" She laughed, appreciating that they could have moments like this even through the difficult times. "They're waiting, my dear."

"DO WE KNOW WHERE he is?" Tristan referred to Alaina's uncle.

"Not at the moment, but Derek shouldn't have any trouble finding him."

"Good. Now in the meantime . . ." Tristan had lost the attention of the room. Their attention had been diverted to the doorway. Tristan's eyes followed their gaze and he smiled. He walked over to his wife and slid her hand into his. Charles and Devon stood to greet her.

"I must say you are an admirable woman, Duchess."

"Thank you, Charles, but please, we're among friends. It's Alaina. No Duchess or Your Grace, please."

He nodded.

"Tristan is a lucky man to have someone of such strength by his side."

"Thank you, Devon, but you sound as though I'm going to need that strength still. What do you know?"

He motioned for her to sit, and they all followed suit. Devon spoke immediately.

"First, Tristan informed us that he told you about what I saw the other night. I want you to know that Derek will return to London this afternoon and find your uncle."

"I'm grateful, Devon."

"Now about the rest." Devon stood and walked over to the desk and returned with a large box, which he set down in the center of the group. "Please accept my apologies. I went through your mother's belongings. What you said about the false bottom in her trunk interested me, and I wanted to discover if there were any more surprises."

He watched Alaina shift uncomfortably, but she said nothing, so he continued. "I found two more trunks built in the same fashion, and in the bottom, I found these." He motioned to the objects in the box. "Foreign currency and land deeds, including a copy of the deed to Claiborne Manor and your mother's cottage in Ireland. The other trunk contained papers and these journals." He lifted one of the leather-bound books from the box and handed it to Alaina.

"I don't understand. We sold the cottage in Ireland years ago. My aunt and uncle coordinated the sale on my behalf."

"We're having someone look into it, but it seems as though the sale never went through or wasn't legal. This is the original deed," said Devon.

"Have you read these journals?" Alaina asked no one in particular.

"No, we thought it should be for you to read them first, but I took the liberty of skimming through one of the books, and they do appear to be accounts of meetings and case details. I imagine they kept two copies. One they passed to their superiors—we all send in reports of our findings and travels. The other is in these journals."

"Thank you for waiting." Alaina opened the cover of the book and skimmed over the pages. "It appears you're right," she murmured, "but I'm reading something about a ship." She flipped through a few more pages. "In fact, they have many entries about the same ship: *The Serpentine.*"

"May I see that?" asked Devon.

Tristan and Charles each took a journal at Alaina's prodding.

"What is it, Devon?" Tristan looked up from the book in his lap.

"I know this ship. *The Serpentine* is a steam transport I've taken myself on more than one occasion."

"For official business?" asked Charles.

"Twice."

"I've never recalled anyone from the agency taking a ship by that name," said Tristan.

"I hadn't either. It wasn't even the usual ship, but on both assignments there had been a last minute change of plans and I was just told to go. The missions went according to plan, and I never questioned it." Devon looked up from the pages of the journal.

Tristan smiled. "This was before our days of rebellion and working by our own rules."

"Precisely."

"Were you on this ship when you went to America?" asked Charles.

"Yes, both times."

"It's possible Alaina's aunt is traveling with Rothschild and his partners. They could have easily doubled back. Neither one of them has been located. It would be simple enough to hide at the docks until the ship leaves," said Charles.

Tristan nodded, agreeing to the possibility.

"Someone needs to be on that transport," added Devon.

"On *The Serpentine*, and the one leaving immediately after, heading in the same direction," said Alaina. All three men focused on her. She explained, "It makes sense to have people on board the other ship. There's always the possibility that they have split their shipment, if smuggling is one of their objectives. For instance, they might choose not to entrust all of their valuables, or whatever it may be, to one crew and thereby avoid suspicion."

"You have a point, my dear," Tristan said, studying her, "but Alaina this is your aunt we're speaking of. Do you understand what could happen if her involvement goes as deeply as we believe it does?"

"No matter how painful the worst outcome might be, I have to see this through. The truth is more important now. My parents, Braden . . . they deserve to be heard. I do not know if my uncle is involved. I pray he is not, but I want the truth. This is why we're going to be the ones on the second ship."

Tristan had been nodding along with her up until the last part. "Excuse me?"

"Tristan, it makes perfect sense. No one is going to suspect a newly married couple on their honeymoon. It is the perfect solution."

Tristan shook his head in disagreement, but stopped when he looked over and saw his friends smiling.

"You two have something to add?"

"I think your wife makes a good point," said Devon.

"Do you, now? And what about you, Charles? Do you believe this insane idea holds merit?"

"It does make sense, friend." Charles smiled when Tristan grumbled. "Listen, you know the people involved better than anyone, and Alaina knows her aunt. You are the best choice, and married couples draw less suspicion. Consider how long the Claibornes ran their operations as a couple. Look at how much they accomplished."

"Exactly," chimed in Alaina.

"What are you suggesting? You wish to join the agency now?" Tristan faced his wife.

"My mother did it and she was pregnant, which probably made her even less suspicious," argued Alaina.

Tristan regarded her curiously for a moment but continued. "Alaina, your parents understood the risks. I don't like the idea of you being involved this much."

"I'm already involved as much as anyone. The kidnappings, the murders, my aunt's involvement. My world as I knew it has fallen apart, and I refuse to accept it was for nothing."

"Even if justice in this case is death?" asked Tristan.

Alaina surprised him again. "Whatever justice there is, I know you will deliver it fairly."

"You have a great deal of faith in the mission."

"No," she countered. "I have a great deal of faith in you."

"Then it's settled," said Charles. "Tristan and Alaina travel on the second ship with Devon. I'll travel with Zachary and Derek on the first ship."

"Won't they recognize you?" asked Alaina.

"They haven't seen my brothers, and Charles here is a master of disguises," Devon answered for his friend.

"Well that's that," said Alaina. "Now does anyone know, by chance, where we'll be traveling?"

Devon answered her. "*The Serpentine* travels only one route—to America."

"Well, darling," Tristan said to his wife. "I hope you like Yankees."

Twenty

"Lord and Lady Claiborne! It is a pleasure to have you aboard *The Queen's Folly*."

"We are pleased to join you for the journey, Captain Lockston," said Tristan. "She's a truly exceptional ship."

"Magnificent," agreed Alaina. "She possesses an unusual name."

"Unusual, but apt," said the captain. "She was originally built for Queen Victoria, but before the ship even left the harbor, the queen declared her unfit. However, I assure you that she is one of the finest ships in England. The queen's loss is the peoples' gain."

"I have faith it is." Tristan kept a watchful eye on the passengers boarding the vessel. They doubted any of their suspects traveling were on this transport, but they couldn't afford to be careless. "Captain, I believe I would like to escort my wife to our cabin. It has been a long journey from our estate."

"Of course, my lord." The captain tipped the brim of his hat. "Your luggage has already been moved to your cabin. I do hope we shall be seeing you at supper this evening."

"You will, Captain, thank you." Tristan placed a hand on the small of Alaina's back and escorted her to their cabin, entering and closing the door behind him. He checked the locks, finding them adequate. He had procured the finest passenger cabin on the ship, primarily because it was situated near a stairwell leading up to each deck. It helped that the cabin had a sitting room in addition to the bedroom and dressing rooms. Tristan didn't especially care for sea travel and was grateful for the extra space.

Luckily, they had managed to acquire the space on short notice.

"It seems my parents never traveled on this ship before." Alaina removed her overcoat.

"It was clever of you to want to use their names. Risky, but clever." He smiled at her and removed his coat before joining her on the small sofa, noticing for the first time the tea tray and sandwiches on the small Tudor coffee table.

"Excellent service," Tristan commented dryly.

"Mmm," Alaina said through a sip of her tea. "I wonder how Devon is faring."

"He arrived before we did." Tristan chose a small sandwich from the tray.

"How do you know? I didn't see him?"

"What Devon failed to mention before is that he is a greater master of disguise than Charles."

"Then how do you know you saw him?"

"Do you remember what he said right before we left him?"

Alaina thought for a moment. "Beware of King Henry's army."

"Very good. You just might make a great agent."

"You had your doubts?" she teased.

"Just worries, my love." He leaned over to kiss her, but she moved back when realization hit her.

"The long gray hair clubbed back and that ridiculous red silk ensemble?" asked Alaina.

"That would be him. Hideous, wasn't it?"

Alaina laughed. "Most hideous." She sobered.

"What's wrong, darling?"

"I'm thinking about my parents. I want closure. Playing at being them is harder than I expected."

He pulled her closer to him and ran his fingers through her hair, loosening the pins.

"It will be over soon, I promise." He slid his hand up and down her back. "Alaina, do you remember the day we met?"

She smiled. "How could I forget? I was furious with you."

"I know. You were a glorious golden angel. I remember seeing you ride that day. I had never seen a woman more capable on the back of a horse."

"Horses are an important part of my life. I miss mine dearly."

"You'll be with them again soon," he promised. "I thought perhaps when this is all over and we return to England, I can take up residence at Claiborne Manor."

She lifted her head and studied her husband. "You wish to live at Claiborne Manor? Why? I am sure you have grander estates."

"They are mere buildings to me. Since the day my father died and I inherited the dukedom, the only thing that changed in my eyes was the title. None of the places ever meant anything to me. Claiborne Manor is important to you, and I have grown fond of the place. It is where we shared our first kiss."

"In the greenhouse."

"A perfect moment."

"Mmm." Alaina laid her head back on his shoulder and closed her eyes. Then one lid lifted slightly and a smile tugged at her mouth when she felt her buttons slowly opening on her dress. Not saying anything, she allowed Tristan to continue his slow and deliberate task until the back of her dress splayed open.

"Have something in mind, milord?"

"Oh, I most certainly do, milady."

Alaina turned herself into him and met his lips. She had so much to be grateful for and too many times she had come close to losing him. Alaina let all of her love flow through into the kiss, and Tristan returned it. He went from a deep idle kiss to nibbling on her lip, and then traced a path down her throat to her shoulder, pulling her dress down over her shoulders. Her head fell back to give him greater access, running her fingers through his thick hair in an attempt to bring him closer and hurry him along.

Taking his time, Tristan slowly removed her gown, kissing his way along her shoulders and arms, enjoying the moans escaping her lips. He picked her up and carried her into the bedroom, laying her gently on the bed. He was determined to cherish as much time as possible with her, and he wouldn't rush.

Alaina helped him to remove his own clothes and then the

remainder of hers. He lay down beside her, starting the process again, kissing and caressing every inch of her body until she begged him to finish.

But still he waited. The pressure building within him was worth the pain because he knew when they did climax together, it would be unlike any other time before. Tristan trailed his lips down her breasts and stomach and farther still until she found her release, and only then did he bring himself back up to capture her lips, sinking into her.

"Tristan, please."

"Hush, my love," he whispered, as they moved together, their hands linked above their heads and their tongues dancing until they crested together.

Tristan collapsed, wanting to take his weight off her but not finding the energy to do so. Their breathing slowed, his breath cooling the side of her neck as she wrapped her arms around him. After the shaking had subsided, Tristan lifted his head and gazed down at her, brushing a damp lock of hair from her brow and kissing her softly. She smiled sweetly and then moved beneath him. Thinking perhaps he was too heavy, he started to raise his body, only to find himself turned over on his back with her straddling him. He quirked an eyebrow up at her in question as much as in anticipation. Alaina leaned over and kissed him deeply, trailing that kiss down his neck, while her hand moved seductively over his chest and stomach. His voice was raspy when he spoke. "No rest, my love?"

Alaina smiled, her voice a husky whisper. "You tortured me, darling, it seems only fair I return the favor." She continued the exploration of his body. "Can you handle it, milord?"

"I do hope so," he said as her mouth captured his once again.

Sometime later, they lay in each other's embrace. A small smile played across his lips as he thought of what had just happened. His wife was full of surprises and proved to be as clever in bed as she was out of it.

His thoughts drifted to the future and what lay ahead. Tomorrow they would launch to sea with no chance of escape, and as he listened to his wife's quiet breathing, he prayed that bringing her along had not been a mistake. *What happens will happen,* he thought, but for now, he was content to hold his wife and dream of their life together when the madness ended.

"WE'RE SORRY TO HAVE missed your company last night, Lord and Lady Claiborne." The captain greeted the couple when they came out on the deck.

"Our apologies, Captain, but my wife took to bed early. First time on a ship," Tristan added.

"I understand," said the captain, then excused himself when one of his men walked forward. "If you'll pardon me, Lord Claiborne, I must see to this matter."

"Of course." Tristan watched as the captain went below decks.

"A fine day for sailing, is it not?" A throaty laugh came from behind them. Smiling, Tristan turned around with Alaina.

"A fine day it is, friend. Any storms on the horizon?" Tristan squinted against the sun.

"Not a one," said Devon.

"Really?"

Alaina gazed out to the calm sea and unseasonably clear sky. She then caught on to the meaning of the conversation.

"I've checked with every crewman and it appears we're to have smooth sailing all the way to Virginia." Devon looked over his friend's shoulder at some of the passengers walking by and nodded to one of the women. He turned his attention back to the pair. "It seems that you just might get that honeymoon."

"Yes, it appears we might." Tristan turned his attention to his wife. "Well my dear, how do you suppose we while away our time at sea?"

Devon chuckled at Alaina's blush. "I'll leave you two alone." Then he added as he studied *The Serpentine,* which appeared as little more than a dot on the horizon, "I do hope the others discover something useful before we reach land."

"They confirmed that my aunt boarded the ship, didn't they?" asked Alaina.

"Yes, they saw them board and stay aboard, so at least we know part of the plan is working," answered Devon. "Well, I'll be off to find myself a little diversion while I'm here."

"You won't find much in that getup," Tristan predicted, drawing a smile from Alaina and Devon.

"Not all of us are as lucky as you are to have such a lovely companion on a long sea voyage. Unfortunately, my diversions will be limited to lightening these chaps' purses. We'll meet tonight at supper. Until then." Devon tipped the red silk tricot over his gray hair, smiled, and then moved to the opposite end of the ship.

"Is he any good?" Alaina watched Devon's retreating back.

"He has the ability to turn the richest man into a pauper and still talk the chap out of the clothes on his back." Tristan recalled the time he had lost a hefty sum to his friend, before he smartened up and refused to play him anymore. "Come, my dear, it's time we begin our honeymoon."

"I thought we started last night."

"That was only a prelude."

"At this rate we'll die from starvation and sleep deprivation."

"It will be worth it."

HOURS LATER, THEY LAY in each other's arms, feeling temporarily sated. Tristan absently stroked his fingers up and down Alaina's arm. She lifted the top half of her body and leaned on his chest, gazing into his half-lidded eyes.

"What is it?"

"A part of me feels guilty for the happiness I feel right now. With everything that has happened and is still happening, I keep thinking we should be spending more time planning strategies, not making love on a ship." Alaina ran her hand up and down his chest and sighed.

"Life is too short for us not to enjoy every moment we have together." Tristan sat up and brought Alaina with him. "We have much to be grateful for, so much we could have lost, but we didn't and that is something to celebrate. There's going to be enough for us to worry about when we reach land, but right now we have every right to enjoy our happiness."

"I know we do and I am happy. I think of my parents and how they lived and died loving each other, giving their lives for each other. I remember walking . . . and watching them . . . and thinking that someday I would have that and never lose it. I heard my father in agony when my mother died, and I know he, too, wanted to die, just to be with her. But you see, I could never be angry with them for that choice. They loved each other deeply. I didn't understand then. I do now."

Tristan brushed a tear from her cheek. "You always wanted what they had."

"I found it with you. If Braden had lived, I probably would have married him. He gave his life for me, and I will always love him for being there, but that was a different time in my life—one that is over but never forgotten. The life I live now and forever is with you, and I wish my parents could have known you. They would have loved you." She let the tears come.

He brought her close to him and settled her head against his chest, embracing her. "I would have loved them too." He held back the moisture in his own eyes.

"Truly?"

"How could I not? They created you, and if there was no other reason to love them, that would be reason enough." He lifted her chin and brought his lips down to capture her mouth in a kiss that spoke not so much of passion but of tenderness and compassion. "You never have to let them go."

"It is you I never wish to lose."

"You won't lose me, either," he promised.

"Tristan?"

"Yes, love?"

"Why did you and the others become agents?" she asked, trailing her fingers casually along his chest. "You could have done many things with your life, yet you chose risk and danger."

Tristan twined his fingers with hers and stared up at the ceiling. "My father was committed to serving his country, and initially I joined to honor him and his service. I came to value the work. Devon wanted the adventure and excitement. Early in our careers, he volunteered for almost any assignment that required him to leave the country—he wished to see the world."

When he paused, Alaina asked, "And Charles?"

"Charles said he joined because of me, but I believe he wished to escape his father's dictates."

"Did his father—"

"Hurt him?" Tristan shook his head. "Charles envisioned a better life for himself, a life different from the one his father chose, so he left home. When his father passed away, Charles inherited the land, wealth, and a title, but he refused to give up the work."

"Will any of you ever walk away from this life?"

Tristan tensed. "Are you asking if I will walk away?"

Alaina raised herself up and leaned on her arm. "Never think I will ask that of you."

"You wouldn't?" Surprised, he looked at her.

"How could I ever ask you to give up something that is a part of who you are?"

Tristan slowly exhaled and his body relaxed. "Thank you." He leaned forward and kissed her softly. "But know that I would."

A STORM CAME UPON them halfway through their voyage, tossing the vessel about, but only setting them a day off course. Three weeks had passed when they arrived safely in Virginia, only half a day behind *The Serpentine*. Once they were on the docks, Devon hired a driver to take them to The Monarch, a hotel where he had stayed on a previous visit. Traffic was bustling, with townspeople and travelers taking advantage of the pleasant weather. The hotel spanned a city block and reached six stories up—a grand edifice, gleaming in the afternoon sunlight. The driver pulled up in front, and a porter from the hotel carried their bags into the lobby. Devon paid the man and joined Tristan and Alaina at the counter.

"Charles should already be here. He was going to make reservations under different names," said Devon quietly and then turned to address the desk clerk. "We have two rooms under Mr. and Mrs. Henry Bothman." Tristan raised a brow at his friend when the clerk checked through his book. Devon merely shrugged his shoulders and smiled, keeping his attention on the clerk.

"Yes, I have a Mr. and Mrs. Bothman plus guest—two suites, fifth floor, with a park view." The clerk motioned for another porter. "He will take your bags to your room." The clerk handed the keys to the young man.

"Thank you." Devon followed them to the stairs. Once inside the first suite, Devon walked through the adjoining door and checked the second suite before returning.

"You're a handy man to have around, Devon," said Tristan, "but Mr. and Mrs. Henry Bothman?"

Devon shrugged again and kept smiling. "We thought a name that didn't draw attention would be best."

"Interesting that you chose the name of the butler who kidnapped me."

"I enjoy the irony, my lady."

"Yes, well, are there any other surprises I should know about? You and Charles seem to be enjoying yourselves a little too much." Tristan hung their coats since they decided it best not to hire a valet or maid.

Devon smiled in answer. "Speaking of partners in crime—" He stopped when someone knocked at the door.

Tristan opened the door to a tall man with jet-black hair down to his shoulders and a beard and mustache. He wore a suit and the most unsightly green overcoat Tristan had ever seen. The man carried an umbrella that doubled as a walking stick.

"I thought you weren't supposed to stand out in a crowd." Tristan stood aside to let him in.

"More fun this way, old man." Charles walked into the room and swung his coat to the nearest chair.

"I thought you left the fun to Devon."

"I have my moments." Charles turned to the other two occupants in the room. "Mrs. Botham, you look ravishing, even after such a long sea voyage." He bowed gallantly.

"Charles? I never would have guessed."

"That's the idea."

"And don't call her Mrs. Bothman," said Tristan.

Charles nodded and turned to Devon. "How was King Henry's voyage?"

"Rather pleasant. Left England a rich man, arrived in Virginia even richer."

Charles shook his head, recalling his own losses when playing cards with Devon.

"Nice ensemble," remarked Devon. "Did you scare the children on the way over?"

Alaina smiled at the banter and leaned toward her husband. "I'd like to freshen up."

Tristan stood. "We'll wait."

"I won't be long." She turned to the other men when they stood. "Excuse me, gentlemen."

Tristan watched his wife walk into the other room and turned back to Charles and Devon. "Do we have any new information?"

"A good deal, actually," Charles paused. "Should I wait for Alaina?"

"I'll share everything with her."

"Very good. Her aunt, Rothschild, and Melbourne came across on the ship. They checked into The Monarch and are staying on the second floor."

"Wait, Melbourne was with them?" asked Devon.

"It surprised me too, but he met them for supper each night. There's more—Lord Croxley was with them."

"Croxley. What could they possibly want with that pervert?" asked Tristan, remembering the way the man had eyed Alaina at the ball.

"I'm not certain as of yet, but he is staying at a hotel across the park," added Charles. "Zachary is keeping watch, but thus far, Croxley hasn't left since he checked in."

"What about Derek?" Devon asked of his other brother.

"He's checking around at the banks, shipping companies, and import and export dealers to see if they have any dealings with Rothschild or the others."

Tristan voiced his own doubts. "A good start, though I doubt they'll say anything if they do in fact know what Rothschild is doing."

"Derek will break them." Devon smiled. "And if not, I'll bend them a little more." He stood to answer the knock at the door and let a waiter, wheeling a large food cart, come in.

When the waiter left, Tristan asked, "Did someone order food?"

"Oh, I was famished and ordered before I came upstairs." Devon rolled the cart over to the other men and began filling a plate. He then sat across from Tristan but rose with the others when Alaina walked back into the room.

"Are you all right?" asked Tristan.

"Would you like us to fill you in?" asked Charles.

Devon continued eating. Alaina sat and motioned them to do the same.

"I'm just fine. I needed a little refreshing after using a washroom on a ship for three weeks. And Tristan can fill me in later." She started to settle back in and then spotted the food. "Bless whoever ordered this." She stood to fill a plate, motioning Tristan back down when he stood to assist her. "Please continue, gentlemen. But I do have one question for you," she said before they began. "Did anyone discover anything new about my uncle? Everyone moved quickly to make the transport, and I realized Derek had returned to the manor without him." She turned to face the three men.

Charles cleared his throat, Tristan kept his eyes focused on her, and Devon shuffled his feet. Tristan finally spoke. "I didn't want to tell you, but Derek couldn't find your uncle. The servants said he left the house in London the day before you were taken, and no one has heard anything from him since." He stood and walked over to her, placing his hands on her arms. "I'm sorry, Alaina."

Her hunger forgotten, she sat back down. "It's not anyone's fault. I just don't understand what happened to him. I realize my aunt is into trouble, but I had hoped Uncle Sebastian had no involvement."

"We don't suspect him," Tristan said.

She looked up, surprised. "You don't?"

"No. In fact, before we left we sent men to continue looking for him."

Alaina sat forward. "It is possible he left after he realized my determination to marry you, with or without his consent." Tristan's warm hands offered her some comfort, and she turned into him. "If only he knew now how much we love each other."

"Tristan, Alaina," said Charles, shifting their attention back to present matters. "I have an idea I'd like everyone to consider."

"You have our utmost attention, old man." Devon took a bite out of a cold meat sandwich.

"There's a charity ball tomorrow night in the hotel ballroom. I took the liberty of procuring tickets from the front desk. Tristan and Alaina will go as Mr. and Mrs. Bothman, the rest of us as ourselves. Derek should have some information for us by tonight."

"How do we know they'll be there?" asked Tristan.

"From the pretty lady selling the tickets in the lobby." Charles grinned.

Tristan nodded. "We'll follow their lead and see what happens. The element of surprise is on our side."

"WHAT EXACTLY IS THIS charity ball supporting?" asked Alaina.

"I have no idea." Tristan guided Alaina through the hotel lobby and into the ballroom.

"The local townspeople want to redecorate their city hall," Charles said quietly to Alaina. "Apparently the new mayor doesn't like the colors or some such nonsense."

Tristan raised a brow at his friend. "You're as bad as the gossips."

"Shameful, isn't it?" Grinning, Charles led the procession into the room.

"Doesn't exactly remind you of home, does it?" Devon commented dryly, moving in to stand beside Tristan, forming a semicircle around Alaina. The room spanned only half the size of the ballrooms in England and lacked British elegance and refinement. Red and gold brocade curtains draped the floor-to-ceiling windows and doors along one side of the room. The opposite wall was papered in red with extravagantly large, gold-framed paintings of men and women, most of whom were too unfortunate-looking to have sat for portraits. Four chandeliers hung low from the ceiling—three too many for the size of the room—giving the ballroom a gaudy bordello appearance.

"Perhaps they should use the money to redecorate this room instead," commented Alaina under her breath.

The men chuckled, nodding in agreement while they watched out for their suspects.

"Excuse me, sirs."

The foursome turned, giving their attention to a short, round-chested man with a square face, half covered by a full mustache.

"May we help you?" asked Tristan.

"Ah, I thought I heard you correctly. English folks, right?"

"Yes," said Devon. "English folks."

The man glanced at each of them and then noticed Alaina. "My dear, I did not see you surrounded by these gentlemen. Allow me to introduce myself. I am Jack Crogswell, police chief in this town." He bowed to the group as far as his extended girth allowed. When no one said anything, he continued speaking. "Seems we are popular with you English tonight. We do appreciate the support from our friends across the sea, though I can't say the same for everyone here. Some folks still think the English should be shot and quartered, but not me. No, you are welcome in my town anytime."

Poor man, thought Alaina. *Didn't he realize how close he was to receiving a black eye?*

"Chief Crogswell." Tristan drew the man's attention. "You've met a few of our fellow countrymen this evening?"

"Yes sir, in fact, it was a group much like yourselves. One woman and three men. Too bad they couldn't stay—you might have known them," said the chief, for he assumed everyone in England knew everyone else.

"They left, you say?" asked Devon.

"Yes sir, they came, looked around for a few minutes, and then got back in another carriage."

"We would like to meet them, fellow countrymen and all. Do you happen to know in which direction they traveled?" asked Charles.

"Well, I believe they went to the east side of town. Only warehouses and docks down there."

"Thank you, Chief Crogswell," said Tristan, and they all left the ballroom.

Thanks to Devon's foresight, their carriage-on-call waited in front of the hotel. They all went out front while Tristan held Alaina back in the lobby.

"What's wrong?" she asked.

"I want you to stay here."

"I am not staying here while you go out there to face those people. This is my fight, too, and my aunt is out there." She stood her ground, but Tristan had another card to play.

"I need you to stay here, Alaina. I won't risk losing you again or the child you're carrying."

Surprised, she asked, "How do you know? It's far too soon to know anything."

"I knew it the night we conceived. I believe in my heart you're carrying our child." He leaned down to kiss her softly. "Please, stay here at the hotel. I'll ask Derek to stay behind."

"That won't be a problem," said Derek, walking up behind them. "The others can fill you in on what I found, and Zachary is still sitting on Croxley—he hasn't left."

Alaina looked from one man to the other. "Seems I don't have much of a choice," she replied dryly, then with a worried look in her eyes, turned to Tristan. "Wait. Croxley?"

"Yes, why? We've spoken of him," said Tristan, wondering what she questioned.

"Not to me you haven't," she said. "My aunt had seemed adamant about my meeting him. Oh my, the other voice. Tristan, the other voice the night my parents died. The face I didn't see. The voice. I remember now—it was Lord Croxley." She grabbed Tristan's arm as he quietly pulled her aside.

"You're certain?"

"Yes. I knew something about that man seemed familiar, but I couldn't place it before."

"We didn't know his involvement went back that far. Alaina, you're staying here, and this time I beg of you not to leave Derek's side." He spoke to Alaina but looked at Derek, who nodded.

"Please be careful. I can't lose you."

Tristan kissed her again and without needing to say anything more, he left the lobby, leaving Derek to escort Alaina back to their room.

"Derek said the man he spoke with probably lied about when the shipments left, but he believed the man wasn't lying about from which dock they had left from." Devon relayed the information his brother had given to him.

"Did his source provide names?" asked Tristan.

"Just Melbourne's, and my guess is Rothschild is using Melbourne to cover himself."

"What exactly do you expect them to be shipping? No one ever discovered anything except the munitions, but he wouldn't come to America for that when other routes would be far more profitable," Charles said.

"I don't know," Tristan answered in growing frustration. "My father believed he was close to figuring it out, but tonight I think we're going to see for ourselves the reason why so many good people had to die." They rode in silence to the docks, and Tristan motioned for the driver to stop a block before the entrance and park behind an old building.

Moving quietly and cautiously toward the number seven slip Derek's source had told him about, the men crouched behind a tall pile of crates and studied the area. Silence shrouded the docks. A light fog conveyed an eerie atmosphere to the area and caused them all to reach for their pistols.

Tristan didn't like the scene. It wasn't unusual for the docks to be quiet this time of night in any country, but at least a few men should be working, loading and unloading cargo freighters. Someone laid a hand on his shoulder, and he turned to look in the direction Devon indicated. He couldn't see anything at first, but he heard the barely audible footfalls on the wooden planks over the quietly lapping water beneath. A man emerged from the shadows and walked in their direction, then stopped in front of *The Queen's Folly,* where another man stepped off the ship docked in the number eight slip.

The three men continued to crouch down behind the crates, careful not to move as they attempted to hear the conversation, but there was a light breeze carrying the words in the opposite direction. Then the conversation grew louder as one of the men's voices grew more forceful.

"You said there wouldn't be any trouble," said the man who had stepped off the ship. The shadows shrouded his face, and Tristan couldn't focus on any discernible features. The one on the dock wore black from the top of his head down to his boots. Tristan noticed the man's tall stature and though the brim of his hat shadowed most of his face, Tristan felt certain that the man was Lord Rothschild.

"There won't be," Rothschild said.

"Then why is that young lad sneaking around asking questions?" the other man asked, his accent undeniably English, though quiet enough not to be recognizable.

"I don't know, though I'm sure he's just someone trying to get some of the merchandise. You do have it well guarded, do you not?" asked Rothschild

"Yes, but I don't like it. Not this close to a launch date."

"Have I ever steered you wrong before?"

"Not yet, but after twenty years, even you are bound to make a mistake," the other man grumbled in response.

Their conversation resumed quieter tones, and Tristan no longer heard what they said. The Englishman pointed to the ship and then walked back in the direction he had come, the other man stepping back to the ship in slip number eight.

Twenty years, thought Tristan. *How many other men and women had died trying to stop them over the past twenty years?*

When silence once again covered the docks, Charles turned to the others. "That was Rothschild, was it not?"

Tristan nodded. "I believe so, and it also looks as though *The Queen's Folly* was the transport ship all along. Since it constantly sets sail only hours after *The Serpentine,* they arrive before their cargo and avoid suspicion."

Devon motioned to the other two and they turned their attention toward the vessel. Someone left the ship and started walking in their direction. They moved farther behind stacks of crates and listened. By the sound of the man's grumbling, he might be the same one who had spoken with Rothschild. Devon looked to Tristan and silently motioned to the ship, indicating he wanted to check it out. Both Tristan and Charles nodded their agreement and waited until the other man was out of sight and his heavy footsteps could no longer be heard on the wooden planks.

The men moved silently from behind the crates, and one by one made their way to the edge of slip number eight and climbed up to the ship.

"DEREK, I HAVE A horrible feeling about what's going to happen." Alaina paced the sitting room of the suite, glancing at the door every few minutes.

Derek dragged a chair next to the window and made himself comfortable while keeping an eye on the streets below. He turned his attention to her. "Tristan asked you to stay here, and you told him you would," he reminded her.

"I realize that, but something is not right. That is my husband and your brother out there."

"Your husband, my brother, and Charles can look after themselves."

"What if they fall into a trap or they stumble onto something they hadn't expected?" she asked desperately.

"They are masters of getting themselves in and out of trouble. You needn't worry." Even as he spoke the words, Derek realized Alaina's concern was valid. He didn't doubt for one minute their ability to handle themselves, but there were some things which still bothered him. He hadn't heard anything from Zachary, and

Alaina had rambled on about them going after a woman and three men by themselves. Croxley would have made the third man, but if Croxley wasn't with them, who was the third fellow? He turned to Alaina, who alternated between pacing the room and sending Derek looks that spoke of frustration, fright, and annoyance. He'd never seen eyes say so much at one time and didn't envy Tristan if she ever became angry with him.

"Dress warmly. It's cold near the water."

Alaina didn't ask questions. She simply nodded and gathered her things, leaving the room ahead of Derek.

He knew he might regret leaving the room with her when he saw Tristan.

AT THE DOCKS, SOME of the same thoughts ran through Tristan's mind. *Who was the third man if Croxley remained in his hotel? And what the hell were they looking for down here?* The ship had been empty of people, which was odd, considering the cargo should have been guarded. They split up, each taking a level of the ship. Tristan went into the lower cargo hold searching the labels of boxes marked as spices and linens—common items shipped between America and England. What bothered him was the number and size of the boxes.

He debated unhinging one of the crates but heard a racket on the upper deck. He stopped to listen carefully, but the area became quiet for a moment. He ran to the stairs when he heard a gunshot. From his vantage point on the top deck, Charles was supposed to have been watching for anyone returning. If something was wrong, something had happened to Charles.

Tristan reached the second level and listened for anything out of the ordinary. A moment later another shot came from somewhere in the direction of the east docks. Racing to the upper deck, Tristan cautiously eased around crates and lifeboats, his heart pounding rapidly at the sight before him. In blazing fury, Alaina walked up to the deck and held a gun directly at the man who was supposed to have been guarding it. The sailor clutched his hand, blood dripping in rivulets to the deck. Derek stood behind her, looking as shocked as Tristan. Charles clutched his side and moved toward the others. Devon had disappeared out of sight. Looking around to see if anyone else had heard the shots, Tristan stepped out from behind a lifeboat. Alaina nearly dropped her gun, and he couldn't find it in himself to be angry at the relief he saw on her face. She managed to level the gun and keep it steady on the injured man. He cursed Alaina in a language she didn't recognize but apparently Tristan did.

"I caution you to watch what you say about my wife. You just might find yourself with a broken face to go along with that hole she shot through your hand."

Derek appeared repentant enough for Tristan to forego a lecture about leaving the hotel. He knew how persuasive Alaina could be when she set her mind to something.

The sailor looked warily up at Tristan, who now had a gun aimed on him, and became quiet. Tristan walked over to Alaina, keeping the man in his peripheral vision. He nodded to Charles whose side was cut open from an apparent knife wound.

"Darling, are you planning to shoot the chap or just make him nervous?" Tristan took the gun from Alaina's grasp, realizing that she was more shaken up than she let on. He handed the gun to Derek and then turned to Charles.

"Are you all right?"

"At least for now," Charles nodded. "But the bloody idiot ruined a perfectly good shirt."

"Where's Devon?"

Charles shook his head. Tristan scanned the deck and then walked over to the man who still bled onto the planks.

"Who are you?"

"None of your blasted business."

"Oh, I think it is. You see, that is my friend you injured over there. I don't take too kindly to that." Tristan remained standing in front of the man, forcing the sailor to look up.

"You're trespassing on this ship."

"I don't really think that's the issue here, man. I was a passenger on this ship, and I forgot one of my trunks. Simple explanation. But as for you and what you are doing here this late at night, it is not simple now, is it?" Tristan glanced over at Alaina but remained alert to act if the man moved.

"I ask again, who are you?" When he still refused to answer, Tristan sighed. "I could always give the gun back to my wife and let her finish you. I think she has enough left in her to do it."

Both men glanced at Alaina, who seemed almost amused but decided to play along. She walked over to Derek and retrieved the gun. Her face showed no emotion when she pointed the gun back toward the man, but Tristan saw the spark of anger in her eyes. He wondered if she could pull the trigger again without provocation. He didn't believe so. The other man didn't know her as well because he chose to finally speak.

"I just sit on the ship and make sure nobody bothers it."

"Who hired you?" Tristan grabbed the collar of the smaller man and yanked him to his feet.

"An English bloke, like you," he stammered.

"What's his name?"

"Claiborne!" the man shouted when Tristan put pressure on his wound. Tristan released the sailor and shifted his focus to Alaina. She had turned white and nearly dropped the gun. Charles stepped forward and took the gun from her limp hand. Derek reached for Alaina, holding her upright.

"How long have you been working for Claiborne?" Tristan turned back to the man.

"Twenty years."

"Then it might surprise you to learn Christopher Claiborne was murdered ten years ago." The man seemed confused and shook his head.

"I don't know a Christopher Claiborne. His name is Justin Claiborne."

The man almost ducked for cover when Alaina shouted, "No! That's impossible." She released herself from Derek and walked to the sailor. Tristan held onto her, but she ignored him and spoke to the man. "Justin Claiborne is dead. You're lying."

"That's what the bloke told me his name was. Now I'm not saying anything more."

"He won't have to." Devon came around the port side of the

ship to the front deck. He took a survey of everyone. "It appears as though you had all the fun without me."

"Where have you been?" asked Charles.

"I found our friend's little stash of surprises. Follow me."

Tristan grabbed the shorter man's collar and dragged him with them, asking Charles to stay back with Alaina. He was only too willing to oblige, considering his side still burned from the cut. His shirt had absorbed most of the blood and clung painfully to the wound. Alaina helped him down the planks and into the waiting carriage, where the driver had watched in amazement.

DEREK GAVE A LOW whistle when he saw the goods. Open crates, packed with weapons, filled one of the larger cabins below deck.

"Seems our friends expected their own war."

"Appears so," said Tristan. He turned to Derek. "Tie this one up and find the port authorities. We don't have jurisdiction here." Derek took the other man and left the cargo hold.

"Justin Claiborne? Have you ever heard of him?" asked Devon.

Tristan shook his head, "No, but Alaina seems to."

"She told me he died," said Devon.

"Someone went through a lot of trouble to make her believe that."

"THERE'S NO TRACE OF the man calling himself Claiborne?" asked Charles. Devon had finished bandaging him up, and he found mild comfort by resting on the short chaise.

"Unfortunately, not even his little friend knows where to find him." Tristan paced the room, glancing periodically toward the closed door adjoining the next suite.

"She's taking this pretty hard."

Tristan nodded but said nothing. After the port authorities had arrived and spoken to everyone, they took possession of the cargo and Mr. Johnston, the sailor Alaina had shot.

On the way back to the hotel, Alaina had said nothing. She wouldn't talk about what happened or about Justin Claiborne. The hollow look in her eyes remained, and Tristan could only hold her.

When they reached the hotel, Tristan immediately took Alaina to their room and helped her into bed to rest. Although he wished to be with her, he stayed in the adjoining room, pacing the floor until a light rap sounded at the front door.

Tristan unlocked the door and let Derek and Zachary walk in. After the hugs and handshakes, they settled down to business. A few hours earlier, Zachary had followed Croxley down to the docks, but when he had seen the commotion, Croxley immediately returned to the hotel.

"I have someone watching Croxley."

"Who might that be?"

"We've met a few reliable men through our travels," said Zachary. "We can trust him."

"How are you holding up?" Derek asked Charles.

"I'll make it back to England."

"And Alaina?" Derek asked Tristan. He was about to speak when the adjoining door opened.

"She's well enough."

Alaina walked into the room and closed the distance to her husband. She placed her hand in his, drawing on the comfort of his strength. Tristan guided her to the edge of the bed, where she faced the other men. "Justin Claiborne was my father's brother. I never knew him. My father told me Justin had died the summer of his fifteenth year during a hunting accident. They rarely, if ever, mentioned his name in my presence. I wish I knew more, but I was led to believe that he died. If this is in fact my uncle, then it pains me to realize he had a part in my parents' death. I don't know anything more."

Tristan squeezed her hand and drew her closer. "The man claiming that name hasn't been found, but there are men searching. At this point, I think it's best to locate the next ship back to England and deal with this on our own ground," said Tristan.

"What about Rothschild and the others? My aunt?" Alaina turned to her husband, but he didn't have the answers she sought. "We've come all this way for nothing? I have to know what happened."

"Alaina, we can't be sure it was your uncle." Tristan absently rubbed his thumb over her palm.

"No one outside of my family knew of Justin. The one time my father spoke freely of his brother, he talked about how his brother held himself off from society. He never went out or attended functions. His family had a difficult time getting him to dine with them. No one went to his funeral. My aunt didn't even know of him because he had supposedly died long before my parents married. Justin Claiborne is the only one who could possibly know about Justin Claiborne." Alaina studied their joined hands and thought through what she wanted to say. "You are all involved in this because my crazed uncle possibly didn't die when he was fifteen, and I have an aunt whose part in this I still don't understand. I won't let any of you be harmed because of something a member of my family has done."

"Alaina, we don't know that."

"I know." Alaina stood and went to the window. She gazed out to the park. With the dawn fast approaching, vendors lined the streets, setting up their street carts. It seemed like another world below, and for just one moment, she wished she were on the street, buying the first apples of the day instead of worrying who would die next.

Alaina turned back to face all five men in the room. Tristan stood but wisely stayed by the bed. She had everyone's attention. "I believe to my soul that my uncle Justin is alive, and he is who that man said he was. A part of me wants to forget about this, return to England, and carry on my quiet life at Claiborne Manor." Alaina absently pressed a hand to her stomach. The gesture was not lost on Tristan. "I have spent too many years of my life afraid to think about my parents and afraid of losing my desire for revenge. I realize now it was because I didn't understand their deaths. A young girl watching her parents die leaves an everlasting mark on her heart. I don't want that mark, or their memories, to go away, but I do want to finish this—for their sake and for the sake of my family's future. You are loyal to duty, but I know your love for my husband has brought you this far. I am eternally grateful." She turned and offered each man a small smile, then focused on Tristan. "I want to go home. That is where these nightmares began and that is where it will have to end."

He walked to her, arms outstretched, while everyone in the room remained silent.

"You'd make a right fine general, my lady," said Zachary.

"She certainly would," Tristan said, then turned and spoke to Devon. "Could you reserve us a few berths on the next ship to England?"

Devon grinned. "Three berths on the *Isadora.* She sails in four days."

"I should have known." Tristan grinned but then took on a somber tone. "When we return to England, none of you has to finish this fight. They've made it personal, and I don't expect any of you to involve yourselves anymore."

Charles swore under his breath, which shot pain through his side, and Derek and Zachary just seemed annoyed. Devon stepped forward and laid a comforting arm on Tristan's shoulder while addressing the couple.

"The case isn't closed, Tristan, but more importantly, if you think we're going to let you be rid of us, you don't know us, friend. Until justice is met, we'll be here for you." He grinned again. "Even if we have to take up residence with you."

"Heaven forbid."

Alaina felt a tear kiss her cheek and released a hand from Tristan to take one of Devon's.

Tristan spoke to all of them. "We would be honored to have you all accompany us. You know we can't do it without you."

"Don't do that again, old man." Charles laughed and then coughed. "About burst my side back open."

Tristan studied his friend. "Are you well enough to make the journey?"

Charles made another attempt at a laugh. "Just get me off this bloody continent. Can't take much more of this Yankee hospitality. Besides, I'm curious as to what awaits us back home."

Tristan squeezed Alaina's hand. "Aren't we all."

Twenty-One

The Virginia night air carried a chill, and clouds had moved overhead, cloaking the streets in darkness. The dim light from the street lamps barely lit the dark night, and the shadows concealed most of their movements. A few drops of unexpected rain moved the still waters of a puddle, and an alley cat meowed, most likely out of hunger. It became colder by the minute, and the breeze coming in off the ocean added to the discomfort. *What was I thinking, coming out here alone?* Thankfully, Tristan and the others had been too tired, and she managed to sneak from the room. But now all of the reasons why she had ventured out alone escaped her.

She wouldn't blame Tristan for throttling her or locking her in her room until the ship sailed, and then again in the berth, and again once they reached England. She was still surprised she had been able to leave the room without waking him. He must have been more exhausted than she realized.

The rain began to fall in soft rivulets, and she had no idea where she was. Alaina had left the comforts of her warm bed and husband to see if she could find her aunt's room and speak with her privately. Perhaps then she might better understand what was happening and ask why her aunt had done all of this. Most importantly, Alaina wanted to know why no one had been able to find Uncle Sebastian before she had left England.

Believing all she needed to do was talk with the desk clerk, Alaina went down to the quiet lobby alone. While in the lobby, Alaina caught sight of her aunt and another man walking out the front door.

The man's face came into her sight briefly, but he seemed familiar. Alaina thought by the time she went back up and told Tristan about following her aunt, it might be too late to find them again. Nodding to the desk clerk when he gave her an odd look, Alaina followed the pair outside and kept what she thought was a safe distance.

Now she berated herself for coming out, and the farther away they walked from the hotel, the closer they came to the docks and the more nervous her stomach became. Clutching a hand to an abdomen that was a long time from growing, Alaina skirted around yet another building. At least she knew where they were—the smell of the ocean became stronger. The salt air grew thicker despite the falling rain.

If wisdom had been one of her greater virtues, Alaina would have turned around, gone back to the hotel room, and told Tristan. But her curiosity won out and she continued on. *Perhaps I'll let them all take turns throttling me.*

When the docks finally came into sight, the pair went into a nearby building. After a tediously long wait, two men exited. Her aunt must have remained inside, but the painfully small windows revealed nothing useful. Alaina grew colder by the minute, wishing she had brought a warmer cloak with her.

Suddenly, a prickling sensation crept slowly up through her spine and tickled the hairs on her neck. Despite the weight from the hair she hadn't bothered pulling up before she left, the chilling feeling reached all the way up the back of her head. She shivered, shrinking into the cloak. She mentally cursed herself for not thinking of bringing a weapon, but then she hadn't planned on venturing out on this escapade. Crouching lower, Alaina looked around the area, and her body froze. She heard a footstep, and then something hard pressed into her back. She didn't even have a chance to turn around.

HE WOKE UP AND found her gone. He glanced to the washroom located across the room. He waited a few more minutes and when she didn't come back into the bedroom, Tristan left the bed to check on her. He opened the door to the small room to find the washbasin, a dressing screen, and her trunk, but not Alaina. A chill crept through him as he walked to the adjoining door and went into the next suite. Alaina wasn't there either. Devon mumbled something as he sat up in bed.

"What's going on?" He dragged a hand over his face and through his tousled hair.

"Alaina's missing."

Devon swore. "Again? I'm tying your wife up when we find her, Tristan, I swear I am."

"You'll have to wait your turn."

Devon climbed out of bed while Tristan went out into the hall and then into the room across the way. He pounded on the door until Zachary opened it. Once he noticed Tristan's enraged expression, he came instantly awake.

"What's wrong?"

"Alaina."

The one word had Zachary going back into the room and waking Derek. Tristan went back to his own suite to get dressed. A few minutes later, the men stood in his room.

"Any idea when she went missing?" asked Charles, gripping his side, which had stiffened while he slept.

"No, and devil take it, I can't believe she managed to leave without waking me. I woke up and she was gone. I know that no one came into this room. I locked the doors and windows before we retired. I have looked around, and her shoes and coat are gone. I don't know why she left, but I'm going down to the lobby to look around. Perhaps the desk clerk saw something. Devon, come with me. Charles, if you and the others could wait here in case she returns, I'd be grateful." Both men nodded and the other two left the room and went down to the lobby.

"Good evening, sir," said the desk clerk.

"Do you remember seeing my wife when we checked in?"

"And tonight, sir."

"You've seen her tonight? When?"

"Well, yes, sir. Almost an hour ago."

"Did you see which way she went?" Tristan leaned into the counter as a sickening feeling came over him.

"They walked east, sir. She didn't ask for a carriage to be brought—"

Tristan and Devon were out of the lobby and in the streets before the desk clerk finished speaking. There wasn't time to pull their own carriage around from the stables, but they spotted a hired hackney half a block away. It took some convincing—mostly with money—but the man agreed to drive them at the dangerous hour to the docks. Tristan prayed that they weren't too late. Never once in all his years of government work had he ever been faced with such strong distractions, such fears. *Is having Alaina in my life interfering with my job?* He was certain of it, but if it came down to choosing, he would never give her up.

The driver pulled to a stop in front of the second slip to let his passengers off, insisting he wouldn't go farther. Noises could be heard a short distance down the wooden boardwalk, but they failed to see anyone. The pair turned when they heard the hired hackney leave at a brisk pace. Obviously, he didn't like what was happening any more than they did.

They heard more commotion and some scuffling and then a scream, quickly stifled. Tristan's heart thudded rapidly, and he urged his legs into a run with Devon following close behind. They reached the farthest docking slip and stopped immediately. There were five people in all. Croxley and Melbourne were still on the dock and had stopped arguing when Tristan came running forward. Charlotte and Rothschild stood on the deck of the ship with someone they assumed was Justin Claiborne. The latter held a gun to Alaina and a cloth was tied around her mouth. A light trickle of blood showed on her forehead. Tristan knew he would have no trouble killing someone tonight.

"Just in time to see us off."

"Justin Claiborne?"

"Well done, agent. Yes, I know all about your work for the government. Your father tried something similar to what you are doing now. Unfortunately I had to kill him, but then again, he didn't have something so lovely with which to bargain." The barrel of the gun nudged closer into Alaina's side, causing her to inch away, only to be pulled back again.

Tristan started to move forward, but Devon held him back. If they died now, there would be no chance for Alaina.

"Luckily for me, I have your lovely young bride here to accompany me back to England. By the time you leave on the next transport, we'll be out to sea."

"It won't matter where you go. I'll find you." Tristan kept his eyes focused on Alaina. She was strong, and would remain strong—for them.

"Not likely," said Justin. "Convenient, though, I'll be able to catch up on family affairs."

"She's your blood. Why do this to her?"

"I killed my own brother. You don't believe I will have a problem with his nuisance of a daughter. You see, my family never gave one whit about me. When they thought I died, they mourned and cried, but it didn't take long for them to get over me. I fooled them, though. It was such a surprise to walk into my brother's home all of those years ago. The look on his face was worth it. He didn't want anything to do with me, but I got my revenge when he tried to interfere with my work."

"Your work? You have killed innocent people. You're a traitor and a murderer."

"Yes, well, the crown never did anything for me. Besides, this pays more than our government ever did."

Justin seemed to be growing bored with the conversation, and Tristan tried desperately to keep him talking until he figured out how to reach Alaina without causing her death. Devon stood behind him, scanning the area, but he also realized they couldn't reach her in time.

"When I return, they'll know your identity. Others will be sent after you."

"This would have been my last run. Since you've destroyed it with your call to the authorities, I'll have to make due with twenty years' worth of payments."

"What about you, Charlotte? Alaina's your niece. You cared for her like a mother. You helped raise her." Tristan saw that

Alaina was losing consciousness but fighting the fall into darkness.

"I love my niece—make no mistake in that. However, she became a liability. Her mother and father wouldn't stay out of my business, even after I left them repeated warnings—indirectly, of course. You see, Justin was always the man I loved, and I wasn't about to let anyone else get in the way of what he had to do."

"You married another."

"Justin was not ready to settle down, and my father demanded I marry then or he would refuse to provide a dowry, and I do enjoy money."

Two thoughts circled in Tristan's mind as he listened to her: the woman had gone crazy, and Justin had used her. He glanced quickly to Justin, who gave Charlotte a look of contempt.

"That's enough talk." Justin interrupted any further conversation and dragged a now unconscious Alaina closer to him in an effort to keep her upright. "If you don't mind, we have a ship to catch. If you try any heroics, your precious wife dies."

"You could kill us now and save yourself the inevitable fight in England."

"It would be my pleasure. However, the docks are beginning to fill with workers, and I prefer to be on my way, no one the wiser."

Melbourne and Croxley climbed up to the deck of the ship, following the others, each one holding a gun on the two men below as the captain slowly guided the ship out to sea. Any hint of color drained from Tristan's face, and he dropped to his knees. He had never failed anyone before. He'd lost people—it was bound to happen with witnesses—but he'd never failed. Devon knelt down beside him.

"It won't do her any good to stay here. We have to get back to the others and find a transport leaving tomorrow."

Tristan shook his head back and forth, almost in denial of what had just happened, and then he composed himself. Standing up, he turned to Devon, the murderous look in his eyes unmistakable.

"There's possibly a smaller ship leaving. Pay whatever is necessary, just get me a ship," said Tristan, and they walked back down the docks.

"I know someone who will travel almost anywhere for the right price. He's a foreigner I met on assignment years back."

"Get him. I want to be gone before morning." They reached the street and found the hired hackney waiting.

"Thought you turned tail and ran, chap," Tristan said as they walked forward.

"I came back for you, didn't I?"

Devon handed the driver a small purse. "Make it a short ride."

They arrived in front of the hotel in quick time. Tristan started for the stairs while Devon walked toward the front desk. Tristan sent him a questioning look.

"The man I spoke of lives in the hotel."

Tristan nodded and went upstairs. It took about ten minutes for everyone to gather what they needed, including Alaina's things, and join Devon in the lobby. He was speaking with a tall man with dark hair. The man's tanned skin attested to hours spent outdoors. He stood with his legs apart and arms crossed over his chest. His clothes were loose and simple.

"You'll take us?" he asked, walking up to them. The sailor looked Tristan and the others over.

"Your friend has offered a hefty purse, but I will also do it because I am a romantic myself and have nowhere at the moment to go. I will take you to England," the man said. "I am Marco."

"Fine," said Tristan. "We leave now."

Marco raised a brow and bowed. "As you wish."

Tristan could only imagine what Devon had offered the man, who bore the look of a pirate more than a sea captain.

In the Middle of the Atlantic Ocean
July 1889

"CAPTAIN!" THE BOSUN YELLED down from the top deck.

"What is it?" The irritated reply made the second in command cringe. It had been a difficult three days at sea. After two storms and many attempted escapes later, there was no sign of the lady calming down anytime soon. The years had been kind financially, but other than wealth, he had nothing of substance to show for his years at sea. For nearly twenty years, he made this same run for the same man, and no one ever questioned him because he had such a stellar reputation among sea captains. His body and mind felt the weight of weariness, and he wondered why he had agreed to this last voyage.

The bosun yelled down again. The captain turned and realized he couldn't hear his reply because the wind was drowning out his voice. Focusing his gaze, the captain saw the other man look through his own telescope and yell back and forth with the sailor up in the top mast. The captain climbed up the companionway to the upper deck, hoping another storm wouldn't keep them any longer than the others had.

"What is all of the yelling about, man?" The captain approached and looked out to sea in the direction the bosun was pointing his looking glass.

"Out there, sir. That ship is sailing a white flag. She came upon us sudden-like."

The captain grabbed the looking glass from the other man and spotted the ship. A smaller schooner moved quickly through the water, gliding like a dolphin making smooth progress in the rough waters. The white flag flew high on the mast, but the ship boasted no other colors. It didn't appear to be a pirate vessel, and the captain couldn't detect any cannons.

The captain knew his current passengers did not want any company, but this was his ship. His client may be paying a hefty sum, but he no longer cared what the lord thought. He'd already been paid.

The captain signaled for the raising of their own white flag, and the crew up on the deck lowered the sails, raised the white flag, and prepared to cross the currents as the schooner picked up speed and glided near *The Queen's Folly*. When the schooner came close enough to the ship, members of the ship crew lowered a rowboat carrying three men. It wasn't long before the small boat was within shouting distance of the captain and his sailors.

"Who goes there?" the bosun yelled down.

"Marco Boisvert!" yelled one of the men from the boat, bobbing around in the water as they tried to keep it steady and in close range of the ship. The captain heard the man and nodded to lower the ladder and bring them up. He didn't know Marco personally, but he knew of him. He was one of the most respected and famous sailors in all the seas who had mastered every known body of water. He sailed for pleasure and enjoyed making profits when it suited him. The captain's curiosity didn't overpower his caution. He stepped back to wait for the men, knowing his own men always took precautions with their benefactor on board.

Two men came up to the deck, the third staying below with the boat. The tall, tanned one with loose clothing looked like a pirate, and the other one, with his pale skin and dark hair, looked like an Englishman. Interesting how this one should come aboard his ship when he carried this particular cargo. Both men saw the captain and met him halfway across the deck.

"Marco Boisvert?" asked the captain, holding his hand out to the darker of the two men.

"Yes, Captain . . . ?"

"Harris," he supplied.

"Captain Harris. I appreciate your hospitality. We ran into a bit of trouble during that last storm and needed to slow down to make repairs with the hope of returning to Virginia. I have some passengers who must reach London. Would it be possible for you to take them aboard *The Queen's Folly*?"

The captain studied the man with him, giving him a cursory once-over. The Englishman seemed to be restless, but ocean storms could make any man who is not used to life at sea uneasy.

"I am sorry, Mr. Boisvert, but my berths are full this voyage." The captain had no difficulty with the lie he had been using in one form or another over the past two decades.

"I understand, Captain, but if you wouldn't mind my asking, where are all of your passengers? I see only sailors on these decks."

"Yes, well, I'm sure you can understand that after the storm, my guests are hesitant to come up until we have reached London." This lie also came easily.

"Of course," said Marco. "We'll be moving along them. I do apologize for stopping you. I'm sure your passengers want to reach their destinations."

"What will you do?" asked the captain, almost as an afterthought.

"My guests will just have to delay their arrival time and return with me to Virginia."

"Yes, well, I am sorry for your troubles." The captain waved them off as the men climbed down the ladder and into the small boat. One of the sailors came and spoke to the captain quietly, causing him to curse and sigh wearily. He knew it would come to this when he dropped sail to let that ship move in on them. Looking up at the sky and the sun that was beginning to set over the horizon, the captain returned below deck, passing sailors who raised the sails and prepared to regain distance on the seas.

The captain's quarters and the cabins on either side were closed off from the rest of the crew. Captain Harris didn't relish giving up his rooms each time Claiborne traveled with him, but the man paid him a great deal of money for use of the ship. Harris reached the door to the cabin, curious as to why no sound came from the other side. Since coming aboard, the woman had yelled at Claiborne or asked for her aunt. He still couldn't believe he was now an accessory to kidnapping. It had taken him by surprise when Claiborne and the others brought a woman hostage on board. She had been kept away from everyone on the ship, but in passing he had heard something about her being a duchess and her uncle being a murdering bastard. Claiborne wouldn't confide in Harris as to the woman's identity. But Harris surmised if he didn't make this his last trip, he just might end up rotting in prison—if he was lucky.

Harris knocked on the door once and then twice until Lord Melbourne answered. Harris never had liked the man. They didn't say a word to each other as Melbourne stepped aside to let him in and then left the room, closing the door behind him. Claiborne was sitting at a small table Harris had picked up while on a trading route to Jamaica. Harris had paid out a good sum for that table and matching chairs.

"Tell me, Captain Harris . . ." Justin began tapping his quill against the table, ". . . did you plan me into your little ship-to-ship communication?"

Harris wasn't about to be intimidated by the Englishman. After two decades of service, the hefty purse Claiborne paid no longer justified the lord's condescension.

"The ship raised a white flag, Claiborne." Harris refused the familiarity of using Claiborne's first name.

"Since when did we become heroes?" asked Justin, as he continued to stare at the other man and tap his quill. "What did they want?"

"Their ship was damaged during the last storm, and they wanted us to take on their passengers," said Harris. "I sent them away, with regrets of course."

"Of course. Who were they?"

"Marco Boisvert captains the ship. He's a wealthy and well-respected, if otherwise notorious, sailor." Harris watched the other man shuffle some papers around the table and then set the quill down. Silence filled the cabin for a minute, and then Justin stood and walked over to face Harris.

"Did he have anyone with him?" A dangerous glint appeared in Justin's eyes.

"There were two other men. One came over on deck, the other remained in the boat. Neither one said anything. They came and they left." Harris wanted to step back but chose to stay his ground. Justin was the one to step back, returning to his table and the papers he had left shuffled in a disorderly manner.

"Your job is to ensure our arrival to London. Nothing more, nothing less."

Justin returned to his papers and ignored Harris as the latter turned and left the room. Stepping out into the companionway, Harris stopped in front of the door where they were keeping the woman and almost knocked. He stopped himself, not wanting to know any more than he already did.

He lifted his arm to knock again. Hesitating, he lowered his arm to his side and walked away. From the shadows, a pair of eyes remained hidden but watched and remembered.

"DID YOU SEE HER?" asked Devon.

"No, but I believe I know which room she's being kept in," Tristan said. "The room is next to the captain's cabin, which is where Claiborne is staying." Tristan had seen Claiborne through the door when Harris came out of the cabin. "I'm not sure about the others, but I imagine they are close by."

Tristan shifted, trying to find as much room as possible in the small crawl space. Luckily, the captain had allowed Marco to come in on the white flag, giving Tristan and Devon an opportunity to sneak aboard. Unfortunately, their clothes were still wet and clung uncomfortably to their bodies. It hadn't been easy to drag behind the boat, considering the temperature and roughness of the water. Marco's diversion proved helpful. *A man possessing his unique skills would be valuable in our world,* Tristan thought. Derek had climbed on board with Marco, both men aware when they had sneaked below deck.

Devon noticed the small smile and couldn't help but comment. "Is there something good about all of this I should know about, friend?" He pulled his wet shirt away from his body.

"No," replied Tristan. "Unless you consider what I'll be doing to Claiborne when this is all over."

"Well, we have a bit of a wait ahead of us. Why don't we figure out how we're going to do this?"

THE ONLY SOUNDS IN the night came from the top deck, where a few sailors remained to keep the night watch. No lights shone from underneath the cabin doors, signaling that everyone had retired for the night. Tristan moved slowly down the companionway to the door on the right side of the captain's room. The rolling of the ship and the sound of the waves crashing against the sides muffled the light footfalls and creaks of the floorboards. Devon stayed back in the shadows, keeping watch.

The room was locked from the outside. It took Tristan only a moment to figure out the lock and open the door with a new set of tools Charles had given him. A thin vein of moonlight shone through the small round window above the bed, which was bolted to the floor in the center of the small room. No other furniture filled the sparse area, and a broken lantern lay in shards just inside the door.

Tristan saw her small form curled up on the side of the bed in the position she slept in during a nightmare. He prayed she wouldn't wake up yelling. He reached the edge of the bed and almost placed his hand over her mouth to keep her quiet when she turned over.

Tristan knelt next to the bed and leaned over to kiss her. Recognizing him, Alaina immediately kissed him back. With regret, he gently pulled away and placed a finger to his mouth, indicating that they had to keep silent. She nodded in understanding and removed the covers to reveal the nightgown and robe she had been wearing when she left the hotel. Holding her hand, he checked outside the door and saw only a dark hallway. On silent bare feet, Alaina followed Tristan down the hall to where Devon waited. He pulled them quickly inside the small compartment. "Good to see you again, Alaina."

She nodded in response, offering him only a weary smile. "I searched upstairs. There are three men on deck and one in the top mast. It looks like another storm is heading in, so we have to do this quickly."

Alaina looked to Tristan, who then turned back to Devon.

"Is there anyone near the boats?" asked Tristan.

"Not that I could tell," Devon said, "but one of them takes a walk around the entire deck every few minutes. Once we get up there, we won't have a lot of time."

"Do we have the lights?"

Devon patted the bag he had pulled out of the small rowboat before climbing aboard the ship.

"All right, let's do this. Alaina, I want you to stay right with me and get in the boat immediately."

"What are we going to do about them?" she whispered. Both men knew to whom she referred.

Tristan answered, "We'll keep close to the ship and find them once they land in England."

"But won't they change course when they realize I'm gone? I tend to make a lot of noise during the day." She smiled unrepentantly.

"We'll worry about that when we need to. Right now I want to get you off this ship." He leaned down to kiss her. "And if you ever do something like this again, I'll tie you to the bed and bolt the bedroom door."

"I would not blame you."

Devon led the group out of the small compartment and up the stairs to the deck. When everything was clear, he motioned them up on deck, Tristan holding Alaina's hand as they moved as quietly as possible across the boards. Alaina felt a splinter stick into her left foot from the wood and cringed. She bit back the cry of pain and continued walking with a slight limp. Tristan turned to see what happened, but Alaina just motioned for them to keep going. Once they reached the boat, Alaina got in and they followed suit, slowly lowering the small boat into the water.

Without warning, a sailor shouted to the other men. Tristan and Devon both swore as they rushed to lower the boat the rest of the way. The pulley stopped about five feet above water level. They looked up to see two men holding the slack line while another took aim with a gun. Tristan covered Alaina as a shot rang out, but luckily the darkness prevented a good aim and the bullet hit the water. They heard more shouting up on deck followed by shots that whizzed past them. Devon pulled a knife from his boot and started cutting through the rope while Tristan did the same with the other side. They had to cut quickly at the same time, or the boat would topple over.

"Hold on, Alaina, we're going to land hard." She grabbed one of the seat planks while the men continued to cut. There was more yelling and then a clear voice came through the rest, unmistakably belonging to Claiborne. Devon and Tristan looked at each other and with one final cut freed the boat. They fell the last five feet to the water, nearly knocking Devon out of the small boat. Devon pulled the small gun from his bag and shot up into nothing.

"I MUST SAY, DUCHESS, I've never been in the company of someone who has had the unfortunate experience of being kidnapped three times . . . by the same people." Charles grinned as he bowed his head from the chair in which he sat. The gash on his side stopped seeping blood, and didn't appear infected, but movement still caused him some pain. Tristan, Alaina, and Devon had safely boarded the schooner as Marco did what he did best and cut swiftly through the waters.

"Let us hope it doesn't happen a fourth time."

"It won't happen a fourth time or any other time." Tristan pulled his wife in closer. "Do you remember what I said about ropes?"

She smiled up at him. "Of course, my dear."

"I do believe it's time we return to England," said Devon. He turned and went to speak with Marco, leaving behind nods and shouts of agreement.

Twenty-Two

On the Shores of County Wicklow, Ireland
September 1889

"I don't see anyone yet." Charles hunched down behind a bush, his finger hovering beside the gun trigger. His wounded side had healed up nicely, but he wanted someone to pay for what had happened.

"They'll be here," said Tristan from his spot a few feet away.

"What about backup?" Devon asked, keeping an eye on the beach below as he knelt beside Tristan.

"Alaina predicted the cargo will come ashore here. We'll hold our position until backup arrives and hope her instincts are correct."

"I adore your wife, Tristan. Really I do. I believe her research skills have put some of the other men to shame."

Tristan smiled at Charles in the darkness. "She's a wonder, isn't she?"

"Perhaps the work is in her blood."

Tristan glanced at Devon and shook his head. "Not if I can help it. Wonder or not, I plan to keep her breathing for the next forty or fifty years."

"Perhaps she . . ." Charles paused. "Did you hear something?"

Charles adjusted his position and turned, his gaze scanning the quiet meadow. The grass swayed with the light ocean breeze, and the trees stood tall, housing creatures that continued their daily lives, oblivious to the events about to happen.

The three men waited for additional agents and the local

authorities, but with everyone more than an hour late, Tristan's irritation grew at the wasted time. He wanted nothing more than to be home with his pregnant wife, confirmed one month ago by his physician, but instead, he was kneeling on the cold ground in Ireland.

Tristan nearly called an end to the mission when a light shone down on the beach. All three men crouched down lower to avoid detection.

Tristan was going to end this tonight if he had to kill every one of them to do it. He waited with the others while another light crossed his view. There were three of them—one a woman—moving toward each other on the beach, cautious to stay away from the water line, which put them closer to Tristan, Charles, and Devon. Careful not to make any sounds, they watched the three as they stood together in silence. After twenty minutes passed, yet another light became visible, this time from the water.

A small boat bobbed its way through the choppy waters and came up on to the shore. One of the passengers climbed out, water reaching to his knees, to pull the boat to the land. Tristan and his friends waited for both men to leave the boat and walk toward them. They were close enough for their voices to carry to the agents crouched behind the bushes. Tristan just prayed their backup stayed in the trees so as not to give away their positions.

Shadows cast by the small lanterns offered the only sign of movement in the darkness, but the voices were immediately recognizable.

"You're late," said Lord Melbourne, who had been in the boat. "We've been here for too long."

"We had to make sure we weren't followed," said Claiborne.

"You never did get that niece of yours back. They know who we are and are probably searching for us now."

"They'll be searching England and perhaps Scotland, but a shipment has never left these northern coasts. They won't find us until we are well on our way to the islands," Claiborne said. "As to my brother's daughter, we did try. Those agents haven't left her alone since they returned to England. They killed one of my men and injured another." Claiborne then turned to Charlotte. "And if you had done your job the first time, when you hired that lout Henry, perhaps you would have thought to pay someone more competent. All those years in your care and still she got away. Fools, all of you."

"Alaina wasn't a threat until she met that meddling duke!" Charlotte shouted. "You idiots didn't think to kill that meddling husband of mine either. Everyone is at fault."

"I thought you adored your husband, Charlotte," Claiborne said.

"Never, love, though I suppose I had enough fondness for him not to kill him myself, but it wasn't for a lack of trying to get someone else to. The fool I hired was supposed to kill him on our last visit to London." She stopped herself before continuing on a rampage.

"It does not matter now, does it, since both Alaina and your pathetic husband still live. We presently have more urgent matters. Is everything ready?" Claiborne asked, turning to their companion.

"Yes," said Croxley. "The new captain is waiting with only enough men to man the ship—fewer to kill later."

"Very good," Claiborne said and then turned to the third person who had walked on the beach with him. He handed him something, and the man left the beach in a hurry.

Devon motioned to Tristan that he was going to follow the unknown man. Tristan nodded back.

The small group made their way down to the rowboat and just when half of them were in, a shot rang out. Tristan swore under his breath and hoped Devon wasn't shot. He and Charles came out from behind the bushes and ran to the beach.

"Stay right there, Claiborne, and the rest of you, out of the boat!" Tristan yelled across the distance between them and the people in the boat.

"Well, this is certainly a surprise," said Claiborne. "I didn't give you enough credit."

"Actually it was my wife who led us in this direction." Tristan held his gun at a deadly aim.

"Ah, yes, well she is family," he said.

"Not a part of yours." Tired of the games, Tristan moved a few steps closer. "Step away from the boat, Claiborne, and one move from anyone will find you with a bullet in the gullet."

"Is it not your job to bring in the traitors, not kill them?" asked Melbourne, smart enough to at least step out of the boat.

"I'll make an exception in this case, you miserable bastard." Tristan couldn't forget what Alaina had told him about this man and what he had done to his son. He then turned his focus to Charlotte, knowing Charles stood just a short distance away with two guns trained on the others. "And you, of all people. She loved you."

"And I loved her, but that was my mistake." Charlotte said nothing more and refused to step out of the boat. Tristan's finger held steady on the trigger, and he turned his gun on Charlotte.

"Step out of the boat. I'd hate to have to kill two members of the family in one night." Even in the dark shadows of night, with the moon shining off the water, the deadly glint in Tristan's eyes was discernible.

"Well, it seems as though you have us," Claiborne said while appearing almost bored with the situation. "What do you intend to do?"

"That's up to you," said Tristan, worried that Devon hadn't returned.

"That leaves us only one option."

Tristan almost missed the small gun Claiborne pulled out of his coat, but the moonlight struck it in just enough time. Claiborne raised the gun and two shots fired simultaneously as both men went down on the sand. Charles yelled out to Tristan, and keeping both guns trained on the others, hurried over to his friend who lay still. Charles bent down to check for signs of life and caught Croxley reaching inside his own coat. Taking no chances, Charles fired and hit Croxley in the chest, killing him instantly.

Melbourne and Charlotte stepped back but did not attempt anything. Charles dropped one of his guns and put a finger to

Tristan's throat. He heard a groan, and then Tristan's eyes fluttered open.

"Did I get the bastard?" he croaked out.

"Yes, you got him. Are you going to make it?" asked Charles, relief flowing through him.

"If my arm stops burning."

Charles glanced at Tristan's left shoulder and noticed a darker spot on his black coat.

"Good. Reinforcements just arrived." Charles helped Tristan stand as Devon came forward with a dozen other men who immediately went to work gathering up the bodies and taking Melbourne and Charlotte into custody. The latter cried hysterically about her niece and second chances while Melbourne refused to say anything.

"Thought we lost you, friend," Tristan said to Devon, who tied a thick cloth he had torn from his own jacket around Tristan's arm to stop the bleeding.

"No chance of that. I ended up having to shoot Claiborne's messenger when he jumped on a horse. Turns out he was carrying letters to someone back in England. I handed them over to Patrick to look over." Devon nodded toward the agents who had arrived with him. "I ran into these gents who got held back on the transport over from England." Devon finished tying off the makeshift bandage and took stock of the scene. "Job well done, chaps." He grinned and slapped Charles lightly on the back.

Another agent came up and told them they had found a ship just off the shoreline and were going out to search it. Tristan and the others nodded and spoke with Patrick, their supervising agent, bringing him up to speed. They watched the other agents load Melbourne and Charlotte into a carriage, hands clasped in front of them. They had a long trip home. *So do we*, thought Tristan, thinking of his wife.

"Let's get out of here."

The three friends turned their backs and walked away from the beach, never once turning around for a second look.

Claiborne Manor, England
October 1889

"HOW IS THE ARM this morning?" Alaina set a tray down beside Tristan, who mumbled about the ointment she had insisted on applying to his wound.

"Could be better if the medicine didn't burn worse than the bullet."

Alaina smiled and leaned over to kiss him. He returned the kiss with enthusiasm and groaned. She leaned back to whisper in his ear. "I think we might be able to find a way to enjoy ourselves without opening that wound," she said seductively, drawing another groan from Tristan.

Alaina knew that if he wasn't careful, he'd rip the stitches open. She moved back and poured him some coffee. He took a scone off the tray and enjoyed a healthy bite. He stared lovingly at his wife. "I should be asking how you're doing." He settled a hand gently on her stomach.

"Perfect, now that you're home and safe and that all of this is finally behind us."

Tristan nodded. "It is thanks to you that we knew where to look," he said, taking a sip of the delicious coffee. "To think that all along, the clues were in your mother's personal journal that she kept beside her bed at night."

"I am sorry for Uncle Sebastian. His own wife, and my aunt, betraying us like that. And I'm grateful to my parents for keeping Justin out of my life, even after they discovered he lived." Alaina helped herself to one of the scones while Tristan opted for a muffin the second time around. "Oh, and Devon stopped by this morning while you were still abed and said they found Henry. He had been hiding away as a butler, no less, at a country estate right here in England. I suppose he thought he could simply disappear back into the life he had tried desperately to escape."

"I'm just glad it's over. And I've been thinking about something I'd like to discuss with you." He sat up a little straighter in the bed and lifted Alaina's hand in his own. "I think it might be time to leave the agency." The pleased reaction he assumed she'd give was not forthcoming.

"Why?"

He hadn't expected this response. "My job got you kidnapped three times and all of us nearly killed because I was more focused on keeping you safe than on the work."

"Tristan, one of the kidnappings was because of my foolishness, and we were all aware of the dangers. You weren't the only agent involved, and you know very well Devon and Charles would be furious to hear you speaking this way." She shook her head when he wanted to speak and continued. "You love your work and you're good at it. I know you've had to do some horrible things in the line of duty, but don't let me be the cause of your giving up the life you have known all of these years."

He couldn't imagine loving anyone as much as he loved her at this moment. Tristan pulled her forward and kissed her softly before speaking. "I love that you are willing to let me continue in that way of life, but the truth is I'm doing this for all of us— me, you, our child, and all the children to come. I don't wish any of you to ever wonder if I'm going to come home at night. Truth be told, I'm ready for a change. I imagine Patrick will let me work in an advisory capacity, but I want out of the field."

Alaina reached forward and kissed him hard, mindful of his injury, and smiled against his lips.

"More children, milord? You know that arm will need healing first, and we still have one yet to be born," she murmured against his lips.

He smiled back and spoke in between kisses. "I thought perhaps we could try some of those things you mentioned earlier. You know, the ones that won't cause too much damage. Besides, we could always practice for the next ones."

Alaina couldn't help herself as she laughed, willing to play the game.

"Well I did have a few ideas . . ." She proceeded to show him while keeping his stitches intact.

Twenty-Three

On the Grounds of Claiborne Manor, England
May 1891

"What did Patrick think about you finally quitting the agency?" Charles helped himself to a glass of fresh lemonade and cookies that the maid had carried outside.

"He yelled for a bit and then congratulated me. He said it was about time but warned he would be calling on me, whether I liked it or not."

Charles laughed as Tristan's gaze moved to the grass and watched Devon trying to teach baby Christian how to play fetch with the new puppy. The lessons weren't going too well for either baby or man. Christian plopped down on his rump when he picked up a stick that was too big for him to carry.

Alaina laughed and left the two on the grass to join her husband, who stood up and guided his arms around her already growing stomach. They laughed together as they watched Devon pick up Christian and swing him high, causing the toddler to giggle with delight.

Alaina turned to Charles. "Do you plan to return as an agent in her majesty's government, Charles?"

"We shall see," he replied cryptically. "I may remain a man of leisure and race horses. Your uncle has an impressive collection of fine horseflesh."

Alaina smiled. "Yes, he does. We add to it every year, filling the stalls, and we'll have to expand soon."

Devon saw everyone had come together, and so he carried Christian over to Tristan, who happily lifted the boy into his arms. Christian began cooing the moment he was safely in his father's arms. The little boy giggled and tried to talk while playing with Tristan's shirt collar.

"What of you and your brothers, Devon? Have you decided whether you'll leave the work and settle down with a lovely lady of your own?" Alaina smiled at their trusted friend.

"I do see the joy Tristan has in retirement, but I won't be giving up the life anytime soon. I'll wager Charles won't be able to stay away for long, and who else is going to retrain the lazy fools when they're called upon again?"

Devon's comments brought guffaws all around.

"Now, who would like a tour of my niece's greenhouse?" asked Sebastian. "They are truly the finest in all of England." His boastful remarks drew everyone's interest, even though Devon and Charles had already had the pleasure. Everyone followed Sebastian across the grass and down through the pebbled paths, talking amicably in the warm spring air. Tristan held Alaina back a moment, still holding their son.

"You are happy, aren't you?"

Alaina didn't look surprised at the question but answered sincerely. "I've never known such happiness. I wish Christian could have known both of his grandparents, but my heart is full and running over with love." Alaina reached up to kiss Tristan, only to have a small fist clamp her hair.

Laughing, Tristan helped disengage their son's fingers. "I promise you'll always have something to smile about."

"You've already given me everything I hoped for. You filled a void in my life I thought would remain empty, but you've given me your love and made me whole again." He kissed her again and together they walked through the gardens to join the others.

Before they reached the greenhouse, the small group turned as a rider galloped up the long drive toward the manor.

"Wait a minute," said Charles as he studied the rider. "Isn't that Jameson, Patrick's aid?"

Tristan looked more closely. "Yes, I believe it is."

"He's only sent out with mission assignments," said Charles, who turned to Devon. "He must be here for you."

The rider saw the group and turned in their direction, moving now at a slower pace. He dismounted and removed a dispatch from the leather bag draped over his shoulder. All eyes were on him as he cleared his throat."

"Your Grace, Lord Blackwood, and Agent Clayton. Your orders, sirs."

Thank You

for reading *Alaina Claiborne*.

Be sure to check out Charles's story, *Blackwood Crossing*, set in Scotland and England, and Devon's story, *Clayton's Honor*, set in Ireland and England. Also available is *The Ghost of Greyson Hall*, set in Northumberland 1782 and 1892.

Blackwood Crossing

Book Two of the British Agent Novels

If you had to make a choice, would it be loyalty or love?

2015 READERS' FAVORITE 5 STAR BOOK
2015 RONE AWARD NOMINEE

Scottish Highlands—January 1892

Torn between loyalty to her family and refusal to marry a laird she despises, Rhona Davidson accepts a dangerous proposal from a man she knows only as Blackwood.

Leaving behind a life of leisure, Charles Blackwood bravely serves his country with honor and the skill of a trained British agent. When his newest case returns him to the wild Highlands of Scotland, he is faced with a choice between killing a man and saving the only woman he has ever loved.

Charles and Rhona join their lives, only to discover that their choices will result in bloodshed, unless they can uncover a truth long buried, deep in the Highland soil.

Author MK McClintock returns with swashbuckling heroes and courageous heroines in *Blackwood Crossing*, a story about buried secrets and second chances. If you enjoy clean historical romance with a touch of intrigue and adventure, then you'll love this "absolute thrill ride of a mystery."

Also available from
Mk McClintock

THE MONTANA GALLAGHERS

Escape to the old west with three classic novels of family, adventure, and love from the Montana Gallagher collection. The Historical Western Romance Montana Gallagher Series

Gallagher's Pride
Gallagher's Hope
Gallagher's Choice
An Angel Called Gallagher
Journey to Hawk's Peak
Wild Montana Winds
The Healer of Briarwood
Christmas in Crooked Creek

PRAISE FOR *THE MONTANA GALLGHERS*

"The Montana Gallagher Collection is adventurous and romantic with scenes that transport you into the wild west."
—*InD'Tale Magazine*

"This author is a talented storyteller and wonderful writer."
—*Nicole Laverdure*

"Any reader who loves Westerns, romances, historical fiction or just a great read would love this book, and I am pleased to be able to very highly recommend it. This is the first book I've read by this author, but it certainly won't be the last. Do yourself a favor and give it a chance!" —*Reader's Favorite*

Also available from
MK MCCLINTOCK

A HOME FOR CHRISTMAS
Short Story Collection

A collection of three historical western short stories to inspire
love and warm the heart, no matter the season.
Set in Montana, Colorado, and Wyoming.

PRAISE FOR *A HOME FOR CHRISTMAS*

"Ms. McClintock has a true genius when writing beauty to touch the
heart. This holiday treat is a gift any time one needs to remember the
true meaning of love!"
—*InD'Tale Magazine, 5 stars and a Crowned Heart for Excellence*

"The cold nips at your face and delicious Christmas cake leaves you
wanting more."
—*M. Ann Roher, Author of "Mattie"*

"If you like the 1800s, like I do, you will love these stories!"
—*Diane Holm, The Reader's Cove, Amazon Vine Reviewer*

**Don't miss the *Crooked Creek* and *Whitcomb Springs*
series, both set in post-Civil War Montana.**

If you'd like to share your thoughts or comments with MK, feel free to email her at her website.

If you enjoyed this book and would like to share your thoughts with others, please consider leaving an online review.

Don't miss out on future books.
www.mkmcclintock.com/subscribe.

THE AUTHOR

MK McClintock is an award-winning author of historical romantic fiction, including the *Montana Gallagher*, *Crooked Creek*, *Whitcomb Springs*, and *British Agent* series. She is also the co-author of *The McKenzie Sisters Mysteries* series. Her stories of adventure, romance, and mystery sweep across the American West to the Victorian British Isles, with places and times between and beyond. She enjoys a quiet life in the northern Rocky Mountains.

Learn more about the author, her books, and find reader extras at www.mkmcclintock.com.

Made in United States
Orlando, FL
27 April 2024

46260410R00145